EGrey

Also by this author


THE CHRONICLES OF JENNA WHITEHAIR
*Kwidatz*
*Return To Kamilon*
*Resurrection*

# EGrey

*Battle for Greylea  Volume 1*

Julie Hancox

ISBN: 978-1-917129-73-2

*Cover by*
*Joseph Witchall*
www.josephwitchall.com

# Chapter 1

Smells always materialise first. Smokey, salty bacon, sweet yeasty bread, and his mother's knock-you-sideways-into-the-morning coffee. They all filtered gently into his gradually awakening mind, as the last vestiges of a river merge with the sea.

Tiny twitches of his nostrils were followed by the flickering of his thick eyelashes as he prized his eyelids apart.

Ribbons of soft sunlight sent dust particles into a sparkling frenzy as they split the curtained darkness of his room.

He snuggled down further into the warm embrace of his blankets, still unwilling to surrender to the day.

"Elijah Grey get your lazy bones down here and eat this breakfast before it gets cold and you end up wearing it!"

He chuckled quietly at her foghorn voice, knowing full well that she would indeed make him wear it if he delayed too long. Then she would cluck on about how he drove her to distraction, but since she loved him, she'd make him more, as breakfast is the most important meal of the day and successful people never ever skipped it!

Groaning just once but somewhat half-heartedly, Elijah stretched his long thin legs out of the side of the bed, wriggled his toes in the soft silky fur that greeted them, shifted his feet so that they came down beside the still sleeping body of his dog, and levered himself out of bed.

Pulling back the threadbare curtains to let in the full blast of bright sunshine, he flexed his shoulders, breathed deeply of the cool early morning air and grinned. It was Saturday!

As he stood with his eyes closed soaking up the warmth, he felt the shock of a cold wet nose on the back of his hand. Pivoting on his heels he was met by the full thrust of his dog's hard head into his chest as he butted him with excitement. He knew that it was Saturday too.

"Elijah Grey, last chance before this breakfast decorates the walls!"

"Coming Burda, just coming!" he called as he half ran half hopped along the hallway from his bedroom, dragging on his jeans at the same time.

# Chapter 2

Leaning back from the table and his wiped clean plate, Elijah smiled at the jiggling figure at the sink. Burda had what would be politely called a well-rounded figure and homely features, less politely but more honestly; she was as wide as she was tall and had craggy features that would probably be totally at home in a scary movie, as the villain, but he loved her as he would a mother.

Dark thoughts of the parents that he had never known began to worm their way into his contentment. They had apparently abandoned him as a small baby; choosing to leave him defenceless and alone in the forest, to be found by Burda's dog Ranger and brought to her door in the dead of night fifteen years ago. The old woman had made inquiries at the nearest town but no one had reported any lost children or kidnappings so she had simply taken him on as her own, raising him by herself in the cosy little cabin in the woods.

Once again he experienced the familiar surge of anger and longing for the family that he would never know. It was as if a cloud of mosquitoes had invaded his head, the buzzing filled his ears and spread to his throat making him feel as if he would choke. Suddenly a cold wet nose was thrust into his clenched fist, shattering his black reverie and bursting the bubble of pain.

Elijah blinked to find two pairs of sapphire blue eyes studying him intently, two faces radiating the same depth of concern.

"Hey that was a great breakfast Burda, shall I help you with the dishes?" He asked to break the heavy silence, hoping desperately that the answer would be no.

"Pah!" She spluttered with her mouth full of left over pancake, running her chubby fingers through the unruly crop of wild grey hair she added with a toothy grin.

"Why break the habit of a life time, go on get out of here and take that flea ridden mutt with you!"

Leaping out of his chair before she could change her mind, he made for the door, then stopped, pulled around and grabbed her in a bear hug about her slouching shoulders and planted a ringing kiss on her warm cheek.

"You're the best Burda, you are, no denying it!"

"No arguments from me, just remember that when I'm old and grey and need you to cook for me!"

"Pah! You are old and grey already, not able to cook, that'll never happen!" he called as he leapfrogged the arm chair to short cut into the hall way and out the door into the already steaming hot day.

Glancing down to check that Ranger, was, as ever at his side he realised that the dog and woman were standing as if in deep and meaningful conversation in the kitchen, squinting and craning his head forward to catch what Burda was saying, all he caught was:

"You make sure you look after him I heard strange noises last night, and have a bad feeling in my water about today, but I know there'll be no stopping him so it's down to you mongrel!"

Ranger whined softly and she patted him roughly on his silken head to take the sting from her words before he wheeled about on his long graceful legs and reached the waiting Elijah on the porch in two loping strides.

The boy just stopped himself from asking a dog what that was all about, after all, Ranger was a wicked clever dog, but he couldn't actually speak right?

Launching himself into the air to skip the three rickety steps he crunched to the ground in a dramatic cloud of dust. Cool, that always made him feel like a super hero with his trusted sidekick at his heels, because of course Ranger had landed soundlessly beside him.

"Come Ranger boy, let us seek out the bad guys and save the world!"

Together, boy and canine entered the shadows of the forest.

Almost immediately the skin on his bare arms prickled with goose bumps, just the lack of sunshine under the lush green canopy he told himself. The muffling of all sound seemed almost complete today, even the twigs and dead leaves beneath his marching feet gave up nothing but silence as they were crushed, it was as if the thick green air was absorbing the noise of their demise beneath his trainers.

He shuddered involuntarily and half thought of turning back, the distant pool of sunshine and the cabin beckoned from behind him strongly today.

"Don't be daft Elijah Grey, you have too much imagination that's your trouble, today is just Saturday, like all the other Saturdays!" he chided himself for letting himself get so creeped out, after all, he'd gone adventuring in this forest every Saturday for as long as he could remember.

The hard warmth of Rangers long bony head suddenly pressed against his thigh, reaching down he stroked his soft muzzle and drew immense strength and comfort from the dog's steadfast presence. He'd be fine because Ranger was there, as always.

They had reached the fork in the path, which way today?

He turned to take the left one but was halted by Ranger firmly planting his streamlined racing frame solidly in his path.

Only slightly puzzled by his dog's unusual behaviour, he shrugged and turned to take the right path, only to be stopped again.

Well now he was a tad shaken, this had never occurred before. Screwing up his eyes and frowning, he looked deep into the brooding blue eyes that were searing into his.

"Okay then, you decide and I'll follow you if that's the way it's gonna be."

Ranger gave a soft whine and launched forward heading straight down the centre between the two paths, leaping over tangled undergrowth like a white gazelle.

"Hey wait! It's okay for you I've only got the two legs. Ahhh!"

Elijah stumbled and fell to the ground outstretched arms plunging elbow deep into the mass of nettles and brambles. Red hot pain flashed like flames up his arms as he heaved himself back onto his feet, using language that would most certainly have earned him one of Burda's bread slicing looks.

Ranger had heard him cursing and returned to stand in front of him, long pink tongue lolling out of his panting mouth.

"Just what's wrong with following the paths today huh?"

Elijah stood rubbing his throbbing forearms and gritting his teeth against the intensity of the pain until it began to subside.

Gently the white dog placed his paw onto his friend's thigh and pressed down insistently. Elijah sighed loudly, shrugged his shoulders and relented, who knew why today it seemed to be so important that he did not follow the paths that he had always done, but Ranger had saved his life when he had apparently turned up at Burda's door in a storm one night with a small baby held gently in his mouth all those years ago and been his faithful companion ever since, if he couldn't trust Ranger, who could he trust?

Brambles ripped persistently at his jeans as if they were trying to pull him back, he was hot and sweating now and the salt stung his raw arms but he plodded on after the white dog's flag of a tail as it waved above the undergrowth like a surrender flag.

He batted away buzzing insects from his ears and inhaled a few with his panting but he kept moving, Ranger's pace was relentless until suddenly he came to an abrupt halt.

"Hah, so even dogs get tired, well I can't say that a rest wouldn't be very welcome, in fact-"

Elijah's next words were stolen from his mouth by the sight of his friend in front of him. Ranger's pointed ears were rigidly erect and flicking side to side like radar dishes, searching for something that eluded Elijah's poor human senses. Every hair from the dog's shoulders down its tensed spine was standing on end like a white crest that ended in his tail which was as stiff as a flag pole.

Elijah's own hairs began to rise and prickle on his neck and it was only then that he really noticed the total silence around him, it was as if the forest itself was holding its breath.

"Come on Ranger quit with the play acting, you're spooking me good and proper now, let's go home, we—"

As he turned to retrace his steps, he froze. Now there was sound, and sound like he'd never heard in the forest before. It was as if someone was using a buzz saw but under the ground, he could actually feel the earth beneath his feet tingling and trembling.

"Oh this is getting better and better, Ranger come on!" He yelled but the dog was already running, deeper into the forest! For a heartbeat Elijah fought with the desire to run back to the safety of the cabin but then the desire to stick with his friend won

6

through and he charged after Ranger, ignoring the thorns that were now ripping through denim and skin.

"They're coming, get him to the clearing, we'll be there as soon as we can, get him to the clearing!"

Elijah physically flinched at the voice that seemed to be coming from just beside his ear; without breaking his stride he glanced over his shoulder to find no one there.

Then another voice, familiar this time but disembodied the same shouted,

"I told you today was the day! Get him to the clearing, I'll cover your backs!"

His heart was thudding so violently in his chest that he thought it would stop, and then came the birds.

Suddenly out of the silence of the moment before there came an eruption of birds, not singing but screeching and screaming, crows, rooks, ravens and jays and he almost stumbled when he realised that he could understand them.

"Run!" they were all screeching at him, "Run!"

So run he did.

Ahead of him Ranger had turned right onto a track just wide enough for the deer and rabbits to use. Glinting out of the viridian back drop, Elijah could glimpse light, could this be the clearing that the voices were talking about, he sure hoped so because his thigh muscles were in agony now and threatening to give way beneath him.

"Keep running and don't look round!"

He couldn't be sure whether the voice was in his head or in his ears but it spurred him on with its undeniable urgency. His lungs burned now and he was feeling light headed and weak. Suddenly the earth beneath his running feet bucked and heaved as if it were alive. It rose up in a soil cloaked mound with Elijah wobbling on the top like a cherry. As he rolled to the ground his ears were filled with a blood curdling screech like a banshee and something sharp gouged down his back, ripping his tee-shirt and scoring the skin of his back like a blade.

"Don't look back and run for the clearing!"

This time he knew that the voice was coming to him from a person, it was Burda.

7

She came crashing through the undergrowth towards him like a stampeding bull rhinoceros, whirling her log splitting axe around her head like a warrior from one of his DS games.

"B-Burda, who-what?" He stuttered as he struggled to his feet on the still heaving ground.

"No talking, duck!" she ordered in a voice that brooked no argument.

Elijah ducked just in time to dodge another swipe of a huge shovel size set of claws, then heard the whistling of the axe as it flew through the air to embed in something large behind him with a stomach churning thud.

"Now do as you're told and run boy!"

This was no longer the Burda that he had known all of his life, which in itself was enough to chill his heart and paralyse his limbs, but the huge black shadow that loomed up from behind him stopped his breathing and drained him of all power to move.

"Run Elijah Grey for your life run!"

The voice was inside his head this time, but the urgent tugging at his jeans was Ranger, who had doubled back to find him. The contact was enough to shatter his stasis, and he stumbled past the soil covered figure that loomed behind him to run with what was left of his strength after the retreating back of the white dog. As he ran there was a tiny part of his mind that was laughing and saying, this is just a dream you fool, wake up, and go have breakfast it's just a Saturday, like any other Saturday.

However, the many erupting mounds that were beginning to form a circle around him, the screeching of the birds, and above all, the sight of Burda out of the corner of his eye, wielding her log splitting axe like a warrior, lopping off limbs and indescribable parts of the creatures, for creatures they were that were pursuing him' made a liar of that tiny voice for good.

Tears began streaming down his cheeks, fear, exhaustion, desperation, anger, all warred within him, at the grunt of pain from Burda behind him anger won and he skidded to a dusty halt, wheeled around and faced the onslaught hell bent on kicking some ass!

Anger was flushed away by terror at the nightmare that met his eyes.

Rearing up out the earth just feet away from him was a sight beyond the imagination, beyond any horror movie that he'd ever snuck in behind Burda's back.

Towering at least his own height again above him, loomed a huge gaping black mouth, out of which jutted two corn yellow curved teeth that dripped putrid saliva down onto his face. The only other features that adorned the giant smooth skinned head were two quivering nostrils; no eyes, ears or hair that he could see. The creature was reared up on its stout hind legs, and waving its front ones around just missing the hair on his head with its scimitar claws. The stench that filled his own nose made him gag and he desperately wanted to move but felt rooted to the spot with fear.

Suddenly a white torpedo impacted on his back, knocking him to the ground where he crouched on his hands and knees, gasping.

"Crawl Elijah, it cannot see or hear it can only smell, crawl close to the ground into the centre of the clearing and wait for me there!"

Not bothering to wonder anymore how he was suddenly hearing words come from his dog, Elijah obeyed, wincing but ignoring the sting of nettles and snagging thorns that ripped into his palms, knees and face. He had rediscovered momentum and was desperate to put as much distance between himself and that monster as possible.

As he reached the centre of the sun soaked glade, he dared to stand up. He felt that he knew what it would be like to stand in the eye of a storm now because all around him creatures were erupting like volcanoes, and their terrible screams of rage filled the air and threatened to burst his ear drums. Burda was swinging the axe in windmill circles around her head, bringing it down on any part of a creature unfortunate enough to be in the way with wet thuds producing spurts of thick black blood, with which she was now covered like one of her signature chocolate coated cookies.

"Wow, I've been living with a superhero!" he thought which ordinarily would have been astounding, but today, well it paled into insignificance. However, she was only one superhero, and

9

there had to be at least a dozen of those creatures closing in on him now, and the end seemed terrifyingly inevitable.

Then from behind him arose an unearthly sound.

"Now what for the love of Pete?" He whispered, before gasping so violently that he almost choked.

The sound was coming from Ranger, who was standing at the dead centre of the clearing, up on his hind legs and howling to the sky. With a jolt Elijah realised that he could actually discern a distinct word in his dog's howl. It was the word "Now!"

# Chapter 3

Standing beside Ranger, craning his neck back and squinting against the bright sunlight to stare up at the almost perfect circle of blue sky above the clearing, despite all of the terrifying sounds as the creatures closed in around him Elijah found a space in his mind that was just filled with wonder.

For as he watched a second sun seemed to grow beside the one that he knew, only this one was blood red like an opening eye.

Bigger and bigger it grew until it had swallowed up the sun into its ruby red universe.

Behind him he could actually feel the hot fetid breath of the creatures on his back, smell their hairless lumbering bodies and anytime now he expected to feel the ripping claws as they sliced him into small strips like a bacon slicer. But he did not look away, his mind was transfixed now by the sudden appearance amid the red perfection above him, of two tiny black dots that were descending down at an alarming rate towards them.

"Stand still Elijah Grey and don't you be worrying, I'll finish these Drillers off for you!"

He glanced towards the voice of Burda, who was still wielding her axe, and completely smeared head to foot in black sticky blood, all around her was the carnage that she had wreaked and still she fought.

A sudden rushing sound from above yanked his attention back just in time to gasp, slack jawed, as the black specks rapidly expanded into figures with outstretched arms descending on what appeared to be bungee ropes suspended in mid-air. With his next breath he found himself wrapped in a pair of those arms, held tightly against a chest and catapulting back upwards at stomach churning speed towards the red hole in the sky.

"Target acquired and coming up to land!"

So at least he understood the language of his captor/rescuer, he couldn't be sure either way at the moment, but one thing was true, he was rapidly leaving the attacking Drillers below him, although what was happening to Burda down there overwhelmed him with fear. He had no more time to worry now as the landing spoken of by the blur of a face above his head turned out to be a very flimsy looking platform made out of what looked twigs!

As they rocketed towards it he squeezed his eyes shut and tensed himself for the impact, he could not believe that they could be travelling at such speed and stop before they obliterated it rather than landed on it.

However, when the stomach churning assent abruptly ceased, to be replaced by the even more sickening falling sensation, Elijah couldn't stop his eyes from opening and he saw that both he and his travelling partner were now quite gently alighting onto the platform, which he realised, now that he was much closer, was indeed made up of interlaced twigs and branches.

Beneath his feet he felt them bend quite alarmingly, but hold, snapping as he staggered away from his rescuer/captor, he still had no idea which, to fall to his hands and knees and bring up the entire contents of his long forgotten breakfast.

"Perhaps we should get him to firmer ground as quickly as possible; the walkers do tend to have that reaction."

Clenching his stomach muscles hard in order to hopefully deter them performing anymore, Elijah tried to wobble to his feet, sweating and swaying unsteadily.

"Firm ground sounds nice .....Please." He whispered, wishing now he had listened to Burda when she had gone on one of her "Things you should always have with you just in case," lectures, he could really do with a handkerchief right now and he was acutely aware of how his red blotchy face and running nose must be making him appear to these people.

As he thought the word people he knew instantly that he was wrong, these were definitely not people as he knew them.

No Dorothy, he was definitely not in Kansas anymore!

Standing before him, swaying gently in unison with the flimsy platform were two tall slender figures. Each was clad in brown, top to toes, with long nut brown hair scraped back into tightly braided pig tails that also swayed in the breeze. Two almost identical pairs of hazel eyes scrutinised him with a mixture of curiosity, amusement and a smidgeon of sympathy. A slow smile spread over their flat dark skinned features displaying even white teeth and pale pink tongues. Suddenly one of them bent down and touched Elijah gently on the shoulder, almost reverently and said.

"Can you stand Elijah Grey or should we carry you as before? For move we must and fast."

In place of a reply Elijah struggled shakily to his feet, the dizzying drop that he could now glimpse over the frayed edges of the twig platform threatened once again to overwhelm his senses but he was determined to move on his own and not have to be carried like some sickly toddler!

"We don't have time for this, they will be here any minute, and you know that sister, if you don't do it, then I will!" The taller of the two snapped, moving decisively towards Elijah.

"NO, you take Ranger I will carry the Elijah Grey until it is safe enough for him to do his own walking." She replied as she grabbed Elijah firmly around his waist before he could protest and swooped up into the air like a swallow.

As the air rushing past his eyes stung so much that he was forced to screw them tightly shut, Elijah had one last glimpse of the rickety platform shattering into kindling and scattering down like brown snow around them. Even in this terrifying situation, that part of his brain that always slightly annoyed him, the part that spoke in the very boring and sensible voice of logic commented almost too calmly.

"So just what was holding that thing up in the air then?"

As Elijah realised with a chill that there was indeed nothing below it and that they were at the moment hurtling towards the ground with nothing to break their fall that he could see through his slatted eyelids. Then, with a gut wrenching jerk upwards, their downwards became a forwards, followed by a sideways with a swerve that felt like the time that he had disobeyed Burda and snuck onto the Roller Coaster at the fairground.

Forcing his eyes to open, Elijah groaned as the blurred images of branches whizzed past close enough to claw those eyes out of their sockets. Gripped by steel strong arms against his rescuers chest, he could hear her heart beating, feel every flex of her muscles as she swung through the air.

Yes, swinging was what she was in fact doing, like Tarzan in one of Burda's flickering old black and white movies, she was looping through the air at amazing speed.

"Yes but there are no vines for her to be grabbing, not that she could as she is holding onto you with both arms, or haven't you thought of that?"

It was that annoying voice again but it was unfortunately correct, she wasn't swinging from vine to vine like Tarzan, so how was she doing it?

"They are above us sister, we must land and take cover, there are way too many for us to fight off successfully!"

Elijah felt rather than saw her nod sharply in response, before dropping like a stone past flashes of tree trunks stark and bare of leaves, to land in a choking cloud of crimson dust.

Released to stand shakily on numb legs and feet, Elijah gaped slack jawed as he watched the slim brown figure straighten up to stand and wait as, what he had taken for a bungee rope as they were descending to grab him out of the clutches of the Drillers, delicately coiled itself around her waist, it was in fact, a tail!

Questions built up like traffic in his poor traumatised brain but were given no chance to escape as Elijah was shoved roughly to the ground and aimed at a large dark opening at the base of one of the tall tree trunks. Obediently he crawled towards it only half registering that the ground beneath his palms and fingers was carpeted in soft red dust that billowed up into his face as he moved, smelling sweet and spicy like Burda's cinnamon cookie mixture.

The image of Burda standing alone against at least half a dozen of those horrifying creatures, armed with just her log splitting axe and caked in black blood suddenly filled his mind and froze his limbs.

"How could he have left her like that? She would never defeat them all on her own, she would surely......."

"Move Elijah Grey or her bravery will have been in vain and then you know what she will do!"

"Ha! Ground me for weeks I'll bet!" He chuckled, willing his muscles back into action and reaching the cool darkness of the opening just in time; for at the moment that he gained its shelter, the air above him erupted into an ear splitting cacophony of sound.

"Do not look up Elijah, just keep moving!"

He again obeyed, diving down into the cool darkness within the tree, not knowing or caring what he would land on or how far he would fall. As he tumbled head over heels downwards the others tumbled with him. Grunting as the air was punched from his lungs and expecting the sickening snapping of bones any second, he felt his descent abruptly halted and lay gasping for breath, his head spinning; her tail wrapped tightly around his waist.

"Are you injured Elijah?"

It was not her voice coming out of the green tinged gloom, and it wasn't that of the other, her brother; tingles of recognition radiated through his brain, he knew that voice, and yet he had never heard it before.

Rubbing the dust and grime out of his eyes he desperately tried to clear his sight enough to look around him.

Slowly his surroundings began to emerge, and he realised that he was somewhat precariously perched on the steeply sloping sides of a huge underground lake, whose slick black waters licked silently at the shore line about four feet directly below him. Squinting upwards, he could just make out the brightly lit entrance through which they had just been thrust so unceremoniously; glimpses of flitting black shapes in the window of red sky sent rivers of ice rippling down his back.

"What's up there?" He whispered, as the sound of rage fuelled screams filtered down into the muffled darkness.

"They are Silff, they are the seekers, they cannot walk on land so are no threat to our immediate safety but they will report back of our whereabouts; we must be as far from here as possible, in the time that your puny legs will allow."

This time he knew that it was her brother speaking, even though he couldn't really see the owner of the voice in the gloom!

"Well I'm ready when you are, um, I'm sorry, didn't catch your names before."

"That is because my brother has no manners and did not tell you! I am named Khizzi and he is Ghelli, perhaps when we are out of immediate danger we can be introduced more fully, I have

15

no doubt that your mouth is choking with questions as well as dirt!"

"Well, yeah, just a bit, but the main one at the moment before we move anywhere is what's happened to my dog?"

For Elijah had acquired enough vision in the half-light to realise that he couldn't see Ranger at all.

A soft cough from beside him made him jerk so violently that it caused Khizzi to almost lose her hold on him and he slithered at least a metre further down the steep dusty bank before she tightened her grip around his waist to halt his descent towards the eerie water.

"Forgive me Elijah but there was no way of telling you before today, I am Ranger."

If there was any of his long forgotten breakfast left to bring up, this would have been the time, for the voice, the one that he had heard minutes before that had so jangled his nerves was coming from a fourth figure on the slope, and this one blew his mind!

# Chapter 4

The young man's head slowly turned towards him, into the small patch of weak light filtering through the dust inside the tree. He had long silky white hair, a bony, angular face, high cheek boned, with a pointed slender nose. As his deep set eyes met with Elijah's a tentative smile curled his thin lips and it was as the tip of his pale pink tongue just for a heartbeat poked out at the corner of that mouth that recognition hit Elijah like a train.

"R-Ranger?" He whispered in a dry croak, all saliva seemed to have dried up in his own mouth, and he felt hot and cold at the same time.

"Elijah Grey, it is good to finally be able to greet you with words instead of licking your hand, which, it has to be said tasted somewhat unsavoury at times!"

All that Elijah could muster was a weak cough before it all became just too much for his poor besieged young brain to cope with and he sank to the dusty floor beneath him, out cold.

"Now see what you've done Ranger, first you bring us a child when we need a leader, then you scare him so much with your hideous appearance that he faints like a girl!"

Ghelli grumbled as he was scrambling down towards the stricken form, still attached by his own tail to the doorway in the tree like an umbilical cord. He reached Elijah at the same time as Khizzi and Ranger, resulting in a red tidal wave of dust that engulfed them all.

Khizzi gently lifted Elijah's head onto her knees, and was clearing the dust from his eyes and mouth as he spluttered back into consciousness.

All three gave a sigh of relief as he jerked himself upright when he became aware of his position on Khizzi's lap.

"I'm fine, just fine, I er we should move right? No good hanging around for whatever those Silff bring after us!"

He staggered up onto his feet, wobbling and swaying unsteadily on the steep sloping inner walls of the tree, but he brushed away the helping hand that Ranger held out and couldn't meet the other's eyes.

"Well, if you're sure that you are strong enough, we need to go downwards, as it is in fact our only choice." said Ghelli, standing still so that his long sinuous tail could once again coil itself tightly around his waist and then plunging forward down into the cool darkness.

"Follow me Elijah Grey and do not allow your pride to prevent your common sense telling you when to cling on to me rather than fall."

The stiffness of her back in front of him was all he needed to inform him that she wasn't too impressed, but Elijah just grunted, what did she know about having a day like this one?

Resorting to sliding down on his backside, he was only slightly surprised by the fact that the dust between his fingers was as cold as ice. Deeper and deeper they descended until the light filtering down from the distant opening was only enough to dimly illuminate the dancing tip of Khizzi's tail in front of him.

Once his limbs had accustomed themselves to the movement, his mind was able to stop reeling and begin to assimilate the bombardment that it had received in what was most likely just the last hour.

Burda was a warrior not a slightly overweight mother figure, his dog was not a dog but a half human half dog thing, they were both from this world which existed, where exactly he couldn't say, he was following two beings who were also half human half some kind of monkey, being chased by Silffs whatever they were and he, well he…"

The jolt of realisation was so forceful that it actually halted all of his movement bringing Ranger and Ghelli crashing into his back.

"What was he? If he came from this world and not Earth, then he must be half some animal too!"

"Elijah, we will explain all to you when we have reached a place of safety, this is not that place, but trust me, I will keep nothing from you."

When Ranger his dog had appeared to be able to read his mind he had thought that it was really cool, but now that Ranger was speaking to him out of a very human looking mouth it sent shivers running up and down his spine like ants.

"Trust you? How can I trust you when you've been lying to me for all of my life, pretending to be my dog when all along you were, you were -"

"I was exactly that Elijah, on that Earth I was a dog with just a few human traits, the opposite of what I am when here, on Egreya. But you have to believe me when I say that in both places I am always your friend."

Staring into Ranger's sapphire blue eyes, Elijah felt hot tears brimming from his own, he was so very afraid and needed desperately to believe that he still had his one true and constant companion with him in this strange and threatening place; but words would not form that could possibly explain his emotions, so he clamped his lips shut and silently turned away to continue with the slippery descent downwards into the bowels of whatever place he now inhabited.

# Chapter 5

Within what seemed to Elijah, mere minutes, even the dim light from the surface disappeared, and he found himself compulsively blinking in a vain attempt to see anything at all. He found himself resorting to crawling on his hands and knees, the complete blackness on the outside of his eyelids making it impossible to tell whether his eyes were in fact open or shut.

As his forehead struck something warm and soft, he sat back on his heels and reluctantly released the words,

"I can't see where I'm going anymore, I need help."

Out of the darkness a small hand brushed against his and a voice whispered.

"None of us can see now Elijah Grey, we will stop here for the night, rest and hope that the going will be easier in the morning."

"But he should be able to see better than all of us, after all he is-"

Ghelli's voice was cut off abruptly by what sounded to Elijah like a hand clamped over his mouth.

"I'm what?" He asked the silky darkness in front of his face.

"Pay no attention to Ghelli, he always gets cranky when he's hungry, we will stop, eat and sleep if we can, although I regret that I did not think to pack a light source which will make both of those more difficult."

There were soft scuffling sounds, with a few grunts thrown in as the four struggled to seat themselves closely together without the luxury of sight. A round object, wrapped in what felt like some sort of leaf, was pushed into Elijah's hand, sniffing it suspiciously he heard an amused chuckle from his left.

"It will not rival one of Burda's cheese burgers with fries, but it is edible I promise you!"

The mention of Burda and the life that he had so taken for granted until this morning brought a lump to his throat but he was so hungry that he ignored it and bit into the spongy contents of the leaf wrapped parcel, swallowing the mouthful of bread like substance without even tasting it.

"Here, there isn't a lot of water left but if we're careful it will last."

From his other side he felt a leather flask pressed into his left hand; fumbling with the stopper, careful not to put it down, as he would never be able to locate it again, he drank a couple of mouthfuls before replacing it and holding it out for the next taker.

"Are you sure that you have had enough Elijah? You have a very tough day ahead of you."

The genuine concern in Ranger's softly spoken question was palpable to Elijah through the thick blackness that surrounded him, rather than allow any of the churning emotions within him to escape with an answer, he merely grunted and curled up like a kitten on the cold ground and squeezed his eyes tightly shut. He did this for two reasons, one was to try to fool himself into thinking that it he could see nothing because of it, and two, to keep the burning tears of fear and loneliness at bay.

"I'll never get any sleep!" Was the last thought that fluttered through his waking mind.

# Chapter 6

Flashing, disjointed images like a badly made music video pounded behind his closed eyes on his journey back into wakefulness.

Burda turning pancakes with a machete instead of a spatula, Ranger his dog tugging at the leg of his jeans as he tried to pull them over his legs, which had suddenly turned into huge black feathered wings, glass shattering inwards from his bedroom window and then floating down like glitter to settle on his hands, yellow hands with one long bony finger, it's hooked end quivering in the air above his face. Struggling to breath Elijah could feel his body responding to the insistent nudging from somewhere out of the suffocating darkness but his mind would not relinquish his dream state.

"Elijah, you must wake up now we have been discovered, we must move!"

As he gasped in a lung full of the dank and musty air his eyes opened, not that it made any difference to the blackness. Then he heard it.

At first he thought that it was a ringing in his ears, but as he became more alert he realised with a surge of hot fear in his stomach that it was coming out of the oppressive darkness that hung above him like a blanket.

"Do you hear it Ranger?" he whispered, his trepidation over riding his unwillingness to talk to his erstwhile doggie companion.

"I do Elijah, stay very still, they will only be able to detect movement at this range."

"They? Who's they?"

"SSSSSh!" hissed Ghelli from out of the void to his left, "They can also hear extremely well remember Ranger or have you been too long away?"

The high pitched almost sing-song trilling sound grew louder, as "They" drew closer to the frozen four, who crouched as still as they could, hugging the cold unyielding surface of the cave like a friend, holding their breath now and waiting.

Suddenly Elijah felt wafts of the stale air ruffling his hair sending electric tingles across his face and neck as whatever was seeking them landed in a flurry of dust and four dull thuds in the area around them. Scuffling noises ensued followed immediately by a thin high pitched voice sizzling into his ears.

"Vibrations in the ground will only attract the Drillers more quickly, we are sent to get you out of the cavern, take help when it is offered or fight them off yourselves!"

"Who sent you, and how do we know that we can trust you?"

Elijah could tell from Ghelli's voice that he was being restrained in some way; which was strange since nothing had laid a finger on him as yet.

"Who sent us is not important, and you don't."

The reply came from another direction and was delivered in a calm and measured tone.

There was silence for what seemed to Elijah far too long in the circumstances, he desperately wanted to get out of this place and into the light, he really didn't care how. He was just drawing breath to speak when the first vibrations below ground reached the soles of his feet.

"Ghelli, we have no choice but to trust them or fight Drillers in this darkness and die!"

It was Khizzi who spoke, followed by Ghelli begrudgingly muttering "Lead on."

Softly a small hand grasped his and he was gently led forward into the darkness, blind and terrified, stumbling over unseen obstacles that his mind made into skulls or grasping hands.

Slowly the velvet blanket of darkness began to lift from his eyes and the dim images of hunched figures emerged from the gloom ahead of him.

He could easily make out Ranger, whose long white hair seemed to glow out of the half-light, and Khizzi's brown back and tightly braided hair bobbed just in front of him, her small hand was still clasping his, and from the shuffling and grunting behind him, he knew that Ghelli was bringing up the rear.

It was the four hunched figures that shambled along around them that riveted his attention and caused his breath to clog his throat.

He could clearly see their bony skeleton moving beneath their smooth, grey skin, but it was definitely no human skeleton! All he could see of the creature's heads were pointed ear tips as they peeked up above their scrawny shoulders, and their long knobbly spines ended in a hairless tail and two very bowed and stunted legs; but it was the arms that threatened to send him running back into the darkness of the cave in panic, they were in fact not arms, but wings, bat-like, with hooked claws instead of hands and soft floppy folds of transparent skin draped between claws and waist, and naked, they were naked!

He couldn't help himself, Elijah gasped and stumbled to a halt shaking and struggling to retain his stomach contents.

With a sharp hissing intake of breath, the four bat things also halted, and as one, four identically hideous faces turned to regard him.

"Elijah, what is wrong?"

He gaped towards Khizzi, how could she ask such a stupid question? Wasn't it obvious?

In the glittering beams of light now filtering into their darkness, the four faces displayed identical expressions of annoyance, although how he knew that he couldn't say. Each had features like he'd never seen before, tiny black eyes like pinpricks, broad splayed noses with huge flared nostrils that quivered constantly and mouths like a paper cut lined with sharp pointed teeth.

"They say that we must keep moving, that the Drillers are not far behind us."

Ranger's voice came out of the gloom behind him, Elijah was about to ask how he knew that, because he'd heard nothing, but then he realised that he could indeed just detect a high pitched sound that appeared to be emitted by the bat things; of course Ranger with his dog standard hearing could hear it and understand!

"H-how do we know we can trust them? They look so-so,"

"We don't but do you have a better idea?" snapped Ghelli, giving Elijah a look of pure disgust before trudging onwards.

No, he didn't, so after taking a deep breath, Elijah forced his still trembling legs back into a shuffling walk behind Khizzi, trying not to see the peripheral image of the bat things all returning to their strange way of moving, clawing along the ground one wing length at a time.

Within a matter of minutes, he heard a new sound, a loud whistling, like the sound you get when you blow across the top of a bottle, and the light suddenly increased to bright blinding and very painful to eyes accustomed to pitch darkness.

They had entered what appeared at first to be a new cave, but as his eyes adjusted, he realised that they were in fact now all standing at the base of what seemed to be a tall chimney carved out of the rock and squinting upwards, he could see a disc of light as bright as the sun, hundreds of feet above them.

Running over to the wall Khizzi began searching the smooth surface desperately searching for a hand hold to use in order to climb upwards.

"They say that there will be only one way to escape the Drillers, to let them fly us up" Whispered Ranger.

Khizzi and Ghelli stood frozen by indecision, they too were obviously reluctant to trust their rescuers completely. The vibrations beneath their feet gave them their answer.

Each of the creatures rose flapping into the air, swirls of glittering dust reminding Elijah of a snow globe that he had on a shelf in his bedroom. As the floor beneath them heaved upwards, ahead of the erupting Drillers, they grabbed hold of shoulders with their talon tipped feet and yanked all four up into the air; arms and feet dangling like rag dolls.

Spiralling upwards towards the opening, the huge leathery wings beat so hard that it thudded against their ear drums.

Peering down between his dangling feet, Elijah held his breath as the open maws of the Drillers snapped futilely at their rapidly rising prey.

Up and up they rose, sharp pain emanated from where vicious talons bit into his shoulders, Elijah closed his eyes against the swirling dust and pain, gritted his teeth and tried vainly to calm the building rise of panic.

Something bad was going to happen, he knew it with a frightening certainty, and the higher he rose up the rocky funnel towards the light, the stronger that feeling became.

"Well of course you're scared, you're about fifty feet up and rising and held in the claws of something out of your worst nightmares!" He muttered to himself, craning his head to one side in an attempt to see the others above him. With a surge of relief he realised that they were already at the top and hovering there for him to catch up, just a few more feet and he would be safe, well at least out of the cavern and out of reach of the Drillers for now. But then with a sting of fear, he became aware that he wasn't rising anymore, that the creature holding him had halted about ten feet below the others and was actually looking down at him.

As he met its jet black eyes, he saw what could only be described as a sneer curl its lipless mouth, and then, before he could take a breath to shout to the others, it released him from its grip to let him fall.

Luckily the shock forced a loud scream out of his throat before he had even thought about doing it; the next thing his terrified brain registered was a sudden tightness around his waist that squeezed his lungs of air as his rapid descent was halted and reversed.

Fighting his body's desire to pass out, Elijah felt himself swaying like a human conker on a string, except the string was in fact Ghelli's tail, and both he and his bat ride were barely managing to continue rising with the added weight. Painfully slowly they cleared the rim of the column and were finally clear to descend to the ground.

Gasping in breath to his starved lungs Elijah rolled away from the creature who had just saved his life as if it was fire.

As all of the others landed around him he crouched to the ground ready to run, glaring at their supposed rescuers with unbridled hostility.

Ranger rushed to his side, searching him all over for possible injury.

Elijah pushed him aside, shouting.

"They're all in on it we can't trust them!"

The other creatures reacted with high pitched sounds and sharp gestures that Elijah did not need Rangers special hearing to understand, they were protesting their innocence.

"They say that they do not know why he let you drop, that it was most likely an accident," said Ranger.

"Oh he knew exactly what he was doing, he waited until we were as high as possible and let me go, he even smiled when he did it!" snapped Elijah, fear and anger forging a new rough edge to his voice.

Silence fell around them as his words struck home.

"Smiled, you said that he smiled, what can this mean Ghelli?" Khizzi's voice was a frightened whisper from behind him.

"It means exactly what you're thinking that it means Khizzi, that he was under the control of Xan and it also means that we have evidently lost our element of surprise."

"Okay, I just know I'm going to regret asking this, but who or what is Xan?"

All three of his companions and the remaining three bat creatures turned in silence to face him.

"We do not have the time to explain that to you now; we are too exposed here, we must find shelter and cover before—"

Ranger's answer was cut short as the ground beneath them began to heave upwards toppling them all from their feet. They all knew what it was, and they all reacted instantly, rolling back onto their feet and running for the cover of a wall of dark trees, their three flying rescuers took to the air like flapping kites.

As the first of the Drillers surfaced they were at least a hundred yards into the depth of the forest, dodging the closely packed moss coated trunks as they slipped and slithered over the uneven rock strewn floor.

With immense relief, Elijah complied when Ghelli skidded to a halt, holding up his hand, finger on his lips to ensure silence, but gesturing that they should stop. Lungs burning the boy slumped to the damp ground, his head swimming and a loud buzzing filling his ears.

For what seemed an age they all huddled to the ground, straining to listen out for the dreaded sounds of pursuit.

Finally Ghelli let out the breath that he had been holding.

"I think that we have lost the Drillers; they will be extremely unwilling to follow us here."

"Well that's the first good news I've heard since |I got here!" said Elijah, standing up to stretch his cramped muscles.

"It's not exactly what you would call good news Elijah."

Elijah wheeled around to glare at Ranger, whose blue eyes met his without flinching.

"Okay, I probably won't like it but why?"

"This is the Forest of Souls, not a place to think of as sanctuary; few who enter get to leave, unchanged."

As the words left Rangers lips, a rustling and hissing sound seemed to suddenly break the suffocating silence around them and Elijah was sure that he could see movement in the deep shadows around them. He swallowed hard as his eyes darted from tree to tree but whatever it was remained elusive.

"We need to move and now, tread carefully and under no circumstances touch the trees!" whispered Ghelli urgently, heading back in the direction in which they had just entered the forest.

Picking their way delicately between the slippery, moss covered boulders, the group approached the fringe of the trees. There they halted and hunkered down to the ground in the shadows.

Each heart sank in their chest as they saw, waiting in the sunlight, four huge lumping figures swayed around on stumpy legs; sniffing the air through gaping nostrils; awaited them.

"So back into the forest then?"

Elijah was eager to put as much distance as possible between himself and these grotesque creatures that may, for all he knew have killed Burda.

Ghelli said nothing, Elijah could see the muscles of his jaws clenching and unclenching with indecision. Khizzi reached out and tentatively laid her long brown fingers on his arm, then gently squeezed. With a sigh of resignation, Ghelli looked deeply into the boy's eyes saying

"Keep behind me, step in my footsteps and touch nothing with your hands especially the trees, do not touch the trees."

28

Elijah had thought that the sight of the Drillers lying in wait for them was chilling enough, but the tone of Ghelli's voice drained his face of all colour; Ghelli was afraid.

As the party entered the gloom of the trees stepping like dancers between the rocks and boulders, his heart thudded so hard in his chest that Elijah was convinced that it could be heard by his companions, and worse still the statuesque trees that seemed to close in around them.

Deeper and deeper into the smothering darkness they picked their way, painstakingly careful not to step on the roots of the giant trees or touch the smooth bark. The silence was complete, even the soft sound of their footfalls seemed to be immediately absorbed by the warm, damp air, it felt like he was wearing earmuffs like the ridiculous furry ones that Burda had given him for his last birthday.

The memory of that day, laughing and gorging himself on the "death by chocolate cake" that was tradition for breakfast on his birthday brought hot tears bursting from his eyes to course down his cheeks. A gentle touch on his shoulder jerked him out of his reverie.

"Burda will have prevailed, do not underestimate her skills as a warrior, they far outweigh her culinary expertise."

It was Rangers soft voice from behind him, and it was as if he could read his mind, just like when-

"When I was your dog?"

"Don't do that, it's creepy!" Hissed Elijah, roughly brushing the other's fingers off his arm.

"I simply know you very well Elijah and can read your body language, you are missing your old life and it's only to-"

They were abruptly silenced by both Ghelli and Khizzi suddenly crouching flat to the ground in front of them, with hands clamped over their ears.

In a split second, Ranger and Elijah followed suit, for the air around them was filled with an ear piercing buzzing that threatened both their sanity and ear drums.

"What is it?" Elijah shouted but his voice was swallowed up before it had a chance to be heard.

"Skorpios are coming for you, you cannot escape; you must touch the tree!"

29

"Who said that?" Demanded Elijah, wiggling his fingers in his ears to try to dislodge the ever increasing buzzing.

"Touch the tree Elijah Grey before the Skorpios kill you all!" Almost without thinking, Elijah got to his feet and reached out his hand towards the nearest trunk, fingers spread.

"NO!" Both Ranger and Ghelli screamed in unison and lurched in his direction to stop him, but with no hope, his fingers made contact with the soft almost skin-like bark, and the world around him exploded.

# Chapter 7

From the instant of his first contact with the skin of the tree, Elijah felt his mind filled with voices, many voices all talking at the same time, in a language that was completely alien to him. He could still hear the approaching swarm, buzzing like a chain saw but it was as if he was inside a giant bubble, muffling the sound. Beneath his feet he could feel the ground heaving and tipping like a roller coaster, knocking him to his hands and knees. Out of his dream state came two pairs of gripping hands, lurching him back onto his feet and urging his unresponsive body into forward motion. Stumbling over the trembling ground, Elijah raised his dizzy head to stare blank eyed upwards, the sight of hordes of huge red and black creatures with snapping pincers impacting on an impassable barrier formed by the canopy of interlocking branches above him, only half registered in his crowded brain.

The voices were all beginning to say the same word and slowly, very slowly, it began to make sense to him, the word was RUN.

But he wasn't running, he was flying, or at least that's what it felt like because he couldn't feel his feet making contact with the ground but the world was whizzing past him in a blur.

Surrendering his mind to the voices, he realised that he was in fact the subject of a heated argument.

"He must be saved, take him to the Waterloggers, they will take him to Ryufu he will be safe there."

"No! Xan will find him there and kill him, he must be taken to the heart of the forest, we can hide him, protect him for her, for when she returns."

"She will not return until he rescues her, and there is no-one in the forest who can show him where she is."

"But dead he is of no use to any of us!"

Elijah desperately tried to make his mouth form words in order to have his say since it was his demise that they were arguing about but he found that he could not even feel his lips let alone use them. Panic threatened to over whelm him, as he realised that, though his

31

mind was acutely aware of every minute sound around him, the creaking and snapping as the tree canopy stretched and writhed in order to form the protective shield that was keeping the angry Skorpios, the laboured breathing of his companions as they struggled to keep up with him, he couldn't feel anything, and had no control over his own body at all.

Squeezing his eyes tightly shut, he focussed his mind on just the voices of the trees, he could see colours and shapes swirling behind his eyelids, and achingly slowly, they began to coalesce into one shape, it was a face.

There was something about the features and especially the coal black eyes that seemed strangely familiar to him, and as they suddenly locked with his, he felt no fear.

"Trust the Forest of Souls, they will protect you my son, but tell no one that you have seen me, and as soon as you possibly can, leave them behind and come to me alone, I will be waiting."

Desperately Elijah tried to form words in his mind, but before he could the image had disappeared into the swirling mist in his mind, and sighing heavily he surrendered to his fate, allowing the moving branches that cradled his body to project him ever onward towards whatever destination they had in mind.

Within seconds he recognised the roaring sound that was increasingly blotting out the voices of the trees, water, crashing roaring water, he was being carried towards what was unmistakably a waterfall.

"We must escape Khizzi, we will not survive the fall and if we do the Waterloggers will finish us off!"

Through the haze in his brain, Elijah heard Ghelli's voice.

"We cannot break through their branches Ghelli, outside are the Skorpios, and I'd rather risk the Waterfall and the Waterloggers than be stung to death!"

Rangers reply drifted towards him as if through a thick curtain, muffling the fear in his voice.

There was no more time for responses, as steel bright light abruptly illuminated their world as all four suddenly broke through the thick protective canopy of the forest and hung suspended for a heartbeat in the crystal clear air at the head of the waterfall; before, with an audible snap, the trees released them, to plummet downwards to the awaiting rocks.

# Chapter 8

As the branches that had been supporting him retracted back into the forest, the stupor also disappeared from his mind, so it was with terrifying clarity that Elijah plunged downwards in the bone freezing column of white that robbed him of the ability to breathe for what seemed like minutes but was in truth mere seconds.

As he hit the surface of the broiling, water bowl, sharp rocks grazed his shoulder and head, the buffeting water pounding the last air from his lungs, and then came utter silence and he felt nothing more.

He did not feel the clawed hands reach out of the cold darkness to grip him like a vice. He did not feel his head break the surface of the churning water and life giving air rush into his straining lungs. He did not feel himself propelled swiftly towards the banks, held tightly against a hard scaly skinned body that swam against the powerful current with awesome ease.

The first thing Elijah was aware of was the hard stones biting into his back and the uncontrollable shivering that had infected every chilled muscle in his body. Coughing and spitting up the last water from his lungs he struggled to sit up, but was pushed roughly back down onto the painful shingle and a voice hissed into his ear that made every hair on his neck stand rigid.

"Keep down and keep still Raven boy if you value your life!"

Scared to move a muscle, Elijah lay, barely even daring to breath, as above him the brightness was suddenly obscured as if the sun had been switched off.

It was not clouds that he saw when he looked up, it was a thick swarm of Skorpios, red and black bodies writhing, inky claws snapping in the air and long whip like tails flicking side to side, spitting out venom in a rain of stinging droplets.

As the venom drops touched his bare skin they sizzled and burned like neat acid. Instinctively Elijah swatted them away with his hand, but found it clamped down motionless against his face and again the rough voice hissed into his ear.

"They respond to movement, trust me, a few blisters will be far better than what you'll get if that lot attack!"

Closing his eyes and desperately focussing on not reacting to the hot stinging pain all over his body, Elijah realised that he could hear a soft grunting coming from close by, telling him that Ghelli, Khizzi and Ranger were also suffering.

After what seemed like an age, but was probably only a matter of seconds, both the high pitched angry buzzing and the stinging rain receded and then disappeared completely. Tentatively, Elijah peered upwards, and, with a silent sigh of relief saw that the sky above them was clear, blue and empty of all but the blood red sun. Slowly he eased his creaking muscles into action and sat up, waited for the fizzing in his head to abate, then stood up on jellified legs.

Looking down over his body, he wasn't surprised to discover that his jeans and sweat shirt were spattered with small round holes, beneath which his skin was red and sore, but he was at least still in one piece!

"Elijah, are you okay?" Ranger's worried face was also freckled with blisters and beside him Ghelli and Khizzi were already starting to rub at their own blisters.

Before he could answer, a large shadow loomed up behind him, reminding him with a jolt that they were not alone.

"Best not to touch the blisters they heal quicker, and best to get out of sight, they'll spot us soon enough if we stand here gabbing."

Turning to look for the first time at his rescuer, Elijah had to swallow hard to prevent crying out loud. The creature standing behind him, seemed to read his mind, as its face split into a distinctly crocodilian grin, exposing sharply pointed teeth, through which it chuckled mirthlessly.

"Yep that's the reaction I was expecting to get from a soft skinned out-worlder, even though I've just risked my own skin, thick as it is, to save his. Now what you must decide Raven boy is whether or not you trust your eyes or your heart; what do you reckon, is Brogan a good guy or bad guy?"

With that he slapped himself on his broad chest and bowed low to the ground with all the sarcasm he could muster.

Elijah narrowed his eyes as he scrutinised the strange creature standing before him. His skin, where it was exposed, looked tough and leathery, and was covered in small wart like lumps and bumps, and yet was the colour of his own skin. What clothes he wore were now in tatters from the acidic Skorpio rain, but his arms and legs, hands and feet were all completely unscathed. Somehow Elijah was not surprised by the long muscular tail that twitched from side to side behind him, grazing the pebbled shore with the soft sound of waves. Finally meeting the creature's unblinking gaze, he smiled.

"The trees told me to trust the Waterloggers, I assume that they were referring to you so I'm going with good guy but with reservations if that's okay with you."

For a heartbeat a black glint glittered in the eyes that met his, then the creature laughed like a lightning crack and slapped his clawed and webbed hand down hard on the boy's back almost winding him.

"Raven boy, against all odds and my better judgement, I think I might grow to like you! Come let us move into the shadows before the Skorpios return and rob me of the opportunity!"

Heading off without a glance towards the others, he strode off towards the sheltering cover of the trees, quickly vanishing into the shadows.

"A good decision Elijah, quickly don't lose sight of him for he will not wait!" Urged Ranger as he took up position behind Elijah, glancing nervously up at the sky.

As he stumbled forward, Elijah realised that the shadows that they were entering were not in fact produced by trees as he had first assumed, but gigantic umbrella shaped leaves, the underside of which were covered in vicious looking spikes, and that the stems on which they swayed were as thick as his thighs. Thankful for the instantly complete protection that they provided, he found himself relaxing enough to concentrate on studying the taut and rigidly upright form ahead of him.

Obviously more at home in water than on land, Brogan was breathing heavily in hissing breaths and sweat glistened in large droplets on his exposed skin before rolling off onto the ground as if off a window pane. His thick muscular neck was so short that it virtually merged with his skull, making movement of his head almost impossible without bringing his broad shoulders into play as well. The bulk of his height, on closer inspection, was achieved by an extremely elongated torso, as his arms and legs were fairly short in comparison, another factor in his movement on land being so laboured.

Curiosity finally got the better of Elijah, and he turned to Ghelli who was loping effortlessly along beside him and whispered.

"Is he—?"

"Yes, and a very sensitive race they are too, so keep any further questions to yourself!" Ghelli snapped back without pausing.

"Oh, right, I just won-"

Elijah swallowed the rest of his response when Ghelli glared silently in his direction.

Khizzi's small hand touched his arm and she leaned her head in close to his ear to say,

"Take no offence from my brother; danger makes him tense and tension robs him of his manners!"

The subtle reference to the fact that they were indeed still in very imminent danger spurred his legs into a new surge of movement, although for all he knew they could be propelling him into a worse situation than the one that he had just escaped!

As the roaring of the white water behind them hushed to a whisper, a smothering silence closed around them to replace it. The light beneath the canopy of overlapping leaves was soft and green, making the straight back in front of him look even more crocodilian.

Scrubbing at the now intensely itchy blisters all over his arms and face, Elijah realised that the other three were also scratching as they walked.

"What was that stuff?" He whispered, to no one in particular.

"Oh don't worry Raven Boy, the blisters'll fade in an hour or so, it was only Skorpio drool, not their venom now that would have taken you entire hide off minutes before you died in agony."

The fact that the owner of the voice showed no signs of any blisters came as no surprise now to Elijah, and just as he was forming another question to ask, their rescuer halted and dropped to the ground. Instinctively Ranger, Ghelli, Khizzi and Elijah dropped too, flat to the ground, holding their breath.

"Now what?" thought the boy, tensing himself for the next assault.

But what followed was a lot of scuffling and muffled grunts as a second Waterlogger appeared out of the verdant darkness and boisterously greeted the first. Slapping him soundly on the back and making soft snuffling sounds that could have been words but not in a language that Elijah had ever heard.

Finally turning to face the other three as if only just becoming aware of their existence, the newcomer bent his long muscular body somewhat awkwardly into a bow before focussing his narrow eyes on Elijah.

"Ryufu is expecting you, the trees sent a message warning that you had already made your presence too widely known for your own good, I am to take you to him as quickly as possible, follow me and tread carefully".

Unwilling to simply obey when so far almost every move he had made had just got him further into trouble, Elijah stood his ground. A gentle touch on his arm, had the same effect as an electric shock; it was Khizzi's small brown hand and she leaned her face close to his to whisper.

"The Waterloggers might look untrustworthy but if the Trees did in fact send you to them then they must be trusted, the Trees do not lie."

Ghelli coughed loudly behind them, he obviously did not share her opinion, and he had after all told Elijah not to touch the trees as they had entered the Forest of Souls.

Indecision froze the boy's limbs in mid-stride. Refusing to glance in Rangers' direction for advice, he huffed out the breath that he had been subconsciously holding, feeling the strange sensation of long hair being puffed upwards from his forehead, he had no idea just how long he had been here, but his hair had obviously grown.

"Well I don't really trust anything or anyone in this place, so following them isn't any more risky than anything else!" he muttered, shrugging his shoulders and launching off behind the Waterloggers. Behind him he could actually feel the indignation radiating from Ghelli, which made him smile, although the slouch of Rangers shoulders spoiled his victory somewhat.

Before very long the canopy of huge umbrella shaped leaves began to thin and finally ended; leaving the group dangerously exposed to the open sky above.

They crouched beneath the last of the protective, staring across the yawning space that opened up before them. Flat and featureless, it offered no cover, and high above they could already hear the distant humming of the Skorpio swarm.

On the far side of the divide was a dark wall of trees, beckoning invitingly, but in order to reach them, they would have to make a dash of at least a hundred yards.

"Don't even consider a dash for the likes of us, we're not built for speed on land," Panted Brogan, sweat now running freely down his face.

"What do you think Elijah?" asked Ranger turning to face the boy, and ignoring the snort of derision from Ghelli.

"Me? Why ask me, I have no idea at all, this is your world not mine!"

Ranger moved closer to Elijah and stared deep into his eyes and whispered.

"But you have talked to the Forest of Souls, what do they tell you to do now?"

With a jolt, Elijah suddenly became aware of a soft voice in his head, almost like one of those tunes that get stuck there for hours when you've only heard them once. Slowly, as he focussed inwards, he realised that he could discern words that were actually saying something to him. Straining to understand them, he suddenly jerked upright and shouted out, "Step back, step back quickly!"

Without question, all of the party did so, and just in the nick of time too, as the ground where they had just been standing seemed to rear up before them like a giant ghoul, with the deafening sound of wood splitting apart in agony.

Up out of the ground heaved the long writhing roots of the distant line of trees, ripping apart the sun hardened soil like soft beach sand, to form the entrance of what appeared to be a tunnel under ground to traverse the gap between the group and the Forest.

"Wow, now that's what I call an answer!" laughed Ranger, starting forward to enter the beckoning darkness.

"Wait!" snapped Ghelli, slapping his arm across Ranger's chest to halt him in his tracks.

"How do we know that this is not another trap?"

"Well my suspicious friend, we don't, but we also have no other choice unless you fancy another tussle with them." replied Brogan, gesturing upwards.

The sky above them was rapidly darkening as the gathering swarm thickened and closed in.

Wordlessly, Elijah took a deep breath, gritted his teeth and stepped down into the cool darkness of the tunnel, not really caring whether or not his companions followed, he had absolutely no intention of dealing with another Skorpio attack.

Behind him he heard them all scrabbling over the floor of the tunnel, and grunts as Brogan and the other Waterlogger bumped their heads on the roots hanging down from the roof of the tunnel.

Within seconds, they were fumbling their way along in almost complete darkness, having to use their hands to feel their way forwards,

The rich smell of damp soil clogged their nostrils, and Elijah could feel the constant soft falling rain of soil tickling his skin. All around him he could hear the straining of the roots as they prized apart the hard ground and held it there for them to pass through, and he realised that behind them, the tunnel was swiftly sealing itself again. Stirrings of claustrophobia threatened to overwhelm him but he marched onwards, knowing that this was his only means of surviving, keep moving, don't falter, and don't look back.

# Chapter 9

As the circle of red sky snapped shut behind them like a camera lens, Burda felt her throat clench and her heart falter. Well, he was there now, after all the waiting and watching, they had been caught napping!

"I knew I should have trusted that feeling in my water this morning, if I had, I would have made sure—the Eye of Ula! He doesn't have the Eye of Ula!"

Physically slapping her blood smeared rocky cheek, she wheeled around to face the last three Drillers left standing.

"Now you my friends are in my way now, I must get back to the house for the Eye of Ula, so,"

With that she forged forward through the knee deep mud, wielding her wood axe around her head and bringing it down on the necks of all three in succession without breaking her stride or even looking back to check that all three slumped to the ground headless.

As she mounted the veranda steps she tossed the dripping axe aside and charged through the door, terror clad her fierce features now, as the door had been open, and she knew that she had closed it.

"Please be there, please be there!" She muttered like a mantra as she headed outside to the back yard, peripherally aware that the house had been trashed by someone looking for the treasure that she hoped so fervently she had hidden well enough. Plunging her long fat arm shoulder deep into the water butt by the back porch, she finally allowed a hot tear to escape her eye. It was still there, safely wallowing around in the water in its waterproof pouch.

Hesitating just long enough to clutch it gratefully to her blood stained chest, Burda took a deep breath and smiled.

"Now, it's just a simple case of getting it to him, no problem for Burda huh?"

Chuckling to herself, and realising that this was the first time she had truly been alone since she was sent here with Ranger to hide the special baby, fifteen years ago; Burda lumbered off down the deer path that led into the heart of the forest and the doorway that she hoped would still be open.

# Chapter 10

Searing light scorched Elijah's retinas as they all suddenly burst out of the tunnel into the shock of day light.

The second shock came immediately afterwards; there was nothing beneath their feet.

As he plummeted downwards at an alarming speed, Elijah felt sand stinging his face and clogging his nostrils, a deafening hissing filled his ears.

"Spread out your arms and legs Elijah, it will slow your descent!"

Above the hissing of sand, he had no idea whose voice he was hearing, but he obeyed, feeling the smooth sand now running beneath his fingers, and his rate of descent slowed as the surface beneath him began to level out like a playground slide.

"Brace yourself for-"

He had no time to obey that one, as his whole body slammed into what felt like a wall, and he lay, totally winded and stunned as a wave of burning hot sand rapidly buried him.

Lack of oxygen began to make his brain buzz in his skull like an angry wasp and panic overwhelmed him as he tried unsuccessfully to move even a hand to free himself.

From out of the suffocating sand enclosing him, Elijah heard voices shouting his name over and over, but he couldn't even part his lips enough to whisper let alone shout back.

Suddenly, as he could feel the life draining out of him, Elijah thought of his dog, Ranger. He had always told Burda that Ranger was not just an ordinary run of the mill dog and that he was so smart that most of the time he knew what Elijah needed even before the boy knew himself. Burda would simply chuckle and shake her head making her chunky shoulders wobble.

"I need you to find me Ranger." He now thought, wishing for all the world that he was back on the porch watching his friend dig frantically in the dirt for a bone long since buried. Suddenly his sluggish brain registered that it was not in fact the soil spray from the dog's digging splattering over him but loose sand, and he heard the words,

"I'm coming Elijah Grey, hold on!"

Out of the smothering heat around his face, plunged a pair of searching hands that grabbed hold of the shoulders of his sweat shirt and yanked him up and out of the sand.

There he knelt gasping in precious breaths, filling his straining lungs with hot air and spitting out sand.

Rocking backwards to sit with his head on his knees he shakily whispered.

"Is everyone else okay?"

"We have all survived, as have you thanks entirely to Ranger, he just seemed to know where to dig."

Cautiously looking up, sand still clogging his eyelashes, Elijah met the gaze of his erstwhile doggie companion. The serious angular features that faced him were frozen in an almost smile.

"Th-thanks Ranger, thanks for finding me." The boy muttered, still not able to adjust to the fact that the faithful dog who had been his constant companion all of his life, now walked on two feet, and was a man.

Rangers smile faded, and he sighed softly as he nodded his head.

"So what in the world was it that I hit?" Asked Elijah to quickly move on from the tense awkwardness of the present situation.

"Pah! This outworlder has to be the least observant creature that has ever walked!" Retorted Ghelli, leaping to his feet in a shower of sand and pointing Elijah's face upwards.

Blinking out the last grits from his eyes, Elijah felt the blood once again drain from his face.

Rearing up out of the red sand, so tall that he couldn't actually see its summit was a tower like none he had ever seen. Its smooth stone walls gleamed like marble reflecting the fiery red of the desert out of which it erupted.

"Behold, Elijah Grey, the Tower of Odora, last refuge of travellers on the Sea of Echoes, and that into which you bumped!"

Brogan's voice reflected the effort his short legged physique had just expended, and he leaned forward, hands on knees to cough and wheeze.

"But this is a desert, not a sea, why is it called that?"

"Always the stupid questions from this boy, get moving before you find out first hand why it is called a sea!" Snapped Ghelli, angrily pushing Elijah towards the base of the tower, and almost sending him sprawling face first into the sand.

As his hands touched the burning surface, Elijah's retort died on his lips as he felt a distinct vibration sizzling up through his palms and resonating in his chest.

"Quickly Elijah you must run!"

This time it was Khizzi who wrapped her brown tail tightly around his waist and virtually yanked him off of his feet, leaving him running through the air like a cartoon character towards the shining walls of the tower.

By the time they reached the bottom of the Tower, Elijah was acutely aware of a loud booming that seemed to emanating out of the sand around them. He also realised that the surface on which he was now standing seemed to be rising up around his feet.

"Where is the door Ghelli, I can't remember!"

The raw panic in Khizzi's voice was enough to send Elijah's pulse racing off the scale. He could see for himself now that the level of the sand around him was rapidly rising, and sucking at his legs as it did.

Ghelli gave no reply, but was frantically running his hands over the seemingly unadorned and unbroken smoothness of the walls. Joining him, Ranger and Brogan skirted the curved base, staggering in the now waist deep wave of red sand.

Suddenly, Elijah heard another sound above the roaring sand around him, he heard the distinct sound of a voice, and it was one that he had been convinced he would never hear again.

"No time to be polite, break it for the sake of Pete!"

Before he could truly register the shock, something large whistled past his ear and thudded into the wall with a sickening sound of breaking glass.

"Get in before it heals itself!"

At least four pairs of hands shoved Elijah towards a large craggy hole in the wall of the tower. He landed in a heap along with the others; winded and head buzzing.

Watching the ragged hole seal itself before his eyes, plunging them all into near darkness, all he could focus on was that voice, he dare not ask, for fear that he might be wrong. Before he had a chance, however, he felt himself pulled to his feet and urged forward until his searching outstretched hands grabbed hold of what could only be a bannister.

"Up Elijah Grey!"

So up, he stumbled.

Step after never ending step, until his thigh muscles screamed in agony and his lungs burned in his chest. Just when he thought that he could go no further, the space around him exploded into light and he collapsed wheezing and blinded, onto his hands and knees. Behind him stumbled his companions, one by one bursting into the blessed relief at the end of the spiral stair case. Rolling over to lay gasping in air and staring at the high vaulted ceiling above him, Elijah took a few moments to recover his breath and slow down his thudding heart. All around him, he was aware of soft, muffled sounds as the others began to struggle to their feet and reluctantly his mind prodded him into the same action.

Suddenly, he heard it again, directly behind him, a ragged grating voice, and its owner did not sound happy!

"What was the last thing I said to you? Look after him mangy mutt, and what do you do? You take him to them damn trees, you throw him into the river and almost drown him, and then to cap it all you try to bury him in the sand!"

A flood of conflicting emotions engulfed him, as he watched the broad lumpy shoulders shake in that oh so familiar way as she stood, hands on hips, berating poor Ranger like an errant toddler.

"Burda, is that really you?" He whispered, fighting to control his urgent desire to cry and hug her at the same time.

Wheeling around, the huge hulk of a woman let out a loud bellow like a bull and launched herself towards Elijah, swept him up into a rib cracking embrace and spun around with his feet dangling in the air.

"Elijah Grey you are the best thing that these eyes have seen since bacon for breakfast!"

Suddenly, all of the supressed fear and warring emotions of the last two days, rose up and crashed over Elijah like a tidal wave. He burst into tears in Burda's arms and sobbed loudly in wracking gasps, interspersed with hysterical laughter.

Lost in the moment they forgot that they were not alone until an awkward cough from Ghelli shocked them apart to stand avoiding eye contact and hastily scrubbing away the tracks of tears from their grimy cheeks.

"Ahem, it's good to see you Burda, I was really worried about you when we left you fighting off those things in the forest." Elijah muttered, rubbing his hands down the length of his thighs, eyes still cast downward in embarrassment.

"Pah, they were no match for my trusty log splitter, damn shame I left it down at the bottom of those stairs! Lost without it I am!"

She replied, slapping him unnecessarily hard on his back, sending him flying across the room and almost flat on his face.

Ignoring the barely stifled sniggers from Brogan and Ghelli, Elijah managed to regain his composure before adding.

"Well when I've got my breath back, I'd be happy to go back down and get it for you."

"And how will you do that Elijah Grey? Please tell!"

Turning towards the voice, Elijah frowned at Khizzi, whose brown face grinned back at his puzzled expression.

Looking around him, he now realised that the trap door through which they had all staggered earlier at the top of the spiral staircase that had appeared to be never ending, no longer existed. The dusty wooden floor was unbroken.

"But-! " He stuttered, searching around determined to find what his heart told him was not there to find.

"It is part of the Towers defences, once ascended, the stairs retract into the sand, and will only reappear for travellers who approach when the tide is out," said Ranger quietly.

"Why do you lot keep talking about tides, it's a desert out there, deserts don't have tides, and waves, they have sand and dunes that's fact!"

Stomping angrily over to one of the open windows that stared out over the surrounding landscape, Elijah jutted his head out and pointed at the horizon, without actually looking.

"See, no waves, it's a desert!"

Glaring inwards, he went from one face to the next, each pair of eyes met his steadily without flinching until he finally reached Burda, who did her one eye brow raise that always meant, stop and think young man.

Reluctantly he turned his head back to look out at the red vista before him, his jaw sagged open and he blew out a sigh of resignation.

# Chapter 11

"It is called the Sea of Echoes and it is inadvisable to look at it for too long Elijah Grey."

"Why Khizzi, will it start talking to me like the trees of the Forest of Souls did, because I think I can handle that!" The boy answered more sarcastically than he had intended and was aware of Khizzi physically flinching beside him, but found that he couldn't pull his gaze from the rhythmic rise and fall of the rolling waves of red sand that rumbled towards the tower and broke in a sizzling shower of sand over its sides.

"Because the Sea of Echoes has claimed many thousands of victims over the centuries, and unlike water, when drowned in sand, the corpse does not decay, but is-"

"Mummified, oh crap, they're mummified!" Cried Elijah, desperate to look away from the visions of horror which had just reared up out of the crest of the latest wave to break over the tower; but his bulging eyes remained glued to the grotesque eyeless sockets and gaping death grin of a skull just feet away from him.

"Unfortunately it is not merely their bodies that the sand preserves, their pain is also contained in the waves, as you can probably now hear." Whispered Khizzi, placing a tentative hand on his shoulder and subtly winding her long prehensile tail loosely around his waist.

Her words didn't register to his ears as they were indeed now filled with a low plaintive cry that resonated through his bones and transfixed his frozen mind. He could almost discern words, but it was like trying to hear someone talking in a storm, the hissing of the sand waves seemed to steal the words away just before they reached his ears. He leaned further and further out over the edge of the balcony, drawn like a moth to a flame, yearning to hear what the ghastly apparitions were telling him. Head after head bobbed ghoulishly atop the waves, dried brown skin stretched tightly over gaping mouths in a frozen scream;

except that now they seemed to be inviting him to join them, and dive in. Slowly the sounds in his head began to change from howls of despair to melodic singing, and in comparison the growing urgency in the voices of his companions took on a sharpness like a saw going through metal.

"I'm coming!" He whispered as he launched himself off the balcony and braced himself for the loving warm embrace of the soft red sand.

As he toppled, he was jerked roughly back inside the Tower by the waist, to roll winded on the floor. Inside his head he felt the hold of the Sea of Echoes snap like a broken elastic band. Full clarity returned with the rather over enthusiastic shaking he was receiving from Burda.

Reaching for her huge hand on his shoulder, Elijah first tapped then slapped until she realised that she could stop shaking.

Struggling to shaky feet, he felt Khizzi uncurl her tail, and realised that she had saved him yet again from what would undoubtedly have been a gruesome end, he smiled shyly and she returned it fleetingly before she turned away, her long brown sinuous tail, coiling itself lovingly around her waist.

"You boy, are far too susceptible to be left alone for a second! From now on, one of us must be keeping tabs on you at all times if we're going to deliver you in one piece to Ryufu."

Brogan was obviously suffering badly in the dry heat, even the effort of speech caused rivulets of sweat to drizzle down his face, stout neck and evaporate on his gnarled shoulders.

"I don't need a baby sitter, but I do need to have someone actually sit down and tell me just where we are, what's going on, and why the hell I've been allowed to live for fifteen years in complete ignorance of it all; and this time no lies, half- truths or sugar coating it to protect me, that's exactly what's nearly got me killed at least three times!"

The silence that followed his demand was deafening, and the panic stricken looks that flashed from face to face around him almost made him choke.

"Well? Surely one of you can at least say something, Burda?"

The huge woman's shoulders bunched beneath her ears and then sagged as she blew out a sigh of resignation.

"Sit Elijah Grey, I will tell what I know, it may not be what is best but I know you well enough to recognise that look!"

Glancing around the circular space, and seeing no place better; Elijah sank down where he stood, folding his long thin legs beneath him. Burda slumped down beside him to his left and one by one the others followed suit until the company was all seated in a circle on the bare dusty floor of the Tower in the fading russet light.

"All I can tell you is the part that Ranger and I have played so far, so that will have to be enough. We were sent through the doorway, with you as a week old baby, we were told to find somewhere safe to live, to protect you with our lives, and to wait and watch for a sign that it was the right time to return. As you know, that plan went to the fan three days ago when those who seek to kill you found the doorway and sent the Drillers to do just that."

He wasn't sure what he had been expecting, but the blunt assertion that someone or something was genuinely trying to kill him; left Elijah literally speechless. Questions buzzed around in his brain, but couldn't find his voice.

"Pha! Tell it how it is why don't you? Or was it your aim to steal the boys tongue and scare him so much that he wets his pants!" Brogan growled, before reaching round Ranger who was seated to Elijah's right, to slap the stunned boy soundly on his back.

"She left out the bit about us all 'aving your back Raven Boy, don't let old rubble face frighten you so much that you make the Tower your final restin' place cos you're being frozen stiff with fear!"

His rough voice, and that slap, broke the boy's stasis and he turned to Brogan.

"And what's with the Raven Boy stuff, why do you keep calling me that?"

Brogan roared out a laugh that echoed around the curved walls,

"Well that one's easy to answer, have you looked at yourself recently?"

"Brogan! Now is not the time to-"

50

"No! Now is exactly the time, what do I look like? What does he mean?"

Elijah watched the same furtive, expression flit from face to face, and not one pair of downcast eyes would meet his own.

It was finally Ranger who spoke.

"Elijah Grey. As you know, when I was living in the cabin with you, I wore the body of a white dog, this was partly by choice, partly not. In this world, the inhabitants all carry some genes that are not human but animal; you yourself originate from this world, therefore, now that you are here…"

It felt as if Rangers words were coming to him through a wall of ice cold water that had just washed over Elijah from head to toe. He felt sick, and light headed, and struggled to breath.

"You mean I'm, that I'm l-like you, part animal, not human, that I—"

Involuntarily, his trembling hand went up to touch his face; what met his tingling finger tips was the last straw, blackness descended over his eyes as Elijah Grey collapsed to the dust covered floor as the last of the red light faded from the sky.

# Chapter 12

All through that night, Elijah slept fitfully, surrounded by his anxious companions. Nightmares about waking up and discovering that he had sprouted wings and a huge chiselled beak caused the boy to grunt and whimper, images of mummified eyeless faces screamed silently out of billowing red waves towards him, crashed over him, robbing him of breath and he could feel himself being dragged down beneath the sand sea by heavy, water logged feathers which now covered his body.

Outside, the Sea of Echoes sent wave after wave of blood red sand to break against the smooth walls of the tower, none of those trapped in the darkness, dared to let their eyes wander out of the windows. The sight of dead hands clawing above the churning surface, or black mouths stretched wide in a never ending plea for help, was not one that any of them wanted; they had enough to contend with inside the tower!

Gradually, one by one, they gave in to exhaustion and by the time that the first rays of morning light slanted across the room, it found six slumped bodies.

Rosy light gleamed softly over the closed eyes of Elijah Grey, a sharp shadow was cast down his now thin features by the main source of his distress, his beak shaped nose that jutted out from a pronounced brow ridge and deeply sunken eye sockets. As he flinched in his sleep, a cascade of raven black hair, now long enough to reach down to his waist, scattered onto the dusty floor like an oil slick. Gone forever were the freckles and snub noise of the green eyed fifteen year old who had set out that Saturday morning for his normal walk in the forest with his canine best friend. He had, in fact, also grown at least six inches in height, giving him an overall long, leggy and sinewy appearance, and in dire need of new, longer trousers!

The loud yowling call from outside had the same effect on all slumbering figures. Jerking upright into ready to fight stance, they instinctively formed a protective circle with Elijah at its centre.

"What was that? You heard it too right?" He stammered, unwilling to trust any of his own senses any more.

Ghelli and Brogan placed digits on pursed lips in unison and motioned to the others to remain, whilst they slid silently over towards the viewing window. Elijah was unaware that he was holding his breath until the tension in both sets of shoulder muscles visibly relaxed and they signalled for the others to join them.

Very reluctantly, after his previous experience, he leaned out over the window sill and gaped.

There was now no sign at all of the Sea of Echoes. Far below him, the surface was once more a flat, featureless desert, for as far as the eye could see. Squinting against the full glare of the red sun, following the direction of their two pointing fingers; at first he saw nothing, just a horizon that could have been drawn with a pen.

Then, on the sultry wind that brushed his cheeks, he heard it again, almost a word but still a howl, lifting and dipping and sending the hairs on the back of his neck prickling to attention. Slowly, what had first appeared to be a small, insignificant dot on the horizon grew larger as it rapidly drew nearer and nearer to the base of the tower. Within seconds, the identity of the approaching dot became clear, and stunned Elijah when he had woken up thinking that this world had no more surprises!

Looking down, he could easily now see the running figure as it raced towards them. It ran on all fours and moved with a fluid speed that seemed to effortlessly skim over the surface of the desert; creating only the whisper of a dust cloud in its wake.

"Who or what is that? Friend or foe?" He asked no-one in particular.

"That is a who, and she is called Kwatili, and she is exactly who we need right now!"

The undisguised tone of utter relief in Ghelli's voice took Elijah completely by surprise.

"Wow," he thought, "If Ghelli actually approves of this person, they really must be something special!"

"And no to the next question about to burst out of that mouth of yours Elijah Grey, this is not the time for more explanations; this is the time for getting the heck down there as fast as possible!" Snapped Burda.

She didn't need to say this, however, as inside his head the voice of the Forest of Souls was urging the same.

"Get out of the Tower Elijah Grey, Go to the stairs now!

"Urm, not that you'll like this, but the trees are telling me to go to the stairs." He said without turning from the sight approaching in the sand.

"Were you not listening Raven Boy? The Tower stairs are a one way street!" said Brogan, ignoring the black glare that his continued use of Raven Boy drew from both Burda and Khizzi.

"But I'm listening to the voices of the trees right now, and they're telling me to-"

Running into the centre of the room, Elijah dropped to his hands and knees, and began desperately searching its smooth surface with his fingertips.

"Ahah, this would be what they're talking about!" He cried in triumph, as he slipped his finger through a thick metal ring that had definitely not been there before, and pulled.

All mouths dropped open in time with the trap door that miraculously now gave way to the dark stairway down.

"Hah Raven Boy, I will never under estimate you or those trees of yours again!" Guffawed Brogan, digging Ghelli so hard in the ribs that the small man doubled over.

Burda said nothing, but a frown wrinkled the already furrowed skin between her tiny beady eyes.

"I suggest we go down sharp like, who knows how long those shrubs can keep this open!" Added Brogan, ushering the group towards the entrance to the tightly turning spiral steps.

"I will go first, you bring up the rear Burda, since you will be the slowest." Ghelli ordered, ignoring the expressions ranging from embarrassment to outrage as he pushed past Elijah to drop swiftly down the first steps and disappear from sight. Frozen for a second of indecision, the rest were prompted into following him, by a new sound from outside the tower, the howling had definitely become a word, and it was run.

As he stumbled down the shallow steps behind Ghelli; the cool darkness entombed him immediately and by the second tight turn in the stairs, Elijah was unable to see anything at all. Fumbling his cold fingers down the chill stone walls either side of him, he could only trust that each time he put a foot forward it would find something solid to step onto.

Down and down they went, remembering the gruelling journey up those stairs the night before, his legs began to tremble with the strain and he longed for light.

Behind him he could hear the others stumbling and suffering too, along with more than a few choice words from Burda at the rear. The claustrophobic darkness and monotony of the descent caused a swarm of questions to infest his mind again, but he forced himself to focus on not falling forward onto Ghelli and shut a mental door on them; but vowed that someone was going to answer each and every one of them!

Abrupt sunlight erupted in front of him as Ghelli launched himself against the door at the end of the steps and it buckled outwards into the sand.

"Quickly, we've got to get away from the tower straight way!" Yelled Elijah, no one now even bothering to ask how he knew this, they all just ran as fast as the knee deep sand would allow.

"Okay, that's far enough!" he panted, his lungs reacting to the scorching air and exertion.

As they all slumped into the desert and looked towards their erstwhile sanctuary, what they saw chilled them to the bone, roasting heat or not.

Beginning with the roof, then rapidly working down the shiny stone walls, the Tower of Odora was turning to dust. Layer by layer, as they watched spellbound and horrified; the beautiful building, which had stood amid the Sea of Echoes for centuries, withstanding its ghoulish pounding waves, was literally crumbling into the desert before their eyes.

Stunned silence hung over the company as they watched the last inches of the walls and stairs dissolve, and leave no sign that it had ever risen resplendent and defiant out of the sand.

"We do not have the luxury of time to grieve for the falling of a building when our whole world is under threat, rise and walk or die where you sit!"

This was a new voice, and Elijah staggered to his unsteady feet and whirled around to face its owner.

The figure that met his eyes was simply the most glorious sight that he had ever seen in his fifteen years of life.

Kwatili rose out of the sand to stand erect and regal before them. Brushing the sand from her arms and hands, her amber eyed gaze was locked on his eyes alone. He had the alarming sensation that she could see what he was thinking, see right inside him. He felt his cheeks flush hot and red, because he couldn't stop himself from gawping like a kid in a sweet shop. Her body, legs, arms and neck were all elongated and slender, and clad head to foot not in clothes of any kind but a soft downy covering of amber fur, dotted all over by chocolate thumbprint size spots. In place of hair her head too, was covered in the same amber fur, although it grew longer into soft tufts that formed a crest down the centre of her head and down the back of her long, slender neck. As if all of this was not enough to take his breath away, his eyes wandered down over her face and an involuntary "Wow!" escaped his lips before he could stop it.

An amused smile curved graciously along her lips, showing brief glimpses of sharp pointed teeth, the golden glint of her eyes was starkly accentuated by the ink black marking that formed a mask across her eye socket and then ran in a broad stripe down her face either side of her flattened nose.

"Kwatili, Princess of the desert, you have no idea how pleased I am to see you!" Ranger strode forward then dipped his head and shoulders in a deep bow before the smiling creature.

"Likewise, and in your true form I'm glad to see Ranger. But introductions must wait until we are safely out of the reach of Xan and his throng of misguided followers, come, Ryufu has set up camp in the Phantom Mountains and is anxious to receive the young one into his protection."

In unison the group all turned their heads to gaze out at the vast featureless desert before them, the daunting prospect of trudging through strength draining sand for what would no doubt be hours if not days descending like a fire blanket on their enthusiasm to get going.

"Do not despair friends, I have no intention of dawdling to keep pace with you, I have a plan!" Kwatili chuckled, as she lifted her head and let out a shrill whistle that was loud enough to cause pain to their ears.

"Wow, the howling was much less painful!" muttered Elijah, rubbing fruitlessly at his ears.

Kwatili cocked her head to one side and scrutinised him with narrowed cat eyes.

"I do not howl Elijah Grey." She said with impossible dignity.

"But before, the howling that woke me up, that told me to run.... That wasn't you?" He stuttered, looking to the others in confusion. One by one they all shook their heads.

"Oh for Pete sake, one of you must have heard it, it was so loud that it woke me up, that's why you were all at the windows of the tower surely, because you heard Kwatili telling you that she was coming!"

"I say again Elijah, I do not howl."

"But then who?"

Khizzi moved to quietly and gently place a small brown hand on his shoulders and whispered softly.

"Since the sounds that you alone hear, seem to always come to your assistance, take comfort in that fact and don't try to understand everything Elijah, some things must just be taken as true without explanation or proof."

Shrugging off her touch he muttered under his breath,

"Sure, that would be a comforting thing to say to someone who hasn't just found out that instead of being a normal human they're half bird, and have a gazillion things out to get them and they're hearing voices in their head!"

"Enough discussion, your transport is about to surface, be ready to dodge them!"

Kwatili had no sooner snapped out the words, when large mounds began to erupt out of the sand around them, sending hissing cascades down to bury their feet in seconds.

As huge smooth grey forms emerged out of the red sand, Kwatili suddenly cried out,

"Close your eyes as they…"

Not quickly enough they all turned their heads and tried to cover their eyes as the creatures shook violently sending a rain storm of sand to shower the company.

Coughing and spitting out grit that had managed to find every crevice he had, Elijah starred in wonder at the sight that met his stinging eyes.

Standing before them, their flanks still twitching to dislodge the last vestiges of sand, were five creatures that most closely resembled earthly horses, with shining silver grey coats and manes. That, and the presence of four legs, wide flaring nostrils and rolling wild brown eyes, was really where the resemblance ended. For these creatures had long flexing reptilian tails that stirred the sand continuously behind them and their long muscular legs ended not in neat hooves but three flattened toes which splayed out as they touched the shifting surface of the desert. All these aspects, however, paled into insignificance, because they were talking!

"Bags I don't get the big one, my back's only just recovered from the last time I had to carry that one!" Grumbled the one closest to the group, rolling his eye towards Burda, who scowled at it and narrowed her own.

"Trust me if it wasn't for the fact that we are being pursued and it would slow us down, I wouldn't go near your bony back with a barge pole, let alone my lovely butt!" She snapped, crossing her huge muscular arms tightly across her barrel chest.

Stepping quickly between them, Kwatili made a wide sweeping arm gesture towards the stamping, restless group of creatures, saying

"May I introduce the Sand Oren, gracious creatures of the desert and our very welcome transport to safety, Oren, please choose your riders so that we can depart before Drillers come upon us and make that decision moot."

Her deliberate emphasis of the words gracious and very welcome plus the timely reminder that they were, indeed, expecting an attack any second, worked like a charm to silence any other resistance from all present. Moving so effortlessly over the shifting sand on their adapted feet that the Oren gave the illusion of hovering rather than walking; one by one they approached the individuals in the party and bent down until it was easy for their chosen one to mount. With his heart thudding so hard that it felt as if it was in his head, Elijah placed his hands tentatively onto the smooth grey hide covered withers and hauled himself up to sit astride the Sand Oren's broad back.

"My name should you choose to use it Elijah Grey is Juno, and you may want to hold on."

With a violent lurch, the Oren heaved itself up out of its kneeling position, throwing poor Elijah forward over its neck and almost unseating him, had he not grabbed frantically at the thick shaggy mane and hugged himself against its hot neck. Eyes tightly shut he muttered,

"Cheers for the ample warning Juno!"

"Welcome," replied his mount, as he shook off sand still clinging to his front legs, again, almost shedding his rider, who wobbled about on the smooth broad surface of his back thinking that this was going to be a long and arduous journey if indeed he survived it!

"Not ridden much, have we? Maybe this will help."

Suddenly, Elijah felt the strangest sensation beneath him, as if he were sitting on a large sack filled with wriggling, writhing snakes, he squealed aloud before he could control himself and was about to dismount as quickly as possible when he realised that what was in fact happening was that Juno's back was actually changing in order to form a custom shaped saddle for him, complete with two bony ridges which grew out from where its ribs were to provide much needed foot rests.

"Wow, um, thanks that's much better." He mumbled, noticing out of the corner of his eye Ghelli, Khizzi, Brogan and even Burda were now seated comfortably astride the other Oren, although the one with Burda on his back didn't look comfortable at all, it was in fact the one who had voiced his desire not to carry her who now, it seemed, had acquired that dubious honour!

"Oh shut your grumbling mouth Brox, I'm half what I weighed last time I had to endure your bony back, you should be thankful to my discovery that eating greenery isn't just for sheep!"

Despite the situation, Elijah smiled to himself, remembering the expression of shocked delight that had lit up Burda's saggy features when she had sampled lettuce for the first time, only now did he register that it had indeed been the first time ever!

As they set off into the desert, Elijah stored the questions, when and why had she travelled by Sand Oren before in the same mental box as how did Juno already know his name when he had not been told it by Kwatili.

As the Oren picked up speed, Elijah was astounded. Clinging on with all his might to start with, he saw only the tossing mane inches from his face; but gradually he began to trust the sureness of his seat and relaxed back, allowing the smooth rhythm of Juno's strides to dictate the rise and fall of his body. Daring to look down, the speed at which they were covering ground became even more impressive, the surface of the desert was reduced to a blur beneath the Oren's flying feet, which barely disturbed the red surface.

Looking swiftly up to ease a sudden wave of nausea, he tried glancing to either side and found himself chuckling, despite the situation.

Brogan was embracing his mount's entire neck with both arms and the poor thing was galloping along with a distinctly strangled expression on its features. Brox, the Oren tasked with carrying Burda again was grimly attacking the endeavour, and had in fact transformed his body into such an accommodating "saddle" that Burda seemed to be almost enjoying her ride and leaned back looking most pleased with herself. Behind them, came Ghelli and Khizzi both making riding an Oren look like an art, of course.

Puzzled, Elijah suddenly registered that there was no sign of the beautiful Kwatili on an Oren.

"Oh, she really doesn't need a ride, she is in front of us Elijah Grey."

Since he was kind of getting used to the inhabitants of this crazy place seeming to be able to read his mind, he let that one go, as he squinted into the searing sun and finally spotted the distant figure, once again bounding with effortless grace over the surface of the desert.

For mile after mile, the five Oren galloped in Kawatili's wake. The blood red sun slowly arched across the sky above them, burning down relentlessly onto unguarded skin until Elijah's face and hands were sore and blistered.

"We will be arriving at the foot of the Phantom Mountains very soon Elijah Grey, they will offer you some much needed shade and protection."

Juno had yet again appeared to read his mind, this time Elijah didn't let it go.

"Okay, how do you do that, are you actually reading my mind? If you are, I'd kinda like my mind back please!"

"Hey don't stress Elijah, Sand Oren are not mind readers as such, we are just adept at reading body language, your brain is safe, well, from me at least!"

"And," he added, glancing round to meet the boys eyes for a second, "Since I felt the tension immediately running through your whole body when I said that, I meant nothing by it, well, not for now any ways, well, all I mean is at this point there's no one who can read your mind, except of course the trees of the Forest of Souls, you did touch them right?"

"Yes, he did, even though I told him not to, he had to go and touch them, and now look at him!" The grumble came from Ghelli whose Oren was now alongside.

Elijah said nothing but his pursed lips and stiffened back spoke volumes.

"Leave him be Ghelli, what's done is done. Who knows, it may turn out to be for the best that it happened the way that it did."

Khizzi had also joined them to ride as a trio, with the two struggling Oren carrying Burda and Brogan hanging back behind them.

"There you go again, what happened? What do you people keep saying things like that for and then not…"

His retort was cut off abruptly by the same bone chilling howl from the morning. It cut through the hot dry air like a knife and this time, they all heard it.

The Oren faltered momentarily, sending up a sandstorm that choked and filled their eyes with burning grit.

Yet again, the howl rose to a crescendo and ended with the clearly distinct word "RUN!"

Not one pair of ears present doubted that order for a second, it was filled with an urgency and conviction that was irrefutable. Each of the Oren took one deep breath to fill their huge lungs, before launching forward over the sand.

The scorching air rushing past his face burnt and lifted his long jet black hair out to stream behind him like a pirate flag. Juno's flying feet barely skimmed the sand but their pursuers gained on them with ease. Elijah had assumed that it would be Drillers erupting up out of the desert that they were fleeing from, but above the roaring of wind past his burning ears, he now registered a chillingly familiar sound. The swarm of Skorpios blocked out the sun as they drew closer, the shrill angry buzzing that the swarm produce invaded his brain with terror.

"You cannot out run them Oren, you must risk going beneath the sand!"

Unnoticed until he heard her voice beside them, Kwatili had dropped back and was keeping pace with Juno while she shouted.

Juno nodded and said to Elijah, "Take the deepest breath that you can Elijah Grey, and then trust me."

As he obediently filled his lungs to capacity, Elijah watched Juno close up his nostrils, before he reared up on his back legs and then plunged down into the sand. Using his strong reptilian tail to thrust his body forward into the sand, followed by all of the other Oren and their riders, Juno dived down deep into the desert leaving the angry swarm to hover over the empty sand.

As the sand closed in around him, Elijah hugged his arms tightly around Juno's neck, squeezing his eyes shut, and struggled against the wave of panic that threatened to overwhelm him. He was underneath the desert, sand rasped over the surface of his body, the pressure building as they plunged deeper and deeper until they left the suns warmth behind and the world turned cold. Fighting the urge to gasp, he pursed his lips closed and replayed over and over in his head the last words that Juno had said to him, "Trust me." It was all he had and he clung to it like a life belt in a stormy sea.

Just as he was thinking that his lungs would burst, and a deafening ringing was filling his head, he realised that they had in fact begun to rise instead of descend, they were heading for the surface!

"Hurry Juno, please, please hurry I can't last much longer!" he thought, hoping that the Oren truly was capable of reading his mind.

Seconds later they burst free of the surface and up into wonderful, breathable air. Gasping, choking and spitting out the sand that had forced its way into his mouth, Elijah slumped back exhausted onto Juno's broad back.

"No time to relax, they are still after you, Juno, the gateway is opening go!"

Still dazed from lack of oxygen, Elijah was only hazily aware that just ahead of them the surface of the desert had begun to shimmer, and as they thundered towards it the ghostly shape of a long narrow bridge had appeared.

As they reached it Juno halted so abruptly that his rider was thrown somewhat unceremoniously to the ground at the foot of the bridge.

"So sorry Elijah Grey, that thing always takes me by surprise, good luck go with you my friend, call me if you ever need a ride across the desert again!"

Staggering to his feet, Elijah stood swaying on unsteady feet, watching each of the Sand Oren eject their riders in much the same fashion, then disappear back below the sand; the last thing he saw of each was the tip of their thrashing tails.

Kwatili loomed tall beside him, and urgently turned him to face the bridge.

"The Oren cannot cross, but we must, and fast!" She said as she virtually pushed him towards it. Stumbling numbly forward, Elijah obediently walked onto the stones that made up the bridge, he was way past asking questions in this place, it was all too much, he just wanted it all to go away and leave him alone, so he walked. It didn't even bother him that when he glanced either side of the flag stones, he could only see swirling fog with strange amorphous shapes floating around like swimmers in a pool. He just walked, one foot in front of the other, mind numb and drained, he just walked.

"I didn't even get to say goodbye to Juno." He mumbled.

"Oh I doubt that it will be the last you see of the Oren Elijah, you'll get your chance."

He could tell from the heavy panting between each word that it was Burda lumbering behind him, that, and the slight shuddering of the stones beneath his feet, as she stumbled!

Ahead of them, there now shimmered a tall arched gateway, which solidified in the air the closer they drew to the now visible end to the bridge. It was no surprise that when he was a few paces away the previously featureless surface, suddenly sported hinges and began to slowly creak open, revealing a dazzlingly bright interior, as if they were entering the sun itself.

His foot faltered momentarily as he reached the gateway.

"Walk, just walk." Said the voice in his head.

As the last of them entered the huge gateway, it closed with a resonating boom, and then vanished into the cool darkness that now engulfed them.

A sudden conviction that he was finally, and for the first time since he had left the cabin three days ago, safe, overwhelmed him and he felt hot tears coursing down his cheeks as his knees buckled beneath him and he collapsed to the ground.

# Chapter 13

The smells reached him first. Smokey, spicy and meaty. Then came the sounds, sizzling, crackling, and, most surprising of all to him, laughter.

Prizing apart eyelids that felt like they were glued to his eyeballs, Elijah blinked until his horizontal view of his surroundings came into focus.

He saw a ring of faces, highlighted red from the central fire around which they were seated. They were all talking excitedly, pausing only to stuff huge chunks of some sort of roasted meat into sideways mouths.

The smell suddenly had a drastic effect on Elijah's very empty stomach, and pushing off the heavy cover draping him, he half crawled, scared to trust his weak legs, towards the group around the fire.

A hush fell as he approached. Into the silence, his stomach rumbled loudly, echoing off walls that were invisible in the darkness.

The nearest pair of red lips split apart and let out a raucous laugh that told him it was Brogan,

"Give that boy something to tame that animal in his belly!" He chuckled, himself reaching forward and filling a small bowl with something steaming from the cauldron suspended over the crackling fire. Holding it out at the length of his outstretched arm he waited for Elijah to join them the way that you tempt a timid dog with a treat.

For the next five minutes, all Elijah could think about was how absolutely delicious the meaty stew tasted, that he was unceremoniously shovelling into his mouth in huge mouthfuls using a crust of bread also pushed into his hand by Brogan. Wiping the bowl clean with the last scrap of bread, he sat back onto his heels and breathed a contented sigh.

"Wash that down with some of this Raven Boy, it'll put hairs on that skinny chest of yours!"

Brogan held out a beaker which was immediately dashed from his hand by an indignant Burda.

"What do you think you're doing offering intoxicating liquid to a fifteen year old?"

"Oh come now Burda, you can't really expect Elijah to obey the rules that applied in another world, another life and to another being, you are not his only guardian now, we all are, I feel that a small amount of something to calm his nerves and steel him for what is to come would be an excellent idea."

Kwatili's voice floated in from the dark edges of the ring, and all he could make out of her tall regal form was her red rimmed silhouette extending a graceful arm to rest her hand on Burda's hunched shoulder. Wordlessly Burda slumped in acquiescence and herself half-filled another beaker from a large black jug, and handed it to Elijah.

Putting it to his lips, the boy tentatively sipped the aromatic liquid, as that small mouthful trickled like down his throat, it spread an immediate sensation of warmth and well-being throughout his body; by the time it reached his stomach he had drained the cup dry.

"Oh no, there'll be no second helping!" Burda snapped as he held out the beaker for more.

"I'm with Burda on that Raven Boy, even Waterloggers have respect for Magma; we don't need to have to carry you up the mountainside!"

Elijah opened his mouth to protest, but snapped it shut. They were both right and he really didn't want to upset Burda when he had just got her back.

"Here Elijah, you may want this if you're going outside."

Rangers quiet voice coming out of the gloom beside him made him jump and the realisation that, now that he came to think about it, he had just been thinking about what the Phantom Mountains actually looked like; how on earth did Ranger still know what he wanted before he did himself?

"Well, thanks but I really don't think I will, even at night, that desert was hot."

He answered, turning quickly, ignoring the offered animal skin, to stumble towards the faintly lit doorway behind him.

"Not the best at taking advice is he Burda?" He heard Brogan say, this too he ignored, the Magma still fizzed warmly in his ears and he felt invincible.

Reaching the doorway which was covered by another heavy drape of hide, he hesitated, what if the Skorpios were still lurking out there in the hot desert sky?

Shrugging his shoulders he took a deep breath and pushed past the hide and out into the desert.

The wall of freezing cold air that hit him robbed him of that breath straight away. Gasping and instantly beginning to shiver uncontrollably Elijah gaped out at the world that met his eyes.

It could not have been any more different to the desert.

The world around him was now blue white frozen ice and snow. The sky merged into the horizon, pale and almost colourless, the sun hung just above that horizon like a giant pearl and he viewed everything through the thick mist of his breath.

Hearing movement behind him, he turned too sharply and felt his feet slip on the ice and would have fallen straight over onto his face had Ranger not grabbed him in time. Holding onto Elijah until he was once more steady on his feet, Ranger again offered him the thick brown hide cloak.

"Thanks, and er, sorry," the boy muttered, still acutely uncomfortable talking to, and meeting the eyes of, his former pet.

"Don't mention it Elijah, you may find these helpful too." Ranger replied, handing Elijah a pair of stout fur lined boots. These he shoved on gratefully, winding the long leather thong around his calf to fasten them securely and very warmly onto his already numb feet. Wrapping the cloak around his shoulders, he turned again to face the new world around him.

Ranger followed him as he walked slowly and carefully forward and surveyed the large grey tent like structure which perched like a giant hunched spider on the flat, featureless ice.

"How can it be so cold when just over the bridge it was so hot?" Murmured Elijah, squinting through the breath haze to find the great gateway through which he had just recently staggered having dismounted Juno and traversed the narrow stone flagged bridge.

"And where has the gate and bridge gone anyway? They were just there!" He cried as he began to slip and slide his way out onto the ice.

"They no longer exist Elijah Grey, these are not named the Phantom Mountains without reason."

Kwatili's gentle voice at his shoulder halted him.

"You should stay inside in the warmth until we are ready to set off Elijah Grey, it makes no sense to remain here and freeze when your questions can be answered just as well by the fire."

Looking up at her amazing face framed by a fur trimmed hood attached to her cloak, he felt like he was drowning in those amber eyes.

As she smiled the black stripe that ran down either side of her nose from eyes to chin curved to accentuate the rare expression.

"Truly you are her son young raven," she whispered softly as she ushered him back into the womblike darkness of the tent.

# Chapter 14

As his eyes slowly adjusted to the dim light inside the tent, Elijah realised that Brogan and Ghelli were missing from the ring of shadowy figures around the glowing embers of the dying fire.

Burda had keeled over onto her side and was snoring loudly like a rhino; Khizzi was nervously poking at the glowing coals with a stick sending dancing fairies up into the roof of the tent and Ranger sat with his head hunched over his knees staring sightlessly into the darkness.

Kwatili threw a chunk of wood onto the fire and lowered herself to sit cross legged beside Ranger with all the grace of a ballet dancer.

"You are needing answers young Elijah Grey, between us," Kwatili paused to nudge the sleeping Burda, not too gently, causing the woman to splutter awake, scrubbing at her beady eyes.

"We will endeavour to give you what you need, in order to face what is to come."

Somehow her words did not make Elijah feel any better, in fact he found himself wanting to tell her not to worry; maybe ignorance was indeed bliss.

"Time and place is what I say to you Kwatili, time and place and this here is neither, we need to get to Ryufu and safety before we start telling stories and scaring the bejeebers out of him, with all due respect of course your Highness!" Rumbled Burda, her eyes never leaving the boy she had raised as her son for fifteen years.

Elijah knew that she was scanning him for the minutest signs of illness or injury, it's what she had done each and every time that he and Ranger had returned from escapades in the forest, but her vigilance took on a new and more sinister meaning now.

Kwatili softly chuckled like a purr and laid her slender hand on the old woman's huge hunched shoulders.

"I demand no respect from one such as you Burda, in fact it is I who have the utmost respect for you and the way in which you have carried out your task all these years; but should he not be more prepared for-"

She was cut short by the sudden and noisy entry of Brogan followed closely by Ghelli, both wide eyed and gasping for breath.

Kwatili was on her feet in a heartbeat, Ranger and Burda followed suit stamping out the remains of the fire as they did so, plunging the tent into darkness.

Out of the gloom came Ghelli's voice.

"We must move and now, Xan has sent Maigrey, many Maigrey, we cannot defeat them we can only hope to out run them!"

"Out run something that we cannot see? We need a miracle!" Khizzi's soft whisper at his shoulder struck terror into his heart.

"What the hell are Maigrey, will someone tell me the truth for once?" He demanded, and flinched as a swift slap was aimed at him through the darkness.

"You will not use language like that young man no matter how scared you might be!" Growled Burda, softening the blow by immediately hugging the boy to her chest and whispering into his black hair.

"You will prevail, we will all happily die for that end my Elijah."

Gulping back the sob that sat in his throat, Elijah gently extricated himself from her giant embrace and said quietly into the darkness.

"I don't want any one of you to even think about giving your life for me, so let's get moving."

"Well said young Ra-Elijah, Ghelli and Brogan, we will follow your lead, keep your eyes open and let someone know the minute you think you see any sign of movement." As she spoke, Kwatili swept aside the heavy door covering and their eyes were momentarily blinded by the dazzling glare of the white snow that awaited them. One by one the company left the relative safety and warmth of the tent.

Out of the corner of his eye, Elijah merely found it curious that the lanky grey tent seemed to gather itself up and fold itself down into the snow.

"Handy," he muttered.

Sloping along at his shoulder, Kwatili drew close so that she could speak directly into his ear in a soft whisper.

"Maigrey are beings of the snow, they can move undetected across the ice, smell just a drop of blood from a mile away, are creatures who kill for the pleasure of taking a life and will do so before you are even aware that they are near. Watch for patches of snow and ice that appear to be moving, that will be a Maigrey."

"Cool, um thanks for that, I feel much better now," he replied swallowing hard, his eyes nervously darting back and forth across the flat featureless snowscape.

"You asked for the truth, therefore I give it." She said whilst also scanning the snow.

"Can't argue with that matey!" Brogan chuckled from the head of the column, just before he halted so sharply that Ghelli almost crashed into him.

Finger to his mouth, Brogan silently pointed over to his right.

Squinting desperately, Elijah could see nothing except white crystalline smoothness. He was just about to say so, when his heart jolted into his mouth and even inside the thick warmth of the hide cloak, he felt an icy chill drench his whole body from head to toe.

One by one, patches of the seemingly unbroken snow surface began to twitch and then creep towards them. Blinking madly in a desperate attempt to focus more clearly, Elijah stood immobilised by fear.

"Move or die where you stand Raven boy!" crackled Brogan's voice into his ear as he felt the Waterlogger virtually lift him off his feet and thrust him in the direction in which the others were all running as fast as the knee deep snow would permit.

"Make for that rock shelf Ghelli, at least they won't be able to hide so well!" Brogan shouted whilst maintaining his grip on Elijah's arm in order to propel him forward.

71

Staggering breathlessly up onto the large rock escarpment that jutted out of the snow, slippery and sharp edged, the group frantically scrabbled as high as they could, at their heels they could all now clearly hear a feral snarling that chilled the blood.

Placing her bulky body in front of Elijah, Burda planted her chunky legs like tree trunks, hefted a huge double headed axe into her hands and shouted."

"No point hiding now you mangy mongrels, we know you're there, come out and fight!" She bellowed, sending a billowing cloud of steam out as she did.

"Your courage is never in doubt Burda, but your tactics sometimes leave a lot to be desired! We cannot fight them off here, we need to climb higher and find a more defensible point." Ghelli shouted as he headed up the steep slippery rock face.

"Climbing is not my strength but you could be right." She grunted as she began to scramble upwards, pushing Elijah in front of her, as she did so.

His hands were frozen numb within seconds of touching the rock, sharp edges cut into his fingers, but he felt nothing except a screaming pain in his thighs from the sudden steepness of his ascent and a rising wave of utter panic as he imagined he could actually feel the breath of a Maigrey on his neck.

Suddenly, it was not his imagination but the ear piercing screeching of multiple sets of razor sharp claws gouging out long grooves in the rock behind him. His breath was coming in short agonising gasps now and he knew that he was rapidly reaching his limit.

"That's me done Ghelli, get him to safety or I'll wrap that tail of yours around your scrawny neck and choke the life out of you, Brogan, are you with me?" Grunted Burda, as she stopped her exhausting climb, and turned about to yet again face the onslaught. beside her equally bent over with the exertion of propelling large, short legged physique up the glassy, almost vertical rock surface, Brogan nodded.

"With you all the way my fair warrior maid, it's about time this blade of mine tasted Maigrey flesh!"

The two stalwarts planted their trunk size legs wide, and stood waiting for the first of the Maigrey to attack.

On hands and knees, Elijah coughed until he could raise himself onto his wobbling legs and then yelled.

"Not again Burda, I'm not leaving you behind again, and you can't-"

His defiance drained from his voice along with the blood from his face at the look that Burda now turned on him.

"You will get up that mountain and you will not look around Elijah Grey, I am still the closest thing to a mother that you have and you will do as I say, because you love me."

"But-"

The sight that now reared up out of the rock behind Burda stole away his reply and the breath that came with it. With a lump of fear and sorrow clogging his throat, Elijah turned his back on Burda and Brogan and the nightmare that now closed in on them to force his tortured muscles upwards and away.

# Chapter 15

Maigrey, the hunters of the ice, were created to be single minded and ruthless. They were far more creature than human and if you survived long enough to look into their dull black eyes before you died, you would see only your own death. They were supremely adapted to their purpose, able to move just above the surface of the snow and ice completely undetected; if you saw them it would be more like when you think you see a shadow deepen in an already pitch dark room.

Covered in a coating of short, slanting stiff hair, which could change colour to suit whatever it was close to, short muscular legs gave them speed as well as strength, and ended in long curved claws able to slice through flesh as if it was paper. Lethal enough, but add to that a flat chisel shape head that was armed with a double set of teeth set in jaws that could dislocate in order to clamp down on a whole head with ease, and you have a Maigrey.

This was what had reared up from the rock surface behind Burda and Brogan when Elijah had been about to argue his point. What had truly frozen the blood in his veins was the fact that he had been left in absolutely no doubt that the leading Maigrey were not, in fact focussed at all on the two defiant figures standing before them, but their death stare had zeroed past them onto him and only him. It was as if, for a suspended moment in time, the universe contained only he, and the Maigrey, and they lusted for his death.

Burda had seen this happen, knew without turning around what the Maigrey were doing, and had put all of her huge heart into her order for Elijah to go.

As she watched him push his long spindly frame into motion, she allowed herself a split second to marvel at the changes already wrought by this world on her erstwhile charge, before winking in Brogan's direction and turning to face the beasts behind them.

"You will get to that boy over my dead body, so do your worst mongrels!"

Flicking their deadly gaze onto her, the four leading Maigrey charged, massive saw-toothed jaws stretching wide in a blood curdling roar, raised up on their hind legs so that they could use their swiping claws more effectively, they were at least two meters tall, towering over the heads of Brogan and Burda who stood, calmly awaiting them.

Up above on the steep rock face, Elijah winced as he heard the sickening sound of blade sloughing off flesh from bone below him.

"Do not look round Elijah, climb for your life, there is a small cave just above that ledge, if we can make it to that their sacrifice will not have been in vain!" Cried Ghelli, lashing his brown tail around the flagging boy's waist and using it to haul him the last twenty or so feet.

Ranger's voice whispered directly into his ear saying, "Do not despair too quickly Elijah, I've seen Burda slay that many Maigrey with nothing but a small dagger before, and she was only fighting for practice then!"

Daring to hope, Elijah clambered over the slippery moss coated stone slabs to collapse, chest heaving, onto the damp floor of the cave. Rolling over onto his back and staring up at the dripping ceiling he lay for the time it took for his head to cease spinning and his legs to feel like they belonged to him once more. Listening to the distant thuds and grunts and snarling sounds, he felt a strange detachment from reality, as if he were just stretched out on the battered old sofa, watching all this happen in a film. But then he heard Ranger stifle a gasp and whisper, "Oh Burda my friend."

In a heartbeat Elijah was squatting beside Ranger staring in horror at the scene below them.

Both Burda and Brogan were still fighting bravely on but it seemed that no sooner had they dispatched one of the grizzly beasts, than it was instantly replaced and they were visibly tiring. Sweat covered their heavy set shoulders in a blue sheen, despite the freezing cold air and the thrusting of knife and axe were getting slower as their distraught friends watched. Blood pulsed from a network of slash wounds and they were steadily being surrounded by the giant staggering monstrosities. Once again Elijah felt his heart stop as one of the huge creatures halted its attack on Brogan long enough to seek out his eyes and tell him of his impending death with just a look.

"We can't just watch them die, we have to go back and try to help them!" He yelled over the rising sounds of slaughter.

"It would be suicide, you must reach Ryufu, this world depends on it, but I too cannot sit here like a coward and watch friends die, Khizzi, the task is yours to get Elijah Grey to safety, I will—"

Before Kwatili could finish, another sound joined the savagery down below them, and she leapt into the cave entrance to crane her neck upwards to the peak of the mountain.

Following her, Elijah saw what at first reminded him of hang gliders against the anaemic sky, but as his eyes focussed and they drew nearer he realised that each shape was in fact made up of two separate beings. One was large, long necked and slinky bodied with a snaking tail, and looked to have four legs, but the fore limbs were out stretched with a rudimentary wing formed by its skin. From its back legs dangled the second part of this duo. All that he could make out, as they glided downwards towards the battle scene, was a human shaped figure who swung precariously from some sort of harness, their legs and feet were almost running in the air, whilst clutched close to their chests was what could only be a weapon.

"Please tell me that they're on our side," Elijah whispered.

"Oh most definitely, they are the Sky Oren, and they carry to our aide the Yehana, come Elijah Grey, we must make the most of their arrival and get out of here."

Kwatili was already scaling the mountainside above the cave entrance, using hands and feet and keeping her long, slender body flat against the rock.

Hesitating long enough to watch open mouthed as the Sky Oren swooped down to release their cargo like bombers upon the Maigrey, who were dropping dead to the ground with sliced throats before many had even had the chance to look up, Elijah felt his throat close up.

"B-but what about Burda and Borgan, shouldn't we wait for them?" He panted, searching desperately for sight of their two bulky forms amongst the growing pile of bodies.

"What did she say to you Elijah? She told to get to safety, trust me it would take many more than a those Maigrey to finish her off, come." Ranger said as he gently urged the boy into motion. Reluctantly he began to crawl up the rock face behind Kwatili, flanked by Ranger and Khizzi, with Ghelli bringing up the rear.

In seconds the frozen surface numbed his hands, and his already strained muscles began to weaken. Overhead, dark shapes cast shadows as they passed; he flinched and instinctively froze against the ground.

"Keep moving Raven Boy, your taxi service awaits on the next ledge!"

The voice came from above him, it was a voice he thought he'd not be hearing again, and he was so relieved that he didn't even mind the annoying nick name.

Spurred on he pushed his exhausted body up the next ridge of rock and there, indeed, waited five of the Sky Oren. Two circled the air nearby, and already had passengers, Brogan and a slumped over Burda were already harnessed beneath their muscular bodies. The others were impatiently snorting hot steamy breath out of large flared nostrils and flapping their forelimb wings.

The four climbers struggled the last few feet and virtually collapsed into the thick leather harnesses recently vacated by the Yehana. Not even waiting to check that they were buckled in the Sky Oren launched off the ledge and out over the giddying drop below.

His long black hair was whipped about his face by each strong down beat of wings, but Elijah dare not loosen his manic grip of the leather straps, from which he dangled like a tree ornament at Christmas, long enough to clear it away from his eyes.

He caught glimpses of the others, and heard the feral sounds of the still raging battle below fade slowly away until all that was left was an almost dream like floating. The rhythmic swaying coupled with the numbing coldness soon sent his body and mind into hyperthermia and he felt himself gradually drifting into a deadly sleep.

Time lost all meaning and he was only peripherally aware of a rising tide of voices that seemed to be coming from his feet, making him chuckle. He thought he could feel warm hands pulling him out of his harness, but then again he may just be dreaming it, he thought that he heard one particularly loud and gruff voice barking out orders for blankets, food and bandages, but that may also just be in his dream. As a soft warmth surrounded his entire body, he realised that he no longer cared what was real and what was not and he let himself truly drift off to sleep.

# Chapter16

Watching the boy sleep he could see so many similarities to his mother, even though the eyes that flicked from side to side were covered by eye lids, he knew that when they opened they would be the same startling jet black, set deep beneath his brow bone, either side of his jutting, chiselled nose with the same narrow flaring nostrils. As he breathed, tendrils of long silk fine hair the colour of a raven's wing floated up and down over his mouth.

A frown wrinkled the forehead of Ryufu, Lord of the Yehana as he remembered. A low resonant growl rumbled up from his throat and leaked out between his parted jaws, lined with sharp and deadly canines. He pushed his body up from its squatting position beside the boy in his care, Xan would pay for his treachery soon, and he looked forward to being the one to extract that payment, hopefully inflicting as much pain as possible in the process. Until then, he would protect this boy with his life if necessary.

"My Lord, the surviving Yehana have returned, they have been taken straight to the treatment tent, all are injured but expected to live."

Without taking his eyes from Elijah, Ryufu nodded his acknowledgment, "Every effort must be put into their care, I will hold you personally responsible for their recovery Adan." He rumbled, whilst bending his thick set, muscular torso to pick up another blanket to gently lay over the recumbent figure.

"Understood, my Lord Ryufu," replied the other nervously as he strode off purposefully to make absolutely sure that he did not incur the wrath of his Lord in any way at all!

A soft chuckle behind him brought Ryufu's attention back to the present.

"I see that your friendly disposition has not changed Ryufu, just as well there are still some who know the real you that hides behind the teeth and the growls."

"Kwatili my friend, it has been too long since you graced my home, even longer since I had a home for you to grace!"

"We share the same lifestyle these days, dare we hope that the arrival of this boy heralds a tipping of the scales in our favour at last?"

Kwatili sighed, gazing at the sleeping figure and tilting her head thoughtfully. A gruff voice cut in from the darkness behind her.

"He knows nothing of his ancestry or destiny, hold off from the victory celebration until he has been told all and still accepts the challenge; in my opinion, he is too young, weak and has been brought here too soon."

Kwatili and Ryufu turned to study the sullen expression on Ghelli's brown features, before risking smiles.

"You forget Ghelli, the only reason that he is here now and not at the time agreed, is that somehow Xan discovered where we were hiding him, and more worryingly, how to get there along with an army of Drillers!"

Ranger had joined them now and beside him Khizzi stood, with her tiny hands on her hips, glaring at Ghelli.

"Brother, we all know your opinion, and we all know why you feel that way, we also know that Elijah Grey is not just any fifteen year old and should be given as much support as we can give him to face the ordeal that is approaching him."

"And what ordeal would that be?"

Elijah's quiet voice startled all five, they had been so engrossed that they had been totally unaware that he had stirred awake and was now pushing back the heavy felt blankets and stiffly standing on his weakened legs.

He chuckled mirthlessly at the worried look that glanced from face to face. "Yep, that's what I expected; you're so quick to criticise me, but none of you has the guts to just sit me down and tell me what the hell is going on here!" He cried, his glare aimed mostly at Ghelli.

"Elijah Grey! What have I told you about using toilet mouth language?"

Burda was struggling in his direction, bandages covering her right arm from shoulder to wrist, and she was leaning heavily on a stout stick, due to a make shift splint that kept her right leg stiff.

79

Sweat beaded her wrinkled brows, and pain was written across her rugged features for all to see. But still, as she neared Elijah she risked over balancing in order to threaten him with her walking stick.

Ryufu threw back his head and let out an ear splitting half howl half laugh, soon echoed by all in the huge cavern.

Elijah was so overjoyed to see Burda still alive that he instinctively ran over to throw his arms around her stout shoulders, hugging the woman who had been his mother for all of his life. For a split second she hugged him back so hard that it squeezed the breath from him, but then sensing that they were now the centre of attention, she coughed loudly and pushed him gently back, patting him companionably on the shoulder.

"Well, I guess that's the second time they failed to get rid of old Burda, let's hope they don't try a third any time soon, and it is time to tell you just what all this is about and how you figure in it; just as soon as you've had a good stomach full of food."

Elijah knew Burda well enough to save his breath and acquiesce to her demand, there truly was no point in arguing. So he seated himself once more on the blanket, and accepted the steaming bowl of stew, and carved wooden mug of something sweet and milky tasting handed to him by one of the Yehana. The reverence and lowered eyes with which it was offered served to raise his anxiety levels, but he was so hungry he decided to ignore it for now, but he was determined to get answers to each and every question that was plaguing his mind.

He studied the beings around him as he chewed and swallowed. He thought it better to think of them as beings rather than people, because, well, they weren't exactly people. The Yehana, like their leader were short in stature, incredibly thick set about the chest, neck and shoulders, and all had the same wiry honey colour hair which grew right down the back of their necks to disappear into the stiff leather jerkin that they all wore. Like Ryufu, all the Yehana, had very rounded black eyes, set far apart either side of a wide bridged nose, flared nostrils and an alarmingly large mouth, well-armed with sharp pointed teeth.

Elijah found them quite disturbing, even though they had all treated him as if he were someone very special from the moment that he had woken up; they were still not normal people, he found that he longed for the sight of an ordinary, boring human, even grumpy old Mr Moore who ran the corner store and always treated him like a criminal, checking his pockets as he left the shop, and muttering about shifty foreigners.

Suddenly things began to start slotting into place in his brain, things that had periodically puzzled him but Burda had always waved them aside with a brusque "If we tried to understand everything in life we'd never do anything except sit and think!"

He'd always just accepted this, shrugged his shoulders and thought nothing more of it, trusting Burda so totally all of his life, if she wasn't worried then there was nothing for him to be concerned about.

But now, now all those weird things, the things that had made his stomach feel like it was full of bees, those things all began fitting into jigsaw holes in his memories.

The first and foremost was that he now knew the reason why there had never been any mirrors in the house, and when he had bought Burda one for Christmas once, she had looked at it for just a heartbeat as if he'd presented her with a live snake. Oh she'd recovered her composure quickly, and thanked him, but he'd found it buried out back the following spring. He'd been hurt and a little angry at the time, but now he realised, she didn't want him to be able to see his own reflection, because he too, was not a normal human.

Tentatively he ran his long slender fingers over his face, feeling the long sharply pointed nose, deeply sunken cheek bones and smooth hairless brows. Reaching behind his head he pulled his mane of raven black hair forward over his shoulder, it reached almost down to his waist now, when it had been chopped short just three days ago!

"It was the contact with the trees of the Forest of Souls that accelerated the process Elijah Grey, it would have taken longer and been easier for you if you had not made that contact."

Khizzi's soft voice and the cool touch of her hand on his arm halted the plunge into a panic pool that had just threatened to overwhelm him.

Without looking at her, he said, "So how much more am I going to change?"

"I cannot answer that Elijah, no-one can, because, well because you're not, um well that is your mother and father were…"

"Your mother and father broke the rules and were of different race, so no-one can really answer your question Elijah Grey, as one such as you has never existed before."

Ryufu's deep voice came from behind him and this time Elijah whirled around to look straight into the deep, dark eyes before him. He saw nothing but truth in those unwavering eyes, and sensed immense supressed strength in the even breaths coming from the wide nostrils.

"You have every right to feel fear, anger, and betrayal, but to give in to these would bring about your death and probably the death of all those you see here, if you are truly your mother's son, you will find within you the courage to accept and move onwards."

Ryufu paused and moved so close to Elijah that he could now feel his breath on his face, eye to eye the two stood motionless, whilst around them all froze and held their collective breath.

Peering deep into Elijah's unblinking eyes, Ryufu relaxed his tensed stance and again let out that loud donkey bray laugh.

"You have your mother's defiance alright. You'll d,o Raven Boy, you'll do!"

A mass release of breath followed by sudden return to motion went unnoticed by Elijah, as he cocked his head to one side and said, "So it was you that was doing all the howling of warnings."

Once again, silence clamped down in the cavern as they waited for a reaction from Ryufu. He cut off mid-laugh and drew even closer to Elijah's face, almost nose to nose and growled.

"A Yehana does not howl Raven Boy, if you heard a howl that could only be…"

"That would be me."

Out of the darkness of the cave strode a tall grey haired figure, clad in black, with pointed features, high cheek bones and startling yellow eyes.

As he drew near, Elijah felt a completely unfamiliar sensation overwhelm him, it was more terrifying than any he had endured since arriving here; he knew without a shadow of a doubt that he was looking at his father!

# Chapter 17

Striding over to stand eye to eye with the newcomer, Ryufu radiated hostility, right down to the hair from head to shoulders bristling on end.

The other merely eased his mouth into a toothy smile, not supported by his glowing yellow eyes, "Ryufu, good to see you, my apologies for crashing the party but it seemed the right time to put in an appearance, other than the odd howl of warning that is!"

"Matthias, at some point I will have to deal with the guard that allowed you to sneak past him," Ryufu paused to glower at his cowering guards who had breathlessly just arrived.

"But, your presence is not required, I have it all under control, so you can just crawl back down whatever hole you entered by."

Matthias smiled again, the smile of a wolf just before it eats you, "So your idea of under control is almost getting the most important being in Greylea sliced and diced by Maigrey, melted by Skorpios and chewed up by Drillers, hmm, don't want to see what happens when you get slack; oh wait, that would be in the next five minutes judging by the pack of Maigrey who are scaling the last hundred feet of mountainside as we speak."

The two stood eye to eye for a moment more before Ryufu broke away, snapping out orders for the Yehana to increase the guards at the entrance and for a party to head out and head off any Maigrey, should they actually be there.

"Um, you might want to post some guards on that hole that I crawled in through too."

Without turning, Ryufu's back stiffened visibly, but he quietly told three Yehana to go to the spot that Matthias was indicating and stand guard.

Kwatili touched Ryufu lightly on his shoulder and whispered softly.

"We both know that the Maigrey will gain entry eventually, the best way to keep Elijah safe is to get him out of here and up to the mountain top, from there the Sky Oren can take him far from their reach."

Ryufu hung his head for a second and then locked her gaze with his own.

"He must have protection, the Rhilion woman and Waterlogger are still recovering, they will stay, you go, along with Ranger, Ghelli and Khizzi, I will catch up with you when we have finished off these Maigrey once and for all!"

Kwatili smiled a gentle smile and answered, "You know that Matthias should be with him too Ryufu, we will need his knowledge of the mountains, and more importantly, his knowledge of Xan."

The intense struggle going on in Ryufu's head manifested in the bulging veins that now throbbed at his temples and the minute clenching and unclenching of his muscular jaws. All around held their breath, except for Matthias who was nonchalantly helping himself to a portion of the now cold stew.

Without looking his way, Ryufu growled between his teeth.

"At the first sign of treachery, kill him Ghelli."

Not waiting for an answer he whirled around and gathered Yehana to him as he marched towards the main entrance to his cave.

"Okay then, we need to leave immediately so grab only what you can carry yourself and let's go!" said Kwatili tossing large canvas back sacks to Ranger, Ghelli, Khizzi and Elijah, Matthias merely held up his own bag when she looked his way.

"But I have to say goodbye to Burda, and don't even try to argue with that!" stated Elijah and he strode purposefully over to where she and Brogan were lying beside the fire, covered with thick felt blankets.

When he knelt down beside her, she opened her eyes sleepily and muttered.

"I strongly suspect that someone has drugged my stew to keep me asleep while you go gallivanting off with that rabble of no-gooders, you make sure that you don't pay too much mind to that Lycana lout, he has an agenda all of his own you mark my words."

Even as she was saying the last word, Burda's small beady eyes closed and she drifted back off to sleep, snoring loudly.

Elijah chuckled affectionately and gently brushed her tough wrinkled forehead with his lips.

"Sleep well Burda, we will meet again I promise and then you can tell me all about this father of mine."

Looking across at Brogan he added, "Look after her for me Brogan she has been the only mother I have known."

"Raven boy, I will guard her with the last breath in this battered body of mine." He replied grinning his crocodilian smile.

Nodding in satisfaction, Elijah stood and hefted the bag, packed for him by Kwatili, up onto his shoulders then the thick heavy cloak, pulling the hood up over his long hair.

"Okay, I'm ready." He said, as he watched the group, intrigued as to who out of Kwatili, Ghelli and Matthias was going to take the lead.

Somehow it didn't surprise him that it was Matthias who took up position at the head of the party as they made their way out of the warm glow of the cave and into the surrounding darkness, he was surprised, however, to see Ranger walking alongside him deep in conversation.

"Hmm, even more to my dog than I thought it seems." He muttered to himself.

"You have no idea Elijah Grey, in fact it might be good for you to know just what he sacrificed in order to go with you to the other realm to be your protector; it may change your attitude towards him."

Kwatili's softly spoken comment caused his cheeks to suddenly flush red with contrition, he had still not found himself able to even look Ranger in the eye, let alone be civil to him.

"Okay, I'm all ears Kwatili." He answered, not taking his gaze from the indistinct cave floor in front of him.

"Ranger was born with the rare ability to switch between the fully animal and semi-humanoid version of his breed; thus he was the obvious candidate for the role of your protector and companion. What he gave up was the role of second in command to Matthias, back when he was ruler of Greylea. This he did without being asked and without hesitation, even though it meant that he would be leaving behind his partner and never see their unborn off spring."

Elijah stopped mid stride and turned to peer into the gloom at Kwatili's shadowy features.

"I do understand I think that you feel a sense of betrayal by him, as he was not what you had been led to believe, but any things that you were told about your history in that realm were always to protect you Elijah Grey, of all the beings in this cave, the one that you can rest assured it is safe to trust with your life is Ranger."

Hot tears of regret burnt the boy's eyes as a wave of emotion broke over him.

"Good, that is a good reaction, remember how you feel now for when it is appropriate to speak to Ranger, and then forgive yourself Elijah, you have more important things to worry about."

With that Kwatili reached out in the dark and gently urged him back into motion before Ghelli and Khizzi caught them up.

Blindly following the amber fur covered heels in front of him, Elijah stumbled along deep in thought. More pieces of the jigsaw slotted into place in his mind, so Burda and Ranger had been hidden in the only world he had thought existed, fifteen years ago, with him as a baby. Of course it made sense now that Burda had insisted that he never venture anywhere without his dog, Ranger even used to walk with him to the tiny little country school, and wait outside the gates all day, to walk back with him to the cabin, conveniently set in secluded woodland.

The other children at the school had always been slightly reluctant to befriend him not because of what he wore or said, but because of his very unusual appearance, he now realised. In fact there had only ever been one local who had shown any interest in him and that had been strange Mr Nax who drove the only taxi car in the region. Shivers ran unpleasantly down his spine at the thought of that man. He had pulled up beside Elijah on the road home, the one and only time that he had walked it alone, because Ranger had got a rusty nail stuck in his paw and had remained at home that day.

The image of Mr Nax leaning over to ask him if he wanted a lift, and tapping the strangely over long middle finger of his right hand disturbingly on the driving wheel came suddenly into his mind. He remembered the man's huge, round, watery eyes, blinking as if the sunshine was burning them, as he had studied

Elijah from top to toe in a way that had made the boy's skin crawl. When the man had begun licking his thin lips as if he wanted to literally devour him, Elijah had blurted out a polite no, and sprinted off towards the path that led to the cabin, praying that he would not hear the car following him. He had panted a sigh of relief when he dared to stop and check, and the car was still sitting on the road, with Mr Nax still sitting behind the wheel watching him but not following.

Could that have just been a weird old man, and a coincidence that the next day and from then on, with Ranger in tow he had never seen him again?

"No Elijah, that was no coincidence, I think that was the day that Xan's search for you reached fruition, I truly wish I'd been there that day."

Ranger's quiet voice beside him made him stumble and almost fall flat on his face.

"Can all people from here read my thoughts? Because—," he stuttered.

"No, it is just a link between us that formed over the years Elijah, I'm sorry I will try to break it but—"

Elijah reached out and put his hand on the other's shoulder and squeezed.

"Not a problem Ranger, after all, what better protector could I have than one that can read my mind and stop me doing dumb things before I even decide to?"

Ranger couldn't speak but the emotion on his face said it all, he nodded and grinned widely before walking on along the tunnel.

Behind Elijah Kwatili smiled, and murmured to herself.

"Your son indeed Egreya my friend.

As the gradient steepened, the walls of the tunnel drew in closer until they were almost touching the shoulders of the company, Kwatili was now having to walk stooped over, and the strain was beginning to show on all of their sweating faces.

"Not far to the top now, Kwatili, will you be able to do your thing when we get there? We don't want to be perched like a cherry on a cake for too long these are the Phantom Mountains after all!" Matthias called over his shoulder.

"No problem," Kwatili replied.

The next second, Elijah and his companions were blinded by a sudden burst of light as Matthias heaved aside a heavy hide cover exposing nothing but sky. One by one they crawled out and collapsed to the ground gasping for breath after the steep climb.

As he went to stand up, Elijah felt Matthias push him firmly back onto the cold rock.

"Stay down boy, do I have to remind you what hunts you?"

Any reply was drowned out by the shrill cry emanating from Kwatili, undulating and piercing it rose up into the steel bright air at the mountain top.

The silence that fell like a fire curtain when she stopped was almost suffocating.

For a second nothing seemed to have heard her, and nothing stirred. Then, from out of the very rocks on which they crouched came a low laughter, chilling and paralysing.

"I sure hope the Sky Oren are as fast as you say they are Kwatili, I don't fancy tackling phantoms with just this!" Ghelli whispered, clutching the bone handle of his dagger grimly his eyes darting from rock to rock.

Kwatili's amber eyes did not leave the pale sky as she nodded.

"They will come Ghelli, the question is whether it will be in time."

All around them now, the laughter became deafening and with sickening dread, Elijah realised that he was seeing many pairs of long bony fingered hands literally emerging out of the ground.

"W-what are those?" he stammered.

Matthias looked at him head to one side and shrugged as he said.

"Phantom Mountains?"

The twitching fingers wriggled as the laughter amplified in response, and arms were appearing, writhing around and feeling about to try to grab anything alive.

"Here they come!" Kwatili cried, pointing upwards at tiny black dots in the sky above them.

No-one doubted that her next shrill call was saying "Hurry up!"

Matthias suddenly leapt to his feet, grabbed hold of Elijah at the waist and hoisted him up above his head. Looking down

Elijah saw that where he had just been crouching a grotesque skull face had emerged, grinning at him and licking fleshless lips.

Swooping down came the Sky Oren, so fast that they could hear the wind whistling over their hides.

"Jump!" The first to reach them shouted. They did, with the Phantoms of the Mountain snapping at their heels with black teeth.

Each of them was scooped up in a leather lasso held between the back legs of the Sky Oren and yanked upwards out of reach.

Soaring upwards until high above the Mountain top, the Sky Oren rode thermals until all of their cargo were secure in their harnesses, then they dived down across the peak that was now crawling with screaming grey figures searching desperately for their prey.

"Head for the Viridian Lake, we can take it from there!" Shouted Matthias, his voice barely audible above the wind roaring past their ears.

Water streamed out of the outer corners of Elijah's eyes and into his hairline and he was sure he could feel his face being distorted by the force of gravity as they plummeted downwards.

"Could we ease up just a bit please?" He managed to push past his gritted teeth.

Instantly his rescuer swung upwards, almost stalling in mid-air, the sudden lurch very nearly regurgitated up his bowl of stew.

As one, all five others followed suit, and began drifting like leaves on a breeze, circling around each other.

"Now look what you've done, we need speed and we need to be out of eyesight pronto, make for the Lake and fast!" yelled Matthias and was instantly obeyed by all save the Oren carrying Elijah.

Bending its horse like head down so that only he could hear, it said.

"Juno says hi Elijah Grey, and he told me to look after you, so that's what I will do!"

Elijah smiled and replied, "Thanks, much appreciated, um…?"

"Goren, my name's Goren."

The boy couldn't supress a soft chuckle as he dangled like a cherry on a tree beneath the slowly descending, Goren the Oren!

# Chapter 18

The Veridian Lake loomed up below, emerald green and shimmering in the limpid sunlight.

The Sky Oren wheeled slowly like vultures circling a corpse until they were low enough to be able to drop their passengers safely on the moss covered shore. They then landed themselves, shaking droplets of water off before folding the skin away behind their forelegs.

Elijah lay his hand gently on Goren's neck, he could clearly feel the thudding pulse of the creature's heart beneath his fingers.

"Great flying Goren, thanks." He said.

"Oh it's more falling with style really, but you're most welcome Elijah Grey!"

"Come Goren, we have a long walk back, we need to get going."

The other Oren had already headed off in the direction of the distant mountains, Goren laid his chin on Elijah's shoulder for a second, then walked awkwardly off after them, almost instantly being swallowed up by the dense vegetation that fringed the lake.

"Um, why are they walking when they can fly, that doesn't make sense?" He asked no-one in particular.

"Not flying, falling with style!" came back a reply from the greenery.

Ranger chuckled and shouldered his back sack once more.

"What's our next move my Lord?" He asked Matthias, who quickly held a finger to his lips, saying

" No longer anyone's Lord, Ranger; plain Matthias will do, and we will follow the shore line for as long as we can and then, see what happens!"

"What about Xan, he will continue to pursue us I assume, won't we be a bit too visible just walking along out in the open?" Asked Elijah, watching with curiosity the strange glances that darted around their five faces like a billiard ball.

"Aha, now that's where we've been sneaky, he will be drawn to the Eye of Ula, which he will assume you are now in possession of, but it is still within the Cave with Burda. The time that it will take for him to realise his mistake should give us enough time to reach a more safe place for tonight."

Matthias sounded supremely confident but his lack of eye contact made Elijah wary, then a red faced Ranger coughed nervously.

"Well, er, that isn't exactly true my-er-Matthias."

Matthias drew in breath slowly, eyes closed before asking quietly.

"Because the Eye of Ula is where?"

Instead of speaking, Ranger reached into his back sack and withdrew a small red leather pouch in a slightly trembling hand as if it were able to bite.

"Burda insisted that it stay with him as it is his by birth, and she, well she was concerned that if anything fatal should befall her it would end up, well, you know."

A terrifying yellow flame ignited in his eyes as Matthias turned to face Ranger, but the other's obvious suffering seemed to douse that fire and he blew out his held breath and laughed heartily.

"Well my Elijah, since it is obviously determined to be in your possession, you may as well take it, but keep it safely tucked away and do not under any circumstances remove it from the pouch until I say to do so." He said, taking the pouch from Ranger and plonking it into Elijah's hand, taking his fingers in his own and closing the boys hand forcefully around it.

Elijah swallowed hard. He could feel a soft pulse in the palm of his hand as if this jewel was alive, resisting the urge to throw it as far as possible, he shoved it deep into his back sack and secured the ties as if to contain a wild animal. There were indeed going to be a lot of questions to be answered now!

"That changes the plan somewhat, we must travel as fast as we can in order to spend as little time as possible out in plain sight, let's go."

Kwatili headed the company off along the mossy coated shoreline, keeping the emerald green water of the lake to their right. The moss was slippery and spongy beneath their feet and the going was slow and hot and humid. With Matthias behind Kwatili, followed by Khizzi, Elijah, Ranger and Ghelli bringing up the rear, they trudged in tense silence, the only sounds being their laboured breathing and the soft licking of waves at the lake's edge.

Steadfastly keeping his gaze glued to the bobbing bag on Khizzi's back; Elijah refused to allow himself to look upward, dreading the sight of Skorpios or worse.

To his right, the muffled plops coming from the viscous lake water sounded almost like voices to his heightened senses, and occasionally his brain told him that he could see movement keeping alongside him as he walked, but he told his brain it was wrong.

It wasn't.

Just below the surface, he thought he saw eyes, and a large shadowy shape was definitely undulating beneath them, keeping pace with him at all times.

Without altering his pace or turning round he whispered to Ranger.

"There's something following us in the water."

"Yes, it has been so since we started." Ranger whispered back.

"Now what? Is it Xan again? Should we stop, run, what?"

Before anyone could answer him, Kwatili halted suddenly, turned to face the water, hands on her hips and shouted loudly.

"If you want to be helpful, frightening the boy is not the way to go Spiro!"

For a second the glassy surface of the lake merely echoed her voice back to them.

Then slowly out of the depths rose a huge head, at least the size of Elijah himself; higher and higher it rose, on a long slender, muscular neck. Large clumps of weed were dropped back into the lake with loud plops and splashes and the transfixed onlookers were sprayed as it expelled water from its fist sized nostrils. Whirling its flat fish like eyes it raised the rest of its bulk above the surface of the water. Floating there like a giant black rubber duck; it proceeded to fix its gaze on Elijah, and bowing its huge bony head it said.

"Juno says to say hi, and that I should look after you very well Elijah Grey."

It was like a bubble bursting in his chest, he spluttered and laughed hysterically as relief washed over him.

"Don't tell me, are you a Water Oren by any chance?" He asked, taking a step towards the floating creature.

It tilted its head to one side and opened its cavernous mouth, lined with sharp pointed teeth, in its best attempt at a smile.

"That I am, Juno told me that you were smart, he was correct it seems."

"So, Spiro, can you help us or are you here merely to hinder our passage, we need to find a place to stay in safety for at least tonight, away from prying eyes." Matthias said, stepping forward to stand beside Elijah.

"Well, I would be deeply honoured to transport the son of Egreya, where to go I'm not sure, I am a creature of the deep and have no knowledge of safe places above the water."

"May I suggest the Glidiri Caves, it will require a brief period of submersion but Xan and his minions will not be able to detect our presence once inside them." Ranger had joined them at the water's edge, as had Ghelli and Khizzi.

Spiro rolled his huge eyes in thought, and then slowly nodded his dripping head.

"I do agree with the white haired one, the Glidiri caves would indeed be a good hiding place if I can just remember how to get to them."

"Well, whilst that slow brain of yours gets to work, how about we get aboard and get the hell off this shore, I'm starting to feel like a target board we're so easy to spot!" Matthias rumbled as he ushered Elijah forward towards the boat size body in the water.

As Elijah stumbled cautiously onto the slippery surface of the Water Oren's back, he found himself wondering how they would all manage to fit and, more importantly, stay put and not slither over board.

Then he remembered how Juno had been able to actually rearrange his body to form a comfortable saddle shape for him to sit on as he had carried him over the desert. As if he'd read his mind, Spiro's broad black back began to dip in the centre and then, as he watched, it widened out until he was left standing in a waist deep boat shape, sunken into the Oren's back, large enough to comfortably accommodate all six with ease.

"Wow, you Oren would make awesome taxis!" He commented as he settled himself down at the end just behind the long giraffe like neck.

"I agree Elijah, as a beast of burden the Oren reign supreme, although unfortunately their brain power doesn't tend to match this, no offence Spiro." Kwatili said smiling.

"Oh none taken at all Kwatili, Princess of the Desert, but if it is of any consequence, this poor old head of mine has managed to remember how to get to the Gladiri Caves, I think."

"That'll do us, top speed please, anywhere fast is preferable now I fear!" Snapped Matthias, pointing up at the darkening sky.

They all saw the undulating swarm immediately, and Spiro gave a massive kick with all four webbed feet, sending them surging forward out into the middle of the lake in seconds.

Fast as he was, however, the swarm of Skorpios was faster. Within minutes they were hissing and spitting out their venom above them as they huddled as flat as possible into the hollow in Spiro's back.

"We cannot out run them, I have an idea!" Shouted Matthias above the angry buzzing, and he wriggled on his stomach over to where Elijah was cowering with his hands clamped over his ears.

"Throw it over the side, the Eye of Ula, throw it as far as you can Elijah!"

"What? Are you mad? Do you have any idea what Burda went through to get this, whatever it is, to me?" the boy screamed back at him, clutching his bag tightly against his chest and glaring at Matthias.

"Trust me my son, do you think you can trust me?" Matthias whispered for the boy's ears alone.

"It is the Eye of Ula, it was created for your mother before you, and now it knows you, it will find its way back to you; but for now, losing it will save your life."

Meeting his father's yellow eyes, Elijah hesitated for a heartbeat more, and then he reached into the bag, grabbed the pouch containing the Eye of Ula and hurled it as far as he was capable into the distance behind them. For a split second it rested on the thick surface of green, and then it sank from sight.

Instantly the Skorpios wheeled around in the sky above them and fizzed off in the direction of the disappearing ripples, and, without hesitation, each and every one of them dove to their death to follow it.

The company sat in stunned silence staring wide eyed at the now mirror still surface. Each of them dreading the sight of Skorpios emerging. With a collective exhaling they finally accepted with great relief that, for now, that threat had been eliminated. Without bidding, Spiro returned to his rhythmic paddling strokes, and the group eased themselves back to nestle once more in the hollow of his broad back.

Lying outstretched on his back with his head resting on his arms, Elijah forced himself to relax, staring upwards at the ever darkening sky above. Beside him lay Khizzi, her soft breathing soothing the last jangles of nerves better than any words.

As the sky behind them turned to aubergine velvet, the stars became brighter and more distinct.

Back at home Elijah loved nothing more than to get out an old pair of binoculars that Burda had presented him with one Christmas, and study the constellations. He had become fairly good at identifying the main ones; but now as he studied these, he frowned. They were completely unfamiliar to him, more than anything else that had happened to him since he had arrived in this world, this fact disturbed him the most and drove home the fact that he was truly in another world to that in which he felt he belonged.

Suddenly as he gazed upwards, the stars shocked him even more; they all moved!

Not by much but each star, as he stared at them, shifted slightly, not uniformly in one direction either but haphazardly, stayed put for a few moments, and then off in another direction.

"It can be very disconcerting at first, but after a while you stop noticing it." Whispered Khizzi, reaching out in the darkness to tentatively squeeze his hand.

Without taking his eyes off the pinball stars, he whispered back.

"Just tell me they're not something else out to get me."

"Oh no, they are stars Elijah, just stars." She answered.

"But stars don't move like that back where I come from!" He said.

"Well, it's not exactly the stars that are moving, more that we are passing through different realms, and it is only visible at night time."

"And by the way, this is where you come from Elijah, the cabin in the woods was just where you grew up until seven days ago."

Rangers had joined them from the far end of the "Spiro boat", where he, Matthias, Kwatili and Ghelli had been in hushed conversation.

"Picture it like the kaleidoscope that Burda gave you for your sixth birthday, as you turn it, different pieces of a pattern fall into place and then out again, and yet your eye remains the constant. We are living in a universe made up of multiple different realms, all revolving slowly around which ever one you are on at the time. There are doorways between them that open and shut at random, thus we, Burda and I with you as a tiny baby, were able to enter the realm where we were hoping you could reach adulthood before Xan found you. Obviously that was not to be, and here we are."

Ranger sighed, he was berating himself for not realising sooner that their hiding place had been discovered.

"Hey Ranger, I should have told you about creepy Mr Nax, but to be honest I'd forgotten all about him by the time I got home, it wasn't your fault, and hey, you got me away safely in the end. So how did you know that a doorway was going to open in the Forest that day anyway?"

Ranger paused for just a bit too long, making Elijah turn to study his long thin face.

"It was not I but you who knew that a doorway was going to open that day, I simply read the signs written on your face."

"B-but I didn't have any idea things like that even existed, I thought it was just an ordinary forest!"

"Consciously yes, but deep down, if you really think about it, is that true Elijah?"

Ranger replied softly, watching the painful internal struggle play over his friend's features.

"No, I guess there was something that felt different that morning, I can't put my finger on it but I do remember feeling strangely drawn into the Forest, especially into that clearing; like there was a picture almost forming in my mind of exactly what happened, but it was all wispy like it was made out of smoke."

"Well, isn't it a shame that you tossed the Eye of Ula into the Lake to be eaten by the fish then? With it that smoke would clear and you'd be able to-"

"Spiro! Hush that weed filled mouth of yours!" Snapped Matthias from the far end of Spiro's back.

"I was only saying -"Spluttered the Water Oren sulkily, spitting out a wayward tendril of weed from the corner of his huge mouth.

"What you should be saying is - oh yes I remember exactly how to get to the Gladiri Caves, after all, I am a Water Oren and that's what I do, take folk to safe places, on the water!"

Matthias grumbled, as he scrambled forward to squat down beside Elijah and Ranger.

"Don't take any notice of him Elijah, you did the right thing trust me, his water logged brain just can't focus on two things at once."

Spiro blew a multitude of bubbles angrily out of his nostrils and ceased his paddling completely, leaving them floating motionless on the gently rocking surface of the lake.

Kwatili huffed out a breath of frustration, glared at Matthias and edged herself close to the Water Oren's long stiff neck.

Stretching up to her full height so that she was virtually head to head with him, she proceeded to converse in a strange series of gurgles and clicks from the depths of her throat. Spiro listened silently, a smile slowly kinking his mouth and his flat fish like eyes rolled to look at Matthias. Finally, snorting loudly and wetly out of his nose, he resumed his strong thrusting strokes, propelling them once more over the flat lake surface.

"Okay, I guess I don't want to know what you said to him, and I probably deserved it whatever it was." Muttered Matthias as he crawled back to his place.

"No you don't, and yes you certainly did." She replied, winking at Ranger and Elijah as she too made her way back to her place.

Much as he felt glad to be moving again, Elijah was still thinking about what Spiro had said, suppose this Eye of Ula thing was the only way that he was ever going to get back home? Suppose Matthias wasn't actually on the level. What if throwing it over board had really been a plot hatched between this Xan person and

Matthias? How did he know that he could trust him? Ryufu certainly hadn't been pleased to see him.

Surreptitiously positioning himself so that he could study Matthias, Elijah watched him staring out over the flat green horizon, one hand absentmindedly toying with some kind of pendant on a chain around his neck, in the fading blush sunlight it glinted like a small pink star.

"He suffers greatly every day that she is gone."

Khizzi's soft whisper came as a shock, he hadn't even been aware that she had moved from her place beside Kwatili.

"She?" He asked.

"The great love of his life, what tortures most must be the not knowing. I can't imagine, I don't want to." Khizzi shivered, clutching her cloak more tightly around her shoulders.

A brisk breeze had picked up around them as the sun dipped beneath the lake. Whipping Elijah's long hair across his face.

"If you'd like I could braid it for you," She said shyly, gesturing towards his hair.

"Oh, yeah, that would be much better, thanks." He replied, turning his back to her, and hunching over his knees.

Teasing out tangles as she went, Khizzi carefully braided his now waist length hair into a long pigtail.

Reaching behind he gave it a tug and nodded.

"Much better thanks, guess it's something I'll have to learn how to do myself now."

Khizzi chuckled, tugging at a tight curl on her own head.

"Swap!" She said grinning.

Suddenly out of the gathering darkness, Spiro said loudly.

"Oh! The Gladiri Caves! I remember now! And hold tight this might get bumpy, we seem to have company!"

All around them the surface of the water appeared to bubble and boil, like stew on a hob. As they strained to see what it was, brief glimpses of shiny silver backs coated in needle sharp spines was all they got.

"Lurchins!" shouted Ghelli "Keep back from sight, if they see you they will fire!"

No sooner had the words left his mouth than a hail shower of spines clattered over them, narrowly missing all targets, but very narrowly. Elijah watched aghast as they wriggled around on the surface of Spiro's back, still searching for soft flesh to embed themselves in, before fizzing into steam and disappearing.

"Dive Spiro, it is our only defence, you can out manoeuvre them under water, every one grab hold of something and take a deep breath!"

Kwatili's order brooked no argument.

All aboard the Water Oren filled their lungs with air and grabbed hold of his loose skin in desperate hand holds as Spiro closed his own nostrils and plunged below the water.

Elijah squeezed his eyes tightly shut as the icy water enclosed him in a numbing embrace. All around him he could feel the Lurchins frenzied attack, and he waited for the sting of a spine piercing his skin. He could sense how much faster they were moving through the water which roared in his ears like thunder and his lungs felt like they were about to burst, the desire to take a breath became almost irresistible.

"Hold on Elijah, do not give in to it, you're nearly there!"

The words were in his head, not his ears which were still full of rushing water, but he held on, although the numbing effect of the cold was beginning to make him feel drowsy and like he really didn't care anymore, he just wanted to curl up and sleep forever.

Just as a high pitched ringing threatened to steal his sanity completely, Spiro erupted out of the water like a geyser and belly-flopped down onto the surface, with all six passengers gasping and coughing and still clinging madly to his back.

"Okay, now that really hurts you know!" He grumbled as he paddled slowly to shore.

Slowly six sets of clenched finger relaxed their grasp on his skin and sat up to gaze in wonder about them.

"The Glidiri Caves, I had forgotten just how beautiful they were." Murmured Kwatili.

Blinking water out of his eyes, Elijah was speechless. They were floating a few feet from the shore, bobbing gently with the softly lapping waves that made a hushed whisper as they washed up over a beach that seemed to consist of huge pearls. The whole cavern was bathed in light, which appeared to emanate from hundreds of tall crystalline structures that stood all around them like pillars in a temple. They stretched floor to ceiling of the cave, and made it difficult to assess accurately the size and shape of the cave, but to Elijah it felt vast and intimidating.

"Come, we're in need of warmth to dry out and food, follow me and don't anyone wander off alone, it is all too easy to lose more than your way amongst the crystals."

Kwatili spoke quietly as she leapt over the side and into the water to wade ashore, but the effect of the crystals was immediate and her voice was amplified and echoed back and forth bouncing of numerous flat mirror like surfaces before dying out.

As he followed her lead, Ghelli stopped to cast a warning glare in Elijah's direction.

"And don't make any loud noises or sudden moves, we obviously want to remain undetected."

Elijah wanted to shout back, "Whatever!" but thought better of it, choosing to drop silently into the warm green water and wade carefully ashore instead. He was pleased to receive a huge grin from Khizzi for his troubles.

Once on the beach, he looked more closely and realised that what he was walking on was indeed very much like perfect round pearls, he reached down and scooped up a handful, letting them trickle through his fingers and marvelling at the silky milk white sheen on each one.

Beautiful they may be, but their silkiness proved tricky to walk over, he slipped and slithered as if he was on ice, and found himself floundering on hands and knees more than once before he reached a part of the shore that was flat and rocky and solid beneath his feet.

Sighing with exhaustion, he could now take the time to look around and study the amazing crystals more closely. He almost fell flat on his back in shock at what he saw.

They were not translucent as he had expected but each was covered by a multitude of flat reflective surfaces, producing a carnival hall of mirrors effect; and what he saw were multiple images of a tall, thin, black haired being, with jet black eyes that stared out from beneath sharply prominent brow ridge and cheek bones, his nose had become so elongated and pointed that it looked more like a beak than a nose.

As he staggered from one to another, being greeted by the same sight again and again, his heart thudded harder and harder and he felt reality escaping with each breathe that he panted out.

How had this happened to him? How could that apparition in the crystals be him? He was just a fifteen year old kid, not some half bird monster!

Sinking to his knees, he covered his face with his hands, he couldn't bear to see it any more.

A warm hand on his neck felt like an electric shock, he kept his face covered, and whispered into his hands.

"I want it to end, I want this nightmare to end I can't do this anymore, I'm just a kid!"

"Raven Boy, I can only try to understand how frightening all of this must be, but contrary to what I would have said a few days ago, you are most definitely not just a kid, and you can do this, in fact, you are the only one who can."

The fact that it was Ghelli who had spoken shocked Elijah out of his downward spiral of panic more than anything else could have done.

He looked up into the other's brown, serious features. As if he was already regretting his words, Ghelli coughed and took his hand away from the boy's shoulder, opened his lips as if to continue, thought better of it, and walked briskly away, his long prehensile tail winding and unwinding itself around his waist as he walked.

Drawing in a deep ragged breath, Elijah rose unsteadily to his feet, carefully avoiding the reflections that mirrored his actions to either side of him. He searched for Ranger, spotted his snow white head deep in conversation with Kwatili at the shoreline where Spiro's large black bulk still bobbed on the gentle waves.

Spiro tilted his huge horse shape head when he spied his approach and his mouth cracked apart in the semblance of a smile.

"If it makes it easier, I personally think you look like a damn cool, funky dude Elijah Grey, and so does Juno!"

Spiros words and his crooked smile made the boy feel like crying and laughing at the same time.

"Now where did you learn language like that? If Burda heard you she'd probably call it toilet talk!" He replied

Thoughts of Burda, yet again left behind and in danger, quickly doused his spark of cheer but he added.

"I guess I know now why we never had mirrors in the house, and why she never put up the one I bought her."

"We both tried to make sure that your life was as normal as we could make it for as long as possible Elijah. Xan discovered our hiding place far more quickly than we had expected him to; all of this was planned to take place many more years into your future."

Elijah turned to Ranger, and nodded.

"So just how did he find us, any ideas?"

It was Kwatili who answered, meeting the boy's gaze steadily.

"The only explanation has to be that he is now in possession of the other Eye of Ula, it is the only way that he could have opened a doorway into your world as he did."

"That cannot be! She would never willingly give it up!" Matthias raged, before falling silent and thoughtful.

"The thought is as abhorrent to me as to you Matthias, but it is a fact which has to be faced and factored into whatever plan we carry out next if we are to have any chance of saving Greylea from Xan." She said quietly, before turning her face up to address the patiently waiting Water Oren.

"As ever Spiro, your kind have served us magnificently, go now with our grateful thanks, but keep an ear turned towards us should we need you again, my friend."

With that she bowed gracefully.

Spiro grinned widely, a rather alarming sight when his mouth could easily have enveloped Elijah's head with no problem at all.

The rest of the company added their own thanks and Spiro turned slowly around before submerging in a flurry of bubbles beneath the verdant fluid, to disappear almost instantaneously.

For some time, they all stood, in silent contemplation of the empty space left on the water with his departure. Then, one by one they trudged back up the beach of slippery pearls to sit in a long row on the flat rocks with their backs to the crystals pillars.

"I see, friend Kwatili, that for this visit you are not alone."

None had been aware of a newcomer approaching and all save Kwatili jerked to their feet in alarm.

Kwatili merely laughed and said, without looking up.

"And I see that you are still as adept at the art of sneaking up on me Maylan, one of these days I will hear you damn it!"

# Chapter 19

Equally as tall as Kwatili, the being facing them stunned all save her into silence.

The two greeted each other like old friends, speaking rapidly in a strange language of hisses and sounds like the grinding of teeth.

Finally, they turned to the others, and Kwatili said,

"I would like to introduce you to Maylan, last guardian of the Gladiri Caves."

Maylan inclined her smooth, hairless head towards them, her pearl white eyes glancing from one to the other until she reached Elijah, on him her gaze rested, head tilted, studying him closely. It was extremely unnerving, for even though it seemed to him that her white eyes must be blind, he felt that she could see right through him.

Drawing in a deep breath, Maylan moved slowly and gracefully towards him, halting just shy of the beach of pearls. Holding out a long slim white skinned arm she offered him her hand,

"Come Elijah Grey, you and I have just enough time to become acquainted, we will sit whilst the others gather the fish for supper."

A puzzled frown wrinkled his forehead and he was just about to ask what fish? When a sudden loud splashing erupted to his left and astounded, he realised that at least six huge silvery fish had just literally thrown themselves up onto the beach.

Kwatili laughed loudly.

"I had forgotten that trick too! I guess this means that somewhere away from the beach, we will discover a fire already set, waiting to be lit?"

Without taking her eyes from Elijah, Maylan nodded and gestured over to her right, where there was indeed a small fire sitting on the rocks.

As the others made their way over to it, each hoisting a fish into their arms, she guided Elijah over to one side, and seated herself, motioning for him to join her.

Close up, she was even more breath taking. Her skin was like smooth snakeskin, and gleamed like captured moonlight. He realised with a jolt that technically she was naked, but her body too was covered in the pearly pale snakeskin, and utterly featureless.

"Poor Elijah, the last week of your life has been, what you would call, a steep learning curve, has it not?"

She ran her fingers gently down the curve of his cheek, in an almost motherly gesture.

"Um, yeah, you definitely could say that." He stammered, unable to meet her gaze now, staring down at his feet, painfully aware of a hot flush igniting his cheeks.

"Alas, time is not a luxury that you have, Xan is gaining power as we speak, I can protect and hide you from him for a short time, but then I will be spent; you bring with you my downfall Elijah Grey."

Her words shocked him so much that he forgot his awkwardness and looked her straight in the face.

"What? No that can't be, I won't let you do that for me!" He cried out.

Maylan again reached out her hand and touched him lightly on the arm.

"The decision is not yours to make, it is mine and I make it freely, I will join the rest of my kind with pleasure as long as I have fulfilled my last task. I am, as Kwatili has said, the last Guardian of the Gladiri Caves, it has been a long and lonely vigil but I have had the constant reminder of my predecessors to hold me to my destiny."

"But you're alone here." Said Elijah glancing around, just to check.

Maylan laughed like pebbles falling down a slide and pointed towards the beach of pearls.

"Did you think that it was just a coincidence that the shores were covered in pebbles that resembled my eyes? No Elijah Grey, those are the eyes of all of the previous Guardians of these caves, who have fallen in their defence since the beginning of time."

No words came to him as Elijah gaped at the shining beach in a totally new light, and felt a sickness in his stomach when he remembered all too clearly the soft crunch that they had made beneath his feet as he had walked over them!

"I'm so sorry, I didn't know!" He finally managed to splutter out.

She shook her head, "There is nothing to be sorry for Elijah, you need to remember why you are here, it is to save this world from destruction by Xan, and that will cost you dearly, it is I who should be sorry for what is to come."

"I want to ask what that is, but I somehow think I don't want to know," The boy whispered, shaken by her words and the tone of her voice.

"Why don't we eat, and see what unfolds, I feel sure that you will gain strength to face all after food and sleep." She rose abruptly, and held out her hand to help him to his feet. He suddenly realised that while they had been talking the others had obviously been busy, as he caught the delicious scent of roasting fish. As they approached, Ranger and Matthias wordlessly shifted to make a space for them both to fit into the circle surrounding the crackling and spitting fire. Suspended on a trivet above the flames were the last three fish, their skins gradually browning, the others were already resting in fragrant steaminess on a large metal platter keeping warm beside the fire pit.

Khizzi stabbed one with her knife and offered it to Elijah, who began to salivate profusely as he reached out for it, but Maylan held up her hand to stop Khizzi.

"Not that one Khizzi, Elijah Grey needs to be given the one at the bottom of the pile." She said calmly.

Not daring to question her, Khizzi obediently replaced that fish with the seemingly identical one from the bottom of the pile on the plate, scooting it's singed tail onto the plate before offering it once more to a bemused but grateful for anything edible, Elijah.

As he teased a finger full of the soft white flesh and sent it down to his empty stomach, all but Maylan set to, eating hungrily and in silence.

Concentrating only on getting the next mouthful ready whilst swallowing the one before, Elijah demolished his meal in minutes, and it wasn't until he had virtually stripped every morsel of flesh from the bones that he stopped and nearly dropped the fish plate and all in amazement.

There, nestled beneath the ribcage, completely unscathed was the small red leather pouch that contained The Eye of Ula!

The circle of faces shared the same expression, except for the serene features of Maylan. She smiled a curl of a smile as she rose effortlessly to her feet to walk away from the fire nodding to herself with satisfaction.

Holding the drawstring gingerly between thumb and first finger as if it was about to bite him, Elijah brushed the last vestiges of fish flesh from the pouch.

"Did I not say that it would find a way to return to you Elijah? Perhaps you will not doubt me so much in the future." Matthias said as he too rose and left the circle, walking off in the opposite direction to the one taken by Maylan.

"So, what do I do with it now?" Elijah whispered, his eyes darting from one face to the next.

"I mean, is it dangerous? Is it safe for me to take it out?"

Taking a deep breath before moving to sit beside him, Kwatili gently but firmly removed it from his hand and untied the drawstring.

"Hold out your hand Elijah Grey." She said, and when he obeyed, she tipped the contents into his waiting palm.

He flinched instinctively as the small round object touched his skin. For some reason he had expected it to feel hot, but it was cold, like a ball of ice. It lay in the palm of his hand like a hole, so black that it reflected no light at all, smooth and utterly flawless. Tipping his hand he carefully rolled it over, it was flawless.

Kwatili leaned in and deftly scooped it safely back into the pouch. Looking deep into the boy's face she said,

"Have no fear Elijah, this is probably not the time for teaching you how to control something as powerful and dangerous as the Eye of Ula. Keep it safe until that time comes."

With that she pushed it into his hands and squeezed them tightly around it.

106

He tried to push it back towards her.

"You keep it Kwatili, I don't want it!" He stammered, suddenly trembling and dry mouthed.

Kwatili gazed at him with her deep amber eyes brimming with tears that tracked their way down her cheeks, following the black stripes down her face.

"Oh Elijah, it breaks my heart to load such a burden on one so young, but truly the Eye of Ula is meant for you and you alone, I couldn't take it from you even if I wanted to. But you must trust me when I say that you will never be expected to carry this weight alone while I breathe."

Then, as if her words weren't disturbing enough, the statuesque Kwatili, stood before him and bowed her head as if he was some kind of king or something! Red faced he shoved the pouch deep into his pocket, and turned away from the fire, taking very special care not to venture down onto the beach of pearls, now that he knew what they really were, he had no desire to step on them! He walked over to where Maylan was now sitting cross legged on a large flat smooth rock, staring out over the lapping green water. Suddenly unsure of himself, he halted and stood awkwardly shuffling his feet, fighting the urge to retreat.

"Sit Elijah Grey." She said in a hushed voice.

Gingerly he eased himself onto the corner of her rock, crossed his own long legs and waited for her to do something.

For several moments, she did nothing, simply stared steadily out over the water with her blind eyes, her chest barely rising and falling so shallow was her breathing. Then, closing her eyes and tilting her head back, she drew in a long deep breath, held it and then sighed it out.

Without moving or opening her eyes, she whispered.

"Drink in the peace Elijah Grey, for it will not last for much longer, you're coming here brings about the destruction of the Glidiri Caves and the last of the Guardians"

"Why? What can I do to prevent that happening?" He cried.

Slowly she turned her silvery skinned face towards him and her lipless mouth curved into a sad smile, she shook her head and leaned forward to take hold of both of his clenched hands in hers.

"What you can do is to stop fighting destiny, yours and ours. It is unfortunate that you have come to this point far earlier than was intended, but, as they say, the best laid plans. What is important is that you are far from here by the time Xan gets here, and that you remain safe until you're able to use the Eye of Ula to bring about his downfall."

"But I can't do something like that, I'm just a kid!" he yelled, yanking his hands from hers.

She held her hand up in front of him and silenced him instantly.

"That is not true and never was Elijah Grey, you are not just anything, you are Elijah Grey, son of Egreya and Matthias and the last hope of Greylea, and your time is now, accept this or we are all doomed."

"But I'm scared Maylan, a week ago, the worst thing I'd ever had to deal with was a spider in my bedroom and the occasional howling of wolves from the forest at night, I can't fight battles or kill things."

"But you are not alone and you have a strength as yet untried and untested, Egreya would have been proud of what you have become."

Matthias's quiet voice at his shoulder made Elijah jump so much that he almost fell off the rock, Ranger saved him just in time from landing unceremoniously on the ground at their feet. They had all silently appeared to stand around the rock, gazes focussed on the startled boy now standing and barely controlling his panic.

Slowly Maylan descended off the rock herself, and placed a cool hand onto his trembling shoulder, but when she spoke, it was the others that she addressed.

"I feel that it would be best for us all, and especially Elijah, to get some sleep now, we will all need to have clear thinking minds tomorrow, I would suggest the back edge of the cave, where the ground is softer."

For a few seconds no one moved or spoke, then, one by one the group turned and began to make their way up the sloping cave towards the darkness at the back.

Elijah followed them because he simply couldn't think of anything else to do, his brain was in turmoil and he was absolutely certain that sleep was the very last thing that he wanted.

Choosing a spot as close to the curving back wall as possible, he lay down on the warm, soft sandy ground. Ranger took up his usual position beside him, which calmed his thudding heart somewhat, he lay there trying desperately to pretend that he was back in his warm safe bed, with his faithful dog at his bedside, with school tomorrow. But that was not going to happen. Tomorrow, what would come would not be Burda bellowing down the hall to get up and eat his breakfast or do the dishes for the next week, tomorrow, according to Maylan, the end of the world that he was now in would come, and it would end because he was supposed to be some sort of hero, but he didn't know how to be a hero, he was just a kid!

"Do not think that your youth is such a bad thing Elijah, in fact it may well be that it is that very thing that will enable you to prevail when I failed."

He glanced around, looking to see if any of the others had heard it, knowing full well that the voice had been in his own head and no one else's.

"Come to the crystal Elijah, I want to see you."

Deciding that this would be no stranger than anything else that had happened so far, Elijah carefully picked his way over all of his now soundly sleeping companions to the nearest of the tall crystal structures.

As he stood before it, at first, he thought that he was just looking at his own reflection. Staring back at him was a slender figure, with long raven black hair cascading over their shoulders, black eyes, deeply set within sharply pointed features, especially the beak shaped nose. Two things slowly dawned on him. Firstly he remembered that his own hair had been neatly braided for him by Khizzi, and secondly, behind him was the silvery luminescence of the cave, whereas behind the figure in the crystal, was what looked like a roaring fire and dark shadowy hunched figures.

"Oh my beautiful son, how I have longed to see you."

Her words filtered into his mind, her lips did not move.

Elijah fought the desire to run away, he fought the urge to scream out loud, he fought back tears that tried to burst free at the sound of her voice.

Struggling to regain control, he forced his brain to form words in his head.

"Is this real? So much has happened to me that's mad and crazy I don't know what's real anymore."

He couldn't see any change to her face but he felt the sadness in her reply,

"Not real as you would understand it, but I am real, and I am alive, I want you to tell them this, especially Matthias, who has been convinced that I died when Xan first captured me. Elijah my son, you must come to rescue me, for only you can. It breaks my heart to ask you to put yourself into such danger for me, but I have no choice, we have no choice."

At her last words, two more figures appeared into his range of vision within the crystal. One was a pale skinned female, with short cut snow white hair, she stared pleadingly unto Elijah's eyes, with eyes as bright blue as a summer sky; the other, much smaller, stood beside her, clinging around her waist, head tucked tightly into her stomach.

"Elijah, this is-"

"Rangers wife and child!" He cried out loud before he could stop himself.

Instantly he heard a flurry of scrabbling and grunting from behind him as all five jerked awake and were on their feet within a heartbeat.

As he turned back to the crystal, he was stunned to see once more his own jagged and refracted reflection and that of the others as they gathered around him.

"What in the name of the Heartland is all the racket about?" Shouted Matthias, re-sheathing the glinting knife that he had drawn instinctively as he had awoken.

Pointing at the crystal, Elijah jabbered excitedly.

"I saw my mother, well I think it was my mother, she looked like me and she called me son, and she said to tell you all especially Matthias that she is alive and then I saw your wife and child Ranger, they're with her, wherever that is, she went before I could find that out, but she said that I have to go and rescue her because only I can or something like that!"

The effect on his audience was not quite the one that he expected.

110

Khizzi gasped and clasped her hands to her mouth, Ranger sank to his knees and sobbed, and Matthias and Ghelli scowled angrily. Kwatili was the only one who actually looked pleased by his revelations. Holding up both hands to halt any retorts from Ghelli and Matthias, she walked calmly towards Elijah and placed her hands onto his shoulders.

"Tell me exactly what happened Elijah" She said, looking deep into his eyes.

Taking a breath, the boy recounted how he had woken up with a voice calling him to the crystal and what he had seen and heard in his head.

Kwatili smiled and released him, to turn to the others saying,

"The boy speaks truly, he was contacted by Egreya by mind meld, only she could have achieved such a feat, and therefore we can trust what he said he saw, Egreya and Rheyana are indeed alive along with your child Ranger; and they need our help."

Ranger staggered to his feet and hugged both Kwatili and Elijah, before silently taking himself off to the quiet gloom of the cave wall to sit with his head in his hands.

Matthias, however, stood in front of Elijah, hands on his hips still with an angry cloud over his features.

"Tell, me everything, what did she look like, where was she?"

Leaning back from him, Elijah stuttered,

"I couldn't see very clearly, she was somewhere big because I couldn't see any windows or walls, and there were loads of other people but they were grey and fuzzy. But I don't think she could move, and she didn't speak out loud."

Matthias stepped back and looked thoughtful for a moment, before turning on his heels and stalking off in the direction of the beach where Maylan was still sitting staring out to sea.

As he approached her, Maylan said, without moving.

"Yes, he has her imprisoned in a Glidiri Crystal, she is alive but immobilised, only able to use her mind as she has just discovered. He keeps Rheyana and her son there as insurance against her trying to escape."

Matthias scattered a shower of pearl stones into the green water as he threw himself down at her feet and forced her to look him in the face.

111

"So you knew this all along and said nothing! What possible reason could you have for being so cruel?"

Maylan rose regally to her feet and replied steadily.

"I knew nothing for certain until Elijah Grey himself found out just now, you forget that I am connected to every crystal in the Glidiri Caves, when Egreya made contact, I too felt it and heard her words."

He stared at her with fire in his yellow eyes, fists clenched by his sides for a moment more, before sagging into acceptance.

"We must get to her Maylan, I cannot bear the thought of her imprisoned and in his hands now that I know that she lives."

She touched his shoulder briefly, and replied smiling sadly.

"Of course you must, you will leave directly I would speak to young Elijah, alone."

Nodding and obediently running off up the slope to where the rest were still sitting stunned by recent revelations, Matthias found Elijah being comforted by Khizzi.

"Maylan would speak with you alone Elijah, the rest of you, we are leaving as soon as possible, get packed up."

"But we don't know where they are being held Matthias, how are we expected to find them?"

Asked Ghelli, frowning as he frantically shoved things into his back sack.

"I realise that Ghelli, but there is no time to waste, we will have to trust to Egreya to guide us through Elijah, its flimsy but it's all we have." Matthias replied whilst wrapping what was left from last night's meal in large sheets of hide.

"Huh! Flimsy indeed if we have only the word of an out world child to go on!" Snapped Ghelli grumpily.

Matthias halted in his preparations to hurl a small rock in Ghelli's direction angrily, narrowly missing the other's head.

"That is no out worlder, Ghelli, that is my son, and he will not let us nor Greylea down, mark my words!"

"You asked for that brother!" Laughed Khizzi, and turning to Matthias she whispered

"For what it is worth, I do not share my brother's low opinion of Elijah Grey one bit."

112

"I know Elijah better than all of you, and have now more to lose if he cannot locate Egreya, and I do not doubt him for a second."

Ranger's quiet voice caught them all by surprise, he had been locked in his private world of agony in the darkness at the back of the cave, where they had all left him alone to deal with it at his own pace. Now he stood before them red rimmed eyes steady, back sack already on his back, radiating calm purpose.

All three turned towards the sound of footsteps behind them to find Kwatili also with a bulging back sack already hoisted onto her long back.

"We needed more supplies I thought." She said with a sly smile, reaching behind her to pat the sack,

"I'm sure that the army camped just above us on the slopes won't miss a thing!"

"Army, of what Kwatili?" Asked Matthias and Ghelli together.

"Such as I have never witnessed before, Xan has been very busy with his breeding program it seems. It narrows down our escape route certainly." She replied thoughtfully looking towards where Maylan and Elijah were talking down on the shoreline.

"Let us hope that he comes back with a plan." With that she hunkered down on the rocks to wait.

# Chapter 20

As he walked down to Maylan, Elijah's legs lost all strength and his heart thudded in his chest. He had a terrifying conviction that this moment, the moment when he reached her, would change his life for ever. He found himself taking smaller and smaller steps to draw it out, dreading what was to come, and desperately clinging to the last few moments of his old life, the old him.

He chuckled out loud. What old him? He had changed completely from the fifteen-year-old boy who had stepped off the porch that day, expecting to have a run of the mill Saturday walk in the forest with his dog and be back in time for lunch!

Suddenly strengthened, he lengthened his strides and straightened his back. After all, he had a mother now, and she needed him!

Watching the slender-framed boy approach, Maylan smiled to herself as she saw this inner struggle take place and be resolved before he reached her. She hoped that she was right about him, that he had in fact inherited his mother's abilities. If he had not? With a tiny shake of her head she dismissed that train of thought, focus, she must remain totally focussed on the task ahead.

Face to face at last, he thought to himself that she was smaller than he had remembered from the previous night; she thought how much he had already grown since their first meeting.

"Come Elijah Grey, I have much to tell you and very little time in which to tell it, hold my hand and close your eyes, the telling will be much more rapid this way."

Not questioning her for a second, he held out his hand and closed his eyes.

She placed his hand palm down on her forehead, and placed her own on his. Instantly the world exploded into light.

"Keep your eyes closed, Elijah; the thought transfer will be too fast for you to understand it at the moment, but it will become clearer with time," she murmured from what seemed to be a great distance away and right inside his head at the same time.

Images and sounds flashed into his mind like time lapse film, at first he instinctively tried to focus on each one but then relaxed enough to let it all just wash over him, absorbing it like a sponge, whilst understanding none of it. He could feel her palm heating up on his forehead, and her skin becoming chilled beneath his own, and then, with an exhausted gasp, the contact was abruptly broken as she slumped to the ground.

Reaching down, he helped her to her feet, shocked at how grey and wan her skin had become, tiny dry cracks ran down her face and the gleam was gone from her pearl eyes. For a few minutes she leaned against him, her head on his chest. He could hardly hear her breathing it was so ragged and shallow, but gradually she rallied and drew herself away from him.

"Well, Elijah Grey, you know everything that Maylan has ever learned, done, seen and loved, there is no longer any reason for me to remain here in my solitude," she said quietly, a hint of a smile flickered momentarily across her drawn features, then was replaced by stern resolve.

"Go now, they are coming, and I will not be able to hold them off for long, go and fulfil your destiny," she added, gently nudging him in the direction of his waiting friends.

"But, we must stay and help you, together we could—" he began to say but she quickly held up a white hand to stop him.

"No, that is not your destiny, it is mine and always has been, do not try to remember all of what I have imported to you, it cannot be hurried, it will become clear to you when it is ready and until then you must trust your instincts and the Eye of Ula. Just two rules apply to that gift, never try to use it for selfish gain, and never question what it tells you to do, even if it seems like madness at the time, the Eye will have a reason. Now, go young man, it has been an honour to meet you, one that I had begun to fear I would not live to experience, I am very glad that I did."

Elijah still could not move away, there were so many questions that he still needed to ask her, and the thought of just leaving her to an army of who knows what was unthinkable.

Kwatili approached them, her steps barely making a sound over the pearl beach. "Maylan my friend, does it truly have to be so?" she whispered, her huge amber eyes brimming with unshed tears.

In reply Maylan threw back her head and laughed loudly, it echoed and bounced around the cavern like the peal of a bell. "Go, quickly before I weaken and come with you Kwatili, for losing sight of your beautiful face will be the worst part. Take the fight to Xan for me!" she called as she turned and strode swiftly down to the water's edge, took up a position with her arms raised above her head and the green water just lapping over her silvery toes.

Kwatili grabbed Elijah by the arms and pulled him away, never once looking back and not allowing him to, by the time they reached the others the water of the lake had begun to boil.

By the time that they had reached the others, standing transfixed, half way up the slope that lead to the back of the cave, Elijah could hear blood curdling screams coming up from the beach. Turning he stared in horror at the scene below.

Up out of the water had risen about twenty huge nightmare creatures, dripping slime and ooze from multiple tentacles armed with spear length spines that they were firing like hail stones at Maylan, who stood defiantly surrounded now by a semi-circle of glowing crystals, hovering just above the surface of the beach. A low humming emanated from them that vibrated through his chest even from this distance.

As each rain of spines touched the glowing aura created around Maylan, they shattered into dust, but those that found the beach exploded and left blackened destruction in their wake.

"We can't just leave her to fight them alone, she won't win against that onslaught!" he cried, pulling against Kwatili.

She held her grip on his arms and, glancing just once down to her besieged friend, she glared back at Elijah. "Do not think that I will ever recover from what I am about to do Elijah Grey, but your escape, with the Eye of Ula, is truly the most important thing for the survival of Greylea and all who live here, therefore it is what we will do, otherwise Maylan's sacrifice will have been in vain."

"There's just one problem with that plan, Kwatili - there's no way out of the Glidiri Caves other than by swimming under the waters of the lake, which is a tad crowded at the moment," said Matthias quietly.

Suddenly, an image flashed into Elijah's head, it was of a burning circle around a dark swirling hole, and behind it, he clearly saw blue veined rock that glowed brightly. Opening his eyes, he realised that he was grasping the leather pouch containing the Eye of Ula.

"Don't ask me how or why, but I have a really strong feeling that we need to head that way," he said, pointing with his free hand to the right.

For a few seconds no one moved or spoke, then, from the beach, they heard Maylan shout above the ravenous screams of the creatures. "Follow him as you would follow me, go!"

It was like an elastic band snapping, they all lurched into action and ran in the direction that he had indicated. There, against the back wall of the cave, where the rock did indeed contain long veins of deep blue crystals, was a shimmering doorway, ringed by flickering flames.

"But we don't know where this will take us!" Ghelli cried, grabbing Khizzi to prevent her from going near to it.

"If it has appeared for Elijah, then it must be that it will in some way lead us towards our goal, we have to trust in the Eye and in Maylan," replied Kwatili striding up to the hovering portal. "Come, we are running out of time." she added, gesturing for the others to go through.

"Well, I for one am willing to trust in Elijah!" said Khizzi, defiantly yanking her arm from her brother's grasp and plunging through the doorway that fizzed softly as she disappeared from their sight. Immediately Ghelli followed, along with Matthias and Ranger, leaving just Elijah and Kwatili in the cave.

"Together, Elijah Grey?" she whispered, smiling sadly as she held a hand out towards him.

He turned to stare down at the beach, Maylan was visibly weakening now, the glow from the crystals around her was so faint that it could hardly be seen and the huge creatures were now wading ashore, just feet away from her, gnashing fang filled jaws and flicking shower after shower of exploding spines down upon her buckling figure.

Once more he heard her tiny voice in his head. "Take the fight to Xan for me."

Looking back into Kwatili's tear-filled eyes, he squeezed her hand, and then together they plunged head first into the doorway, just as the cavern behind them imploded into non-existence.

# Chapter 21

A soft carpet of moss met his fall as Elijah tumbled forward and sprawled on his face out of the doorway. He lay there, gasping for breath and listening to Kwatili's muffled sobs beside him.

Gradually other sounds filtered into his awareness, sounds that jerked him upright in astonishment. Gazing around him in wonder, he forgot for a moment the horror that had just befallen them.

The dark, gloomy, dankness of the cave had been replaced by a verdant lush jungle, bedecked with vines like Christmas tinsel, vibrant flowers dangled like baubles and all around them buzzed insects as big as birds.

"What the—"He whispered.

"Yeah, the multiple realms thing, when it's safe to stop for the night, I probably should try to explain." Muttered Matthias as he gathered their scattered belongings and handed back sacks back to their owners, as, one by one they got to their feet.

Last to rise was Kwatili, who remained sitting head bowed, absorbed in her grief. They stood respectfully waiting until, with a heave of her chest, she too rose to her feet, straightened her back, shouldered her bag and turned to Elijah.

"Do you have any strong thoughts as to which way we go Elijah Grey?" She asked.

"Me? No I don't even know where we are, how would I know which way we should go?" He said, glancing unhappily from one expectant face to another. Why did they all suddenly see him as the leader all of a sudden, he was just a kid!

"Because Maylan put all of the knowledge that you will need in order to save your mother, my wife and child, and defeat Xan into your mind before she, well, before she died Elijah. It may seem like a shattered jigsaw at the moment, but from now on, any hunches or ideas that pop into your head, may well be what saves all our lives." Ranger said giving his friend's shoulder a squeeze to soften the blow.

"No pressure then!" the boy replied, pulling a face.

"Yes, lots of pressure Raven Boy, but get used to it!" Laughed Ghelli, slapping him hard on his back.

"So, which way, Mr Fount of all knowledge?" He added, hands in the air.

Elijah closed his eyes, cleared his mind as best he could, and waited for inspiration.

Nothing. Not a thing came into his mind except the sound of some creature that sounded like it was laughing at him.

"Even the animals think I'm a joke!" He shouted in frustration.

"What animals Elijah? We hear nothing except the buzzing insects." Asked Khizzi, moving so close that he could feel her breath on his cheek.

"Um, the laughing ones, over that way, sounds sort of like Hyenas." He stuttered, moving slightly away from her so that she didn't notice the sudden pink flushing on his cheeks.

Matthias slapped his thigh and howled loudly.

"See Ghelli, my son will not fail us! He hears Ryufu, he must be in this realm somewhere, with his Yehana, that old laughing boy will be a sight for sore eyes even if he does hate my hide!"

"Oh well, if that works for you, it sounds like it's coming from that direction." Elijah said pointing.

"Well done Elijah." Khizzi said as she touched him lightly on the arm before moving off behind Ghelli and Matthias.

Elijah swallowed nervously before picking up his back sack, his reaction to her touch was totally out of order.

A soft chuckle behind him from Kwatili made him jump.

"Easy young Elijah, your secret is safe with me!" She said grinning widely, baring all of her sharply pointed canine teeth.

"And with me!" Added Ranger, also enjoying the boys discomfort a little too much for Elijah's liking.

"Don't know what you're talking about!" he grouched as he stomped off after Khizzi and the others.

Behind them, like the closing of an eye, the doorway suddenly winked shut, leaving no trace that it was ever there.

# Chapter 22

After an hour of forcing their way through tangled undergrowth, and contemptuously swatting away swarms of biting insects intent on feasting upon every inch of exposed skin; they were all exhausted, drenched in sweat and extremely irritable.

Stopping to lean heavily on a moss coated tree trunk, panting hard, with droplets of perspiration dripping off the end of his nose like rain drops, Matthias held up his hand for them all to halt. They needed no encouragement, even Kwatili's peach fur skin was slick and flushed, and both Elijah and Khizzi sank thankfully to the ground.

"I guess it would be asking too much for another vision from you Raven Boy, it would make such arduous walking conditions a little more bearable if we had some sort of assurance that we were heading in the right direction." Ghelli said moodily squishing and smearing insects over his arms and face.

"I have no idea how all this works let alone how to control it Ghelli, stop being a jerk!" Snapped Elijah, glaring at Ghelli with his fists clenched.

"Now let's not let the heat and the flies set us at each other's throats. We have enough enemies out there already!" Kwatili said silkily, moving to stand between Elijah and Ghelli until the two visibly relaxed.

"Can I suggest that we seek somewhere to set up camp soon, I personally do not fancy sleeping at ground level here when the sun goes down?" Ranger added, hauling himself wearily upright once more.

"Couldn't agree more Ranger, I suspect these little biters are the least dangerous of the inhabitants here. Perhaps we should split up, you go that way with Elijah and Khizzi, Kwatili, Ghelli and I will go this way, first to spot higher ground whistle, or, especially for you Elijah, howl!" Chuckled Matthias, enjoying his own wit far too much.

"Good plan Matthias, but I think that I should stay with Elijah, since I am the only one who has any hope of interpreting any signs he receives from the Eye of Ula." Purred Kwatili quietly, holding her long slender arm out to pull the boy up onto his wobbly legs.

Matthias merely nodded before heading off in the direction he had chosen, followed closely by Ghelli.

"Come Elijah, you can lean on me if you need to." Whispered Khizzi as she came up beside him.

"Nah, I'm fine!" He spluttered, then added "But thanks for the offer anyway." On seeing her hurt expression.

Ranger fell in the other side of him, and Kwatili walked ahead, forging a pathway through the dense vegetation.

He wasn't sure what he stumbled on, but suddenly, Elijah found himself on his hands and knees. As the palms of his hands sank through the soft springy carpet of moss, they met the unyielding surface of rock. A hot tingling sensation fizzed through his veins and up his arms to his head, filling his ears with a deafening ringing that slowly transformed into voices.

"Kwatili!" He gasped, fighting the nausea that rose rapidly from his stomach.

Leaping fallen trees and vines she was by his side in seconds.

"Is it happening again Elijah, try to remain calm and let it wash over you, don't fight it I am here, I will protect you." She whispered urgently into his ear as he crouched, eyes closed, twitching and breathing in shallow gasps.

As her words filtered through the others in his head, he managed to calm his thudding heart and forced himself to listen and allow whatever wanted to invade his mind, to do so.

One voice immediately prevailed above the others, and it stood out because of the undiluted vitriol laced within it.

"Just how does one small and ineffective child manage to run rings around the so called elite of my force? No that does not require an answer, I know the answer; you are all under estimating the misguided mongrels who are aiding him!"

This was greeted by a muffled mumbling in Elijah's head, and grey fuzzy images fading in and out of focus, some humanoid, some most definitely not.

Suddenly the whole scenario shifted, lurching from face to face, giving Elijah close ups of snarling mouths lined with filthy teeth, bulging blood red eyes and pounding fists. It felt as if he was an insect, flitting erratically around a vast space with no control what so ever over where he looked next. Nausea became a real sensation amidst the surreal scene inside his mind.

"Kwatili!" He cried, not sure if he had made any sound out loud or if it had just been in his head, Elijah quailed at the response to his cry.

From within the dark centre of the space in which he was trapped, two scrawny hands thrust outwards and upwards to halt all sound which was instantly snuffed out, Elijah realised with a chill, that one of the hands was sporting an elongated, bony finger, twice the length of all the others, ending in a curved claw, it twitched with a life of its own.

"Mr Nax." He whispered through clenched teeth.

"So, the little boy is gaining power is he? Well bring it on child, you and your bedraggled entourage are still no match for Xan!"

Struck dumb, and rapidly losing his fight to keep the contents of his stomach where they were, Elijah collapsed flat to the ground, raising his hands to grip his burning forehead, with Xan's laughter ringing in his ears as he broke the contact.

He was vaguely aware of a multitude of hands trying to raise him up off the ground and a chorus of muffled voices urging him onto his feet.

As his head cleared and the uncontrollable shaking subsided, Elijah drew in some deep breaths before he turned to Kwatili and Matthias.

"Teach me what it will take to make sure that never happens again unless I want it to." He stated flatly, his dark eyes meeting theirs without flinching.

Kwatili leaned towards him and gently brushed his shoulder with a hand.

"It pains me to tell you that as far as I know, the only being with that knowledge perished, but hours ago, along with all of her kind in the Glidiri Caves. I know very little of your powers and those of the Eye of Ula."

Elijah's shoulders sagged at her words, the outrage that had filled him from his contact with Xan trickled away and was rapidly replaced by despair.

Seeing this, Matthias play punched his son's arm and added, "Now that's not how Egreya would expect her son to behave, she would expect him to buck up and soldier on, never give up while you have a breath to take, that's what she used to say, and you are so like her Elijah- you-"His false cheeriness faltered as he spoke, and he blinked away tears as he turned brusquely to Ranger.

"Did you and Burda get any instructions when you left with him as a baby?"

Elijah laughed at the expression of disbelief that flashed onto Rangers face.

"You make me sound like a new toaster Matthias, I don't think I came with an owners- manual!"

"Burda was the one given the role as mother, she was told what to do with the Eye of Ula, when he would be ready to receive it, and what signs to watch out for as to when he should return to Greylea. I was simply given the role of constant companion and protector, and friend."

Ranger kept his gaze on the ground at his feet, unable to meet any eyes on him.

"It was a role that you fulfilled admirably my friend, and Matthias did not mean any disrespect I am sure!" said Kwatili, flicking Matthias deftly with the back of her hand as she walked past him.

"What? Oh no course not!" He muttered.

"Besides, that plan didn't exactly work out thanks to Xan getting hold of the other Eye, and what not." He added, slapping Ranger on the shoulder.

Elijah moved to stand close to Ranger, and whispered quietly into his ear.

"For what it's worth, to a kid, his dog is the most important friend in the world, Burda made great pancakes, but you were why I was glad to wake up every morning Ranger."

His friend's sapphire blue eyes shone with pride as he smiled back silently, straightened his back and shouldered his back sack once more.

Kwatili also smiled as she watched this exchange, and murmured to herself.

"Truly you will be proud of him, Egreya."

"So, we must assume that Xan knows by now what realm we are in, and will be bending all of his will towards finding a doorway that is open to it. We need to get moving fast, but as to which direction, there I am open to suggestions." Said Matthias

Each waited for another to speak, before Elijah pointed into the denser part of the forest to their left and said shyly,

"Well, don't ask me why, but my gut tells me that we need to head that way."

Matthias studied the boy intensely for a few seconds before pursing his lips and nodding assertively.

"If that's what your gut tells you to do then I for one am willing to trust it, let's move."

Marching decisively off into the dense undergrowth, steadfastly ignoring Ghelli's attempt to stand in his way and dispute the matter, Matthias almost instantly disappeared into the gloom.

Silently following in his wake, the others fell into line, with Ghelli stomping along at the rear, slashing needlessly away at vines to disperse his frustration.

Within minutes of entering the forest, the air around them became thick and heavily scented, they were surrounded by huge white flowers the size of dinner plates with long dangling anthers, coated with a sticky red substance that plucked at their skin and clothes as they tried to forge their way through the undergrowth.

Each time they brushed against these sticky strands, more and more of a heady fragrance was released, clogging their lungs and nostrils, and they pulled at their skin and clothes like grasping, dragging fingers.

Matthias stopped panting heavily and leaned over, head hanging down and his eyes closed.

The others did the same, exhausted already even though looking back, Elijah could still see the clearing that they had just left; they had only managed to cover about a hundred yards.

"Do not even begin to doubt yourself Elijah, your instincts have always been correct, remember when somehow you knew that there was a wild bees nest in the trunk of the tree near the cabin, it had never been there before, and you climbed it almost every evening to watch the sun set, but that day you knew they were there even though I heard nor smelled anything new."

Ranger's soft voice triggered a vivid image of that evening, the old gnarled tree that grew by the porch had always been his vantage point, he had built a rough and ready platform half way up on which to sit and contemplate the world according to Elijah Grey.

It had been as if a voice spoke to him that night as he walked towards it, the bees had been silent, completely hidden, but a voice said "Not tonight." And a vision of himself and Ranger smothered in a swarm of angry stinging bees had flashed before his eyes, knocking the breath from his lungs like a punch to the chest.

With a gasp he realised that he had forgotten what else he had seen that night. When he had halted and turned back towards the porch followed by a puzzled Ranger, he had looked back just once and seen, or thought he'd seen a tall black clothed, black haired woman standing between him and the tree, she had smiled sadly before vanishing. He'd thought he's been mistaken then, but now he knew differently, his mother had saved him then, maybe she could do it now?

"The flowers are dangerous, try not to breath in their scent and avoid the sticky stuff if you can." He said, getting down on his hands and knees and continuing forward by crawling beneath the level of the flowers.

It did somewhat surprise him to see that all the others, even Ghelli, immediately adopted a crawling position and followed him, but he didn't have time to enjoy the sensation for long as the same tingling began to burn in his hands where they were in contact with the forest floor.

Jerking to his feet he stood frantically rubbing his palms together to rid himself of the conviction that there were ants crawling over his skin.

Kwatili was at his side instantly, anxiously searching the surrounding trees and bushes for threats.

"What is it Elijah, was it Xan again?" She asked urgently.

"Dunno, I stopped it before it really got going, I'm sorry, I know that we need to know what he's up to but I just can't-"

Matthias hushed him with a raised finger, they all froze to listen.

At first he thought that they were all just listening to the ever present buzzing insect life, but then Elijah realised that the sound was getting louder and changing as it did.

The sound was now focussed in a spot in front of a particularly large tree, bent over like an old decrepit man, leafless and stark, and he realised that he could now hear actual voices coming from a strange patch of mould that seemed to be expanding as he watched, horrified.

It was a voice he recognised only too well by now, it was Xan.

"Here I come Raven Boy ready or not, running time is over!"

The patch of churning shadow on the trunk of the tree rapidly expanded now, and hissed like an over boiling pan. Around its edge flickered blue flames and in the centre they could all discern shadowy figures growing bigger and bigger, clearer and clearer.

Elijah felt fear blowing up like a balloon in his chest, choking his throat and lungs. Then that fear changed to anger, steel bright anger. This thing was the source of all of his pain, the reason that he had grown up not knowing that he even had a mother and father, it may even have killed Burda, the only mother that he had known, and it wanted to slaughter all those around him simply because they were with him.

Red rage slammed down like a trap door in his head, and he swung his arm out towards the opening doorway with all the force he could muster and yelled.

"No!"

And the doorway closed.

# Chapter 23

Deep within her frozen mind, Egreya could feel his power growing. The once tenuous connection between them was rapidly strengthening, becoming more and more accessible. At first, when he was small and in the other realm she had only been able to get flashes of his life, like windows in a long black tunnel, and she had not had any control over when it happened; but it had been enough to sustain her life and keep her from simply letting go of her life force and drifting off into oblivion.

Then, when Xan had first discovered his hiding place and a doorway to it, he had come to gloat over her before he left, to stand before the block of crystal in which she was imprisoned and smile that twisted smile as he lay his long fingered hand on the surface of the ice, tapping the elongated finger with its yellow nail.

"Oh poor lonely Egreya, worry not, for you will soon have the company of your mongrel offspring."

A wave of panic had risen in her chest at his words, but she refused to succumb to it. She trusted Burda and Ranger, they would protect him; inside her frozen mind she forced herself to smile back, even though she knew that her face would show nothing.

Xan threw his head back and laughed a loud shrieking laugh as he sensed her defiance.

"Even now you foolishly place so much faith in that bumbling duo, how I will enjoy proving you wrong my lady!"

Performing a deep exaggerated bow, he had stormed off to find the doorway before it closed.

She had felt the fear in her son when he had been attacked in the forest by the Drillers, and when he had faced the Maigrey on the Phantom Mountains, but it had been that night in the Glidiri Caves that the connection between them had finally become fixed and to her great delight she had been able to see him for the first time since he was whisked away from her after his birth.

The sight had filled her heart with true hope and pride for the first time in fifteen years. Looking back at her had been her own dark features, but his father's ferocious courage, for even though he had been terrified, she could see his inner strength blazing out like a flame.

She and Matthias had both known what the consequences might be when they had fallen in love, but they had been young, wilful and swept away by the strength of their emotions.

By the time that Elijah had been born, the council of Elders had decreed that it would be too dangerous for him to remain in Greylea and that two chosen guardians should take him to a hidden realm and bring him up in secret until they felt that it would be safe for him to return.

It had torn her heart from her chest to let go of him, knowing that there was a very real chance that she would never see her son again, given the rise of Xan and two attempts on his life already, so she had placed him in the strong arms of Burda that night, and closed her eyes as the huge woman had walked away with him, telling herself that she was saving his life, over and over again until the sounds of his tiny cries faded.

Within an hour of his going, Xan had attacked the Isle of Tears and ransacked the entire settlement in a desperate and blood thirsty search for the child that he believed to be the missing element to his plans. He had based his whole campaign on some old documents that he had unearthed in the Phantom Mountains, which told of a hybrid being who would be able to use both Eyes of Ula to not only predict where doorways to other realms were going to open, but cause them to open. This would enable Xan to not only conquer Greylea but all other realms as well, and so the power crazed creature had become completely obsessed with finding Elijah and forcing him to comply with his demands. To that end, he had captured Egreya in the hope that when he finally found Elijah, he would be able to use her as leverage. Fortunately, she hoped, Xan had no real knowledge of the power contained within the Eyes of Ula and didn't realise that even though she no longer possessed both, because they had been attuned to her at birth, she could still access the one that she had sent with him from within her crystal prison cell, and he had no idea that her mind had remained completely active for the long fifteen year wait.

Alone she had suffered, not knowing whether her son or her beloved Matthias were still alive even, but she had tried to remain strong and believe that they would both find their way back to her.

And now they had, and together!

Her blank sleeping face showed not a sign of the volcanic excitement that was building up in her heart, both of them, together, father and son, coming to rescue her and over throw Xan.

Inside her mind she smiled, she would look forward to vacating her crystal prison for him.

# Chapter 24

All six mouths still gaped open as their owners stared stunned into silence by the slamming shut of the doorway.

Matthias was the first to regain a sense of urgency, shaking his grey shaggy head to clear away the after effects.

"That was a good trick, but in my experience with those things, it won't stay shut for long and then we'll have an angry Xan and his hoard charging through. So, young Elijah, what does your gut tell you? Which way? And make it a quick decision I suggest!"

He stood with his hands on his hips, yellow eyes staring straight into those of his son, but Elijah's were shifting and flinching from the contact.

"Um, well I'm not sure now, I had thought that this was the way we should be going but then that happened-"

He muttered, gesturing towards the gnarled tree trunk, now minus the whirling doorway.

Khizzi stepped towards him and gently laid her hand on his to steady it and said quietly but assertively.

"I for one still trust your instincts Elijah Grey, if you were told to go this way, then that is the route we should continue to take."

"Well said Khizzi!" said Kwatili smiling widely.

"Come, this is as good a decision as it gets, at least let us put as much distance between ourselves and the re-opening doorway as possible." She added, striding forward into the dense undergrowth once again, forging a path through the clinging sticky vines for the others.

One by one they followed, with Matthias bringing up the rear. All straining to hear the first sounds of pursuit, all dreading what would follow.

Elijah walked as if sleep walking, his mind still compulsively reliving the moment that he had closed the doorway. The memory filled him with fear and excitement in equal amounts.

Did he truly possess some kind of power? If not how had he done it?

One thing that occurred to him as he went over and over it was the sudden spark of realisation that at the very point that he had unleashed whatever it took to slam that doorway shut, he had in fact been holding the pouch containing the Eye of Ula in his hand, and it had been burning that hand even through the leather.

Stumbling slightly as he looked down to the pouch as it swung side to side as he walked, he was sorely tempted to take it out but was too afraid now.

"It was destined for you Elijah, therefore it will never bring you any harm, do not fear it."

He jumped as Matthias spoke, he had not been aware that he had come so close.

He was just opening his mouth to answer when up at the head of the party Kwatili abruptly halted and held her hand up for silence.

Her sharpened hearing had heard it first but gradually they all did, water, running water and close by too.

She turned to look questioningly at Elijah, he gulped nervously, how come all of a sudden he was being treated as the leader? He was just a kid after all.

"Follow the water to its end, help will come."

He glanced around to see if any of the others had heard it, knowing full well that the voice had been in his head. Oh well.

"We should follow the water to its end, help will come?" He muttered and shrugged his shoulders.

Disconcertingly Kwatili simply nodded and surged forward, following the gurgling sounds to her left.

Elijah's legs were weak and shaking as he fell in line behind Khizzi, this was all happening too fast, his reeling brain just couldn't keep up and he was fast losing his battle with panic.

"There, it's a river, maybe there are Waterloggers coming, it looks deep enough." Shouted Ghelli over the almost deafening sound of the fast flowing river that now heaved and crashed beside them over boulders and fallen trees.

Matthias shook his head thoughtfully, "Too rough for them, I seriously doubt they'd risk it!"

"Keep going, help is coming but it will be a leap of faith."

Elijah's quiet words were of no surprise now and keep going they did, stumbling along the muddy and slippery bank they drew closer and closer to the inevitable sight that caused them all to quail.

About fifty strides ahead, the river disappeared.

It disappeared over the edge of a deep vertical drop and exploded into a boiling cloud of spray, one by one the company sank to their knees in despair.

"We will have to go back and try to find a way around the falls." Ghelli said, exhaustion making his voice rough and thin.

Without words, each began to drag their aching bodies up out of the mud, but even as they did so, they felt the ground beneath them begin to vibrate, in a way that was painfully familiar.

"Drillers!" Kwatili cried, bracing for the inevitable eruption out of the ground.

"Into the river, it's our only chance, we will not survive a driller attack here!" Matthias shouted, giving Elijah no chance to argue as he pushed the terrified boy sideways into the raging current as he did so.

The shock of the ice cold embrace of the water as it engulfed him, emptied his lungs of air. His blurred vision told him that his friends were all cannon balling into the river around him, sending balloons of bubbles up to the surface. Completely disorientated by being tumbled in the torrent like a sock in a washing machine, he struggled futilely to control his body enough to break the surface. Just as he felt sure that his lungs were about to burst and his head was fizzing, he felt something coil tightly around his waist and drag him upwards to erupt spluttering into breathable wonderful air.

"Thanks!" he spluttered to Ghelli as he felt the safety rope of a tail uncoil, his rescuers brown features were barely visible above the churning white water and all sound was swallowed up by the ever increasing roar that filled their ears.

Using his hands to attempt to stay on the surface, and sculling as best he could to turn and face in the direction of the current, Elijah immediately wished that he hadn't.

Rapidly getting closer and closer was the end of the river. A dead white line on the horizon was all he could see, and the water fall was sucking him towards it as if it wanted to devour him.

Panic took over and he began to flail his arms and legs frantically trying to fight the inevitable.

"Don't fight it Elijah, just keep your arms high above your head and hope!"

He had no idea whether that voice was inside his head or was one of his companions, but he obeyed all the same, and as he was swept over the edge and thrown out into the spray choked abyss beyond, he closed his eyes and waited for the stomach wrenching drop, with his arms above his head.

Suddenly a huge black shape loomed above him casting a shadow over his closed eyelids. As he prized them apart something snatched him out of his fall and swung him upwards by his wrists like a juggling trick. As he flopped down into some sort of cup shaped basket, a huge horse shaped head hung down inches from his face and shouted over the roar of the water fall.

"Juno says 'Hi!'"

# Chapter 25

Each one of them had been neatly caught like fish in a net as the force of the river had spat them out into mid-air to plummet to their deaths below.

Laughing hysterically as the terror that had built up within him sought release, Elijah allowed himself to flop in the cradle slung below the soaring body of Goren the Sky Oren. As the wafting breeze dried off his hair and clothes, caressing his face like a kiss, his mind wandered deliriously.

Warm sunshine replaced the dampness of the permanent mist cloud that shrouded the falls.

Rolling over so that he could peer downwards through the leather lattice work, he was shocked at how high up they were. Far below them he could just make out the mouth of the river where it pooled out to become a huge glassy lake, so vast that it could have been a sea. The surface was so incredibly still and smooth that he realised that the strange dark shapes travelling across it were in fact the reflections of the five Sky Oren with their passenger as they rode the air above it. Circling slowly on the thermals, they were gradually getting lower.

"Hey Goren, nice catch, how did you know that we needed you, or did you just happen to be flying past?" He asked, smiling as he watched the strange horse like features take on an almost Cheshire cat grin displaying a mouth full of chunky white teeth.

"Why thank you young Elijah, always glad to be of service. It was in fact a message from Ryufu that told us that you may need a bit of help but he'll tell you himself soon enough, better not let my old lips flap too much and say things I shouldn't!"

He made a sound that was less a chuckle, more a snort and bent his long neck down so that he could look Elijah straight in the eye and perform an exaggerated wink.

Elijah winked back and asked, "Before your lips stop flapping, Burda and Brogan - are they okay too?"

Tilting his head slightly to one side, Goren hesitated long enough for Elijah's heart to falter.

"Humph, take more than a few Mongrel Maigrey to put Burda out of action!" He said, exactly mimicking the woman's gravelly voice.

Elijah sagged back in relief and sighed.

"Yep, that's my mum alright!" He said, but even as he heard the words leave his mouth, he realised that it was not actually true anymore. Burda had been his mother for fifteen years, and he had never had cause to think anything else, now, he was having to come to terms with the fact that she was in fact not even related to him, and that his real mother was a half raven, half human being who was trapped inside a crystal, and waiting for him to rescue her!

"I think you'll find that Burda will never willingly relinquish her role as your parent, so if you carry on calling her that, she will be happy, and we all prefer a happy Burda; as for rescuing Egreya that is not a task that you will be expected to undertake alone, you really ought to have got that by now!"

"Hah! What I really should have got is that slightly creepy way that you Oren have of reading my mind!" Elijah chuckled, then added looking down at the flat surface below.

"So is that where we're heading, to wherever she's being held? Is it down there?"

He could now see a number of small islands like freckles on the vast expanse of silver water. As they passed over the first, he could see what looked like one huge rain cloud sitting above the island like a giant grey cherry on a cupcake. Sparking periodically out of it shot forks of blue lightning.

"That is the Isle of Tears, and yes, that is where we think that Xan has Egreya imprisoned, but no, that is not where we are heading, that would not be safe or sensible at the moment. We're going to try to make it to the Isle of Sighs, that's where the meeting is being held."

Goren replied, snorting loudly out of his wide nostrils, producing two billowing clouds of hot steam in the chill air.

"Um, sorry but was that the word try I heard? Not sure I like the sound of that, just how far is it to this Isle of Sighs?"

"Oh not that far, I'm sure we'll make it!" The Sky Oren said cheerfully, smiling a wide and very fake smile down at his passenger.

"Right, well I feel so much better now!" The boy muttered, returning to squinting downwards through the leather webbing of his cradle beneath the huge creature.

"Jubilations! Juno said you were very brave for a young one, he was not incorrect it seems. Sky Oren always try our best to deliver our passengers in one piece, you just relax and enjoy the view!"

Lower and lower they glided, until the racing reflection keeping pace below them was so clear that Elijah could actually see details now.

"I think you should maybe fly a little higher Goren, there's no island in sight and we're getting so low I'll be able to catch a fish for dinner soon!" Elijah called up, somewhat alarmed now by a sudden descent towards the lake surface.

"Ah, if only I could Elijah Grey, but you forget, Sky Oren do not fly, we fall with style!" came the reply from above.

Elijah swallowed hard.

"Of course, forgot that, well can you maybe fall a bit higher and maybe faster so that I don't end up in the drink for the second time today, I haven't dried out from the first time yet!"

"Sure thing here we go, hold onto something!"

Goren bellowed as he gave a huge thrusting beat with his bat like wings, which jolted Elijah backwards onto his backside it was so forceful but it did the trick, it gained them at least fifty feet in height and allowed him to access a thermal that drifted them further upwards.

"Phew, don't want to do that again, now let's find your Island before I run out of puff completely, cos then we're in trouble!" Goren wheezed, obviously close to exhaustion.

"What about that one!" Elijah cried excitedly, pointing down at a small isle that appeared completely white and totally featureless, like a dinner plate wiped clean.

"Nope, that's the Isle of Shivers, made of snow, brrr!" Goren said.

"What about that one, the little yellow one to the left then," Elijah was getting desperate now, they were once again dropping from the sky rapidly and Goren was looking frighteningly drained now.

"Nope, that's the Isle of Burns, all day, all night burning sun and sand, no shelter, you'd last ten minutes before you were a red wrinkled dried up Raven Boy raisin!" Panted Goren, dropping another few feet closer to the glistening surface of the lake.

"Okay, okay, listen Goren, I don't want you killing yourself to get me there, just set me down as gently as you can and get yourself to safety, I can swim pretty well, I'll find the Isle of Sighs I'm sure, I mean it you look like hell!" Elijah shouted up at the Oren, who was now only feet above the water and indeed looked close to death.

"And there he goes using toilet language again Brogan, I told you it would happen if he spent too much time with that father of his!"

The gruff voice from below whipped Elijah's head round with instantly.

There directly below him in a long narrow boat was Burda, holding her two stout arms up towards him and beckoning.

"Jump Elijah, I will catch you!"

Without a second's hesitation, he worked his legs and torso free of the straps of the cradle and allowed his body to drop like a stone towards her waiting arms, at the same time yelling,

"That was falling with great style Goren!"

As he landed with a thump and a loud grunt from Burda, he heard Goren reply.

"Ever at your service Elijah Grey!"

His words faded as he used the last of his strength and the loss of Elijah's weight to soar upwards and then swerve into a high spiralling thermal until he was a tiny dot against the sunshine.

"Full steam ahead please Brogan!" Burda shouted as she made sure that Elijah was securely seated at the boat's pointed prow.

"Already on it mate, hold on tight!" Came an answer, from where Elijah couldn't figure, but the small craft suddenly surged forward as if it had an outboard engine, a silent one.

Elijah's expression evoked a spluttering cackle from Burda, who gestured towards the far end of the boat and added.

"If you go carefully you can look but no rocking this thing, it's not big enough for me as it is!" She said.

"I'll say! And you're not the one pushing it!" Came the voice out of nowhere.

As he edged tentatively down to the far end Elijah gaped in astonishment.

The boat did have a motor, it was called Brogan, true to his Waterlogger genes he was virtually submerged behind the boat, and using his muscular body and tail to propel it through the water. As Elijah leaned over the side, Brogans wide mouth cracked into a broad toothy grin, but his speed did not falter.

"There we are, the Isle of sighs, about five minutes more at this speed Brogan!" Burda called, ushering Elijah back into his safe position in the middle of the long narrow boat, behind her.

"Where? I see nothing except, oh-"

Elijah had spotted a tiny pointed lump of land that looked more like a pimple on the horizon than an island. But as they drew closer, he began to pick out more detail.

Rising steeply from its centre was one funnel shaped mountain, out of which wafted a thin column of purple smoke. As he watched it grow larger as they approached, he found himself rubbing at his eyes to clear them, he thought his eyes must need clearing.

Burda chuckled and touched his hand gently.

"No, you can trust what you see, why do you think it is named the Isle of Sighs young one?"

The island was in fact rising and falling as if it were a living thing that was breathing, and closer still he could now make out a different sound to the thrashing of Brogan's tail in the water, he could hear, well, he could hear the island sighing.

"But is it alive?" He asked, unable to take his eyes off the eerie sight.

"Well, now there's a question alright!" She answered, then set her mouth in that way that he had learned at a very early age meant, "But I'm not going to give you an answer no matter what you do."

For some strange reason, he found her familiar behaviour so incredibly comforting that he decided that he didn't need to know, he would find out himself soon enough, because they were close enough to the shore line now for the end of the boat to be grating on the surface of the beach, and coming to a halt.

Burda clambered out and waded the last few feet, dragging the boat behind her as if it were a mere pillow. When she beckoned for him to join her, Elijah jumped ashore and was immediately taken by surprise at how solid the ground felt beneath his feet, he had been expecting to sink into sand. Stumbling after her, he had to put his hands down a couple of times to steady himself, the surface felt much colder than he had expected too.

They reached the top of the sloping beach and stopped to wait for Brogan on his short stocky legs to catch them up. He slumped down beside them, panting heavily and a pool of water slowly formed around him.

"Phew, out of condition or what?" He gasped, coughing up the last of the lake water.

"Hah! Never in condition if you ask me!" Snorted Burda, clapping him hard between the shoulder blades.

Elijah stood looking around him, suddenly worried and feeling guilty that he had completely forgotten about his friends.

"Oh they're fine, got here before you, their Sky Oren must have taken a shorter route I suppose."

Elijah scowled at Burda, who shrugged at his expression.

"Is there anything in this place that can't read my mind?" He said sulkily.

"Oh I don't read your mind my lovely, don't need to, raised you for fifteen years, changed your nappies, fed you, bathed you and sorted you out when you needed it, can read you like a book, one written in dirty great big letters too!"

Brogan barked a laugh but swallowed it back when he saw the response on Elijah's face.

Coughing away his laugh, he said very seriously.

"We need to get below and out of sight as soon as possible, Xan has eyes everywhere."

Then to Elijah's surprise he stamped his right foot hard three times, paused then repeated it.

Just as Elijah was opening his mouth to ask what on earth he was doing that for, the ground beneath his feet began to tremble and vibrate, grabbing hold of Burda's stout arm to stop himself from toppling, he gasped, as the Isle of Sighs rose slowly up out of the water.

"Quickly Elijah, hold on tightly!" Burda said as she staggered unsteadily towards the edge.

"What is this thing?" he shouted as he crouched onto his hands and knees in order to prevent himself sliding over the sloping edge that was now clear of the water.

"Well there's a question I can't wait to hear answered!" Chortled Brogan, suddenly diving onto his stomach to grab hold of the end of a rope that had just appeared. Burda launched herself forward to latch onto his feet as he slipped over the side, gripping Elijah by the wrist in a vice like hold as she followed him.

All three now dangled like bunting flags from the rope which originated from a large hole at one corner of what now appeared to be some sort of creature rather than an inanimate island.

As they rose further up into the air, with water running like small waterfalls from its perimeter, Elijah realised that what they had been standing on previously was in fact a gigantic turtle like creature, with its feet and legs now withdrawn within its shell, leaving just a long swan like neck ending in, why was he not surprised, a huge horse shaped head with whirling eyes that grinned back at him and said.

"Juno says hi!"

"Elijah, meet Ayobi, the last of the Time Oren, now, swing until they can reach us!" Burda shouted, heaving her massive bulk back and forth in unison with Brogan causing their little string of baubles to swing closer and closer to the cave sized leg-hole, out of which the rope emerged and Ranger, Matthias and Ghelli now dangled precariously, stretching out to catch hold of the rope and hoist them "aboard"

"Got you!" Matthias yelled as he got his fingers around the rope and began to haul them in, Ghelli and Ranger hauling him from inside Ayobi.

With a large amount of grunting and scraped skin, Burda, Brogan and Elijah were safely landed like flopping fish into the warm darkness.

"Okay Ayobi, you can submerge again now!" Matthias cried, slapping the inner surface of the Time Oren's shell.

"Hold tight little fleas!" came a distant reply as Ayobi descended once more onto the surface of the lake, and then withdrew his breathing tube before sinking down below leaving behind a mere ripple as evidence that it had ever been there.

As they entered the silence of the lake, Ayobi sealed up his shell, and withdrew his long neck and head to create a completely water tight refuge.

In the enveloping darkness, Elijah heard footfalls approaching, and Kwatili and Khizzi appeared, wide eyed and grinning.

"See Khizzi, I told you that Goren could be trusted to get him here safely, he's just, a bit slower than his brethren that's all!" laughed Kwatili, rubbing Elijah's shoulder in an attempt to show affection, obviously an unfamiliar behaviour for her. Khizzi had no such restraints and launched herself into a tight hug, squeezing the gasp of breath out of the startled boy's mouth as he took it.

At a starchy cough from Ghelli, she stepped back away from the profusely blushing fifteen year old; but refused to stop grinning in wide happiness.

"Well, now that we are all assembled, I feel the need for food, sleep and then, a plan!" Matthias announced, heading off with the others in agreement behind him.

Elijah reached out to Ranger, touching his friend's arm and whispering.

"Is it worth me even asking what the hell a Time Oren does and why he/she is the last one?"

Before Ranger could answer, Burda snapped over her shoulder,

"All in good time Elijah Grey, and less of the toilet language!"

In the dim light, Ranger's blue eyes twinkled and he chuckled.

With an exasperated sigh Elijah fell into line behind him.

After a walk along the narrow gangway between what was apparently Ayobi's body and shell, stumbling frequently as they rocked from side to side occasionally as it came to rest on the lake bed, the company finally arrived at a large open space at the front of the Oren, where his head and neck were.

"Ah, there you are, I was getting worried that you had gone the wrong way round, as the items of sustenance are here, please seat yourselves and partake until your hunger is defeated." He said in a low rumbling resonant voice that echoed softly around the cavity in which they now stood.

Smiling broadly, exposing her rows of sharp teeth, Kwatili bowed low and graciously saying.

"Dear Ayobi, you are still the most welcoming host in all Greylea, we thank you!"

Gesturing to the others to follow suit, she lowered herself gracefully to the floor, and sat, cross legged beside a huge up turned shell and began passing round small wrapped packets to them in turn.

As he unwrapped his, Elijah sniffed at the green strips that it contained.

He jerked in shock, it looked just like seaweed, but it smelled exactly like bacon!

Glancing around, he watched as each of his companions made the same discovery, grinned and tucked in with gusto.

Popping the end into his mouth, he chomped down to experience delicious juicy texture and the taste of not only bacon but eggs fried just how he liked them all piled onto crispy fried bread, it had always been his favourite, made by Burda as a special treat on Sunday mornings

"But how?" he asked, mouth stuffed.

"Manners Elijah, no talking with your mouth full!" Muttered Burda, with her mouth full.

"I trust that your Oarweed is to your tastes, I conducted very thorough research in order to cater to each of your needs and desires?"

"Oh it truly is to my taste thank you Ayobi, you did your research well!" replied Matthias shoving the last of his Oarweed into his mouth.

"You like bacon, egg and fried bread too?" Elijah asked Khizzi, he had to admit that he was shocked, he had thought that both she and Ghelli would definitely be vegetarians.

She giggled and held her portion out for him to sniff. Cherries! Her Oarweed looked exactly like his, but it smelt of cherries!

Ranger and Kwatili and Matthias held theirs aloft together and said in unison, "Juicy steak!"

Looking towards Burda quizzically, he ventured a guess. "Chocolate Chip muffins, by any chance, Burda?"

Still chewing, she nodded.

Ayobi's deep voice cut in, "Oarweed provides perfect nutrition, but tastes like muddy water, so I make it taste of whatever my guest desires, easy entertaining really since it grows everywhere like grass!"

"So, healthy and tasty then!" Elijah cried, tucking in even more enthusiastically, much to the other's amusement.

Once the last morsel was consumed he turned his attention to the liquid in a large bulbous flask.

"So, I guess that this looks like ordinary water, but tastes like Pepsi?" He said as he uncorked it and took a gulp.

"Oh no young Raven, that is water that tastes like water, I can't perform miracles!" Ayobi chuckled richly as he spotted the expression on Elijah's face.

"But if it helps, it has had all of the wild life filtered out of it," he added with a wink towards Kwatili.

Elijah glanced from one unreadable face to the other, decided that if there was an in joke going on he was too tired to bother to find it out, and took another few swallows, recorked the flask and yawned pointedly.

"You need to sleep now I see, if you retrace your steps you will find a sleeping facility sufficient for you all I hope." Ayobi said, promptly closing his own huge brown eyes.

One by one the company walked back along the "corridor" which was in fact the space between Ayobi's body and the inner surface of his shell and discovered six hammock type structures attached to the shell wall.

"Wow, his middle name should definitely be hospitality!" cried Elijah as he eagerly climbed up into the first hammock and lay down. Closing his eyes and relaxing into the comforting support of the soft fabric, the last thought to enter his mind was that he was too highly charged up to actually sleep, but at least he could really relax for the first time in days.

# Chapter 26

After the third sharp poke in the ribs, Elijah reluctantly rose to the surface of sleep and grumbled, "Okay I'm up, I'm up Burda!"

"Hah! Not Burda but up is good Raven Boy!" rapped Ghelli as he turned quickly on his heels to head back to the front end of Ayobi, adding as he walked. "Important meeting in two minutes, don't keep them waiting sleepy head!"

"Hmph! Might just as well be Burda!" the boy muttered as he flopped unceremoniously onto the floor and staggered after Ghelli, rubbing his eyes furiously, in an attempt to appear wide awake even if he was not.

"Ah, welcome Elijah Grey. Breakfast is served. Again, I trust that I did my research thoroughly enough," said Ayobi smiling so broadly that his huge teeth gleamed in the soft morning light.

Grinning and taking a large bite Elijah nodded vigorously and swallowed before saying, "Banana pancakes with maple syrup, and the taste would rival yours, Burda!"

"Glad to see that's all it takes to cheer you up. Good move, Ayobi!" Matthias said reaching up to pat the long coiled neck above their heads.

Chewing thoughtfully, Elijah began to frown, studying both his surroundings and the strangely beautiful face of the Time Oren.

"Uh oh, here it comes, I can see the questions forming in that head and I do not need to be able to read his mind to do it!" chuckled Burda.

"Well he has been promised answers from the day he arrived and has been given none that really explain anything, I feel that it is time."

Kwatili stood and walked over to the great head of Ayobi, laid her hand gently on his broad forehead and said quietly.

"If you can bear it, old friend, I believe that showing would be easier for Elijah than telling; but I do not underestimate what I ask of you."

144

His deep brown eyes rolled to look into hers and were filled with such sudden sadness that Elijah wanted to jump up and tell him that whatever it was that he was being asked to do, not to do it, but Ayobi was already nodding slowly and replying.

"It would give my life the meaning that it has lacked for so many years, and I am tired of hiding, it is time for the last Time Oren to act. It would be safer to vacate this area until I have arrived, might I suggest the sleeping area." He rumbled as he began to uncoil his long neck towards the sealed front opening in his shell.

Without a word, they all stood quickly and retraced their steps back to where the hammocks had been. These had now been replaced by loops of rope for the passengers to hold onto, presumably it was expected to be a bumpy ride.

"Where are we going?" Elijah whispered to Kwatili as she took her place beside him.

Without turning her head, she whispered back, "It is not so much where, but when."

"I don't understand, how—"

"Time Oren? Does the name not give you a clue, Raven Boy?" Ghelli snapped from behind him.

Elijah's lips formed an "oh," but he made no sound.

Suddenly, they all felt their knees buckle slightly as Ayobi thrust towards the surface, broke surface then continued upward into the air above it. They were all jolted again as the ascension halted abruptly and remained hovering for a few seconds before slowly moving forward.

Letting go of her handle on the wall, Kwatili rubbed her wrist and said, "We can go forward now, we don't want to miss it."

Following her along the corridor Elijah was quickly aware that the further forward they went the lighter it got, and by the time they were once again in the front chamber, it was flooded with sunlight.

Around the edges of Ayobi's neck they could clearly see the rippling surface of the lake flashing by beneath them and a coastline was rapidly looming up on them.

From his vantage point beside the Oren's neck, Elijah could see immediately that this was not an inviting place and aptly named the Isle of Tears, for that had to be what he was looking

145

at. A thick veil of grey fog hung over the entire island, cloaking it so effectively that he really couldn't discern any features save the rim of black sand that was the shore. In his chest he felt a heavy weight of despair descend and a chill spread throughout his body.

A tiny cold hand found his and interlocked fingers squeezed his. "I feel it too, Elijah Grey," Khizzi whispered softly into his ear.

Ayobi stopped about a hundred meters from the shore line and hovered just above the water level, looking down Elijah could see the strange reflection of the Oren in the glassy surface.

"So is that where we have to go to rescue my mother?" he asked, finding speaking out loud difficult with such a dry clenched throat and mouth.

"Yes, and no," Kwatili answered.

"Yes it is the place where she is right now, but it was not always thus, it was once a place of beauty, which is the Isle we must travel to, when it was called the Isle of Song, fifteen years ago."

"But how? Oh, Time Oren, oh! TIME OREN!" Elijah cried as the penny finally dropped.

"Time Oren can travel through time - cool!"

"Not exactly travel, young Raven, Time Oren can open doors that take them to another time zone, you will be the one travelling through it," said Ayobi, his deep voice sounding very different without the resonance of the inner chamber.

"But first, I will float, while a few decisions are made and instructions given," he added as he descended onto the lake.

Once they were bobbing gently on the waves, Kwatili and Matthias gathered them all together, the atmosphere suddenly becoming deadly serious. Ghelli in particular was looking extremely anxious, not at all his usual arrogant self, which probably alarmed Elijah more than anything else!

"What happens next will be pivotal to the survival of Greylea and probably all other realms, and I'm very much afraid to say that it all has to rest on your shoulders alone Elijah Grey" said Kwatili, her warm amber eyes staring deep into his very soul as she spoke.

He could only swallow hard and nod in response, this he had not expected, he had assumed that whatever happened, he would have the support of these amazing creatures; the thought of going up against Xan on his own was terrifying.

"You must understand that if there were any other way we would not have it so my son, but where, and more importantly when you will be going, we all exist already, and we cannot risk meeting ourselves from another time, the consequences would be catastrophic. You are the only one who will not already be present, and even then, we must time it to the second for it to be safe and under no circumstances must you interact with anyone except Egreya."

Matthias's voice cracked momentarily as he spoke her name, it was blatantly obvious to all present that the thought of her being this close and not being able to see her himself was painful beyond bearing for him.

Somehow his father's pain helped steel Elijah to his task and he straightened his hunched shoulders and said, as confidently as he could muster, "I'll be fine, just tell me what I've got to do and I'll try not to let you all down."

It was too much for poor Burda, huge hulk that she was, she let out a loud sob and crushed him breathless in her arms.

"Oh my brave boy, if only I could go with you. Or someone. I can't bear to think of you facing this alone, it's just not right!" she cried, her gruff voice muffled into his hair.

"Well, actually, he does not have to go alone" Khizzi whispered shyly, stepping out from behind Ghelli, who's face crumpled as he heard her.

Kwatili and Matthias both closed their eyes and smiled in obvious relief.

"I was not born fifteen years ago, I cannot meet myself; therefore if Elijah will have me, I would be honoured to accompany him."

Behind Khizzi, Ghelli's shoulders slumped in submission; he had known, as had the others, that this was the case, but had been desperately hoping that his little sister would not offer to go, and that Kwatili and Matthias would not feel that they could ask her.

"Well yeah, of course that would be great, as long as you're sure," Elijah replied, trying not to let too much of the immense relief he was experiencing be evident in his response.

Khizzi grinned and moved to stand beside him, her decision clearly made.

Kwatili took a deep breath and said, "All is good, I have no doubt that you two together will accomplish what must be done." Turning to address the awaiting Ayobi, she added, "It is time to open the door Ayobi, the task will be easier to explain then I think."

Ayobi nodded his heavy head and slowly rose up above the water once more. "Haven't done this for a while, I may be a bit rusty so I advise you all to hold on to something," he called back as he began to spin around in the air, slowly at first but rapidly gathering speed until the horizon with the view of the Isle of Tears became a stomach churning blur.

Sweat coursed down Elijah's face and his heart felt as if it was about to burst through his rib cage, just as his legs were about to buckle beneath him, everything stopped and a muffled silence descended.

"Phew, that has definitely not improved!" muttered Brogan, as he grappled himself upright.

"My apologies but I did warn you. Many years in hiding have taken their toll, but we are at our destination," Ayobi said, exhaustion having drained his voice to a rasping whisper.

Once his vision had returned to normal, Elijah moved forward and peer around the Oren's neck.

"Wow!" he gasped.

"Behold Elijah Grey, the doorway to the exact time that you departed this realm fifteen years ago!"

"It's so different, it's beautiful, all green and—" he stuttered as his eyes took in the transformed vista before him.

The island was bathed in bright golden sunshine, and wheeling in lazy circles above the lush green canopy were a multitude of rainbow coloured birds.

One by one the travellers squeezed past Ayobi's neck to drop down onto the soft white sand of the beach.

With a worried expression on his huge features, the Time Oren manoeuvred his bulk until he was floating just off shore.

"Please remember that the present and future as we know them depend completely on how careful you are not to interact with anyone other than your mother Elijah, do not under any circumstances give in to the temptation to warn Burda or Ranger about the Driller attack in the forest."

His rolling eyes suddenly focussed solely on Elijah's and he paused, the only sound was the soft whisper of the waves breaking gently on the sand.

Elijah sank to his knees and rocked back to sit hugging them to his chest. "I-I'm not sure that I can do this, what if I screw up, I'm just a kid!" he muttered, unable to meet that gaze.

Ayobi huffed loudly from his giant nostrils, sending a gust of air to scuff up the sand and shower the group assembled before him.

"I am unfamiliar with what a kid is, but you are the first of your kind Elijah Grey, you have power that has never existed before, your mother, your world and all others need you to be strong and believe in yourself as I do; you will not screw up!"

Elijah risked looking up into those deeply wise eyes, he flinched and jumped up to his feet, crying.

"What power? What is it with you people, you drop whoppers like that into conversation like you'd tell someone to come down for dinner, not that the whole damn universe suddenly depended on them!"

As Burda opened her mouth, he added sharply,

"And yes Burda, if I'm expected to save the world I think I'm entitled to use toilet language!"

Silence descended like a blanket, and all present stood in awkward indecision as to who to look at or what to do next.

Ayobi lowered his head in a semblance of a bow to Elijah, a large round tear drop welled up in both eyes and dripped onto the sand to be immediately blotted up by it.

"Forgive me Elijah, I think I now have a better idea of what it means to still be a kid. Being two centuries old myself, it has been a very long time since I felt any of the emotions that you must now be experiencing."

Turning to Matthias, he narrowed his eyes and continued in a low voice.

"Have you not, as his father, spoken to him about the circumstances and consequences of his ancestry Matthias?"

Matthias sighed deeply and hung his head like a scolded school boy.

"I see, all is clear now. Sit, Elijah Grey. Before you embark on your task, the bare essentials at least must be told."

They all obeyed, and sat around Elijah in a protective circle. Ayobi settled onto the sandy surface and took in a long deep breath that he released slowly as a soft sigh through his breathing tube.

"In the realm of Greylea it has always been forbidden to reproduce with a creature not of your kind, as you already know, all Greyleans are human except for one gene in their DNA. Thus we have the amazing creatures surrounding you and many others.

Your parents, however, chose to break the rule, they fell in love across two species and the result of their love, was you Elijah Grey. You are a complete unknown, a first, a never before. This makes you a glorious and exciting gift to most, but a terrifying threat to a few; one of which is Xan. He has long desired a tool by which he could depose those in power and gain that power for himself. You are that tool Elijah, he used the fact that Matthias and Egreya broke the rules to turn enough inhabitants against them and outcast Matthias and, well Egreya you will see for yourself soon. He searches for you frantically, because he fears what you may be, and knows that you possess the Eye of Ula.

What he does not know, however, is that there are in fact two Eyes of Ula, and that it takes both to fully control their power, which is to open doors into other realms at will."

"And if he got a hold of it," Elijah whispered, subconsciously grabbing the small leather pouch around his neck, "He would be able to go anywhere he wanted and no living creature would be safe!"

"Not without the other of the pair Elijah, remember that both are needed for the power to be wielded," said Kwatili quietly.

"And where is it? Where's the other one?" he asked, almost dreading the answer.

"At this point in time, where we are now, your mother still has it, this is why we are here, so that you can take it from her before, well before she makes it impossible to do so."

Elijah jumped to his feet and paced back and forth along the beach, still clasping the Eye of Ula close to his chest.

"But back there, in the forest, when the door started to open in the tree, I shut it. How did I do that if I didn't have both of them?" he asked Ayobi, standing inches from the Oren's huge head and staring him straight in the eye.

"I was not there to witness that occurrence Elijah, but I would guess that what came into play were the unknown powers of which I have spoken," replied Ayobi steadily.

Elijah sank weak kneed down to the damp sand, his heart thudding and his ears ringing.

Matthias and Kwatili both leapt to his side, Burda, slower to stagger to her feet, pushed them aside to encircle him in her thick arms.

"Enough!" She cried gruffly, scowling around like an angry rhino protecting her calf.

Then leaning away from him to look Elijah hard in the eyes, "You are afraid that you have something bad inside you, something that you cannot control. That is not true Elijah Grey, I have known you from the moment that you were born, I know your mother, and father and there is nothing that they could create that could be bad in any way. You have a good heart and you have always made good choices, granted I haven't always said so, but you have, and that is not going to change."

Elijah remained stiff and panic stricken for a moment more, before letting out a held breath, and deflating in her arms as he relaxed visibly.

Nodding to herself, Burda patted him heftily on his shoulder before walking away, hoping that no one noticed her hastily swiping away a tear from her tiny beady eye.

"I think that's enough information thanks, it's probably best to find out the rest myself, or remain in blissful ignorance who knows, but I just want to be doing something now, if that's okay?" Elijah said, wiping his sweaty and sand encrusted palms on his trouser legs, and steadfastly not meeting any sets of eyes.

Khizzi walked over to him and stood silently beside him.

"I am ready Elijah Grey." She said timidly.

He smiled shyly to himself and looked up into Ayobi's huge face.

"So what now?" he asked.

Gesturing over towards where the jungle ended at the beach, the Time Oren said.

"If you enter where the trees part and follow the path, you will come to a vantage point where you will be able to observe without being seen. It is crucial that the only person that you interact with is Egreya, you must wait until she is alone, and then convince her to give you the partner Eye of Ula, before she makes it impossible to do so, I cannot emphasise enough how imperative it is that you do not change what happens next Elijah, no matter how much you may want to."

Turning to look at Khizzi, he said, "Your role, young Khizzi, is to keep him strong in this, and remind him of my words should it prove necessary."

She nodded and immediately headed off towards the tree line.

Elijah hesitated momentarily, before following her, trotting to catch up and together they entered the jungle and disappeared from sight within seconds.

On the beach, Kwatili, Matthias, Burda and Brogan climbed back on board Ayobi, each silent and deep in thought.

Ayobi rose once more into the warm air above the water before withdrawing his long neck and head, sealing the hole and submerging beneath the glistening green lake, to wait.

# Chapter 27

As they entered, the dense canopy closed overhead like a sunroof. Both blinked furiously, in a futile attempt to see more clearly and it took at least a minute for their eyes to adjust to the emerald gloom.

Standing together in the muffled silence, listening to their own breaths and the soft rustling of the breeze caressing the leaves high above them, Elijah finally looked round at Khizzi and whispered.

"I'm really glad that you're here with me Khizzi, I don't think I could make myself go any further if I was on my own."

In answer, she reached out and quickly squeezed his hand.

Taking a deep breath, he forced his feet back into motion, treading carefully so as not to make too much noise; he had the definite sense that something or someone was watching every move they made.

As their eyes adjusted to the gloom, they spotted a narrow winding path, worn away in the dense undergrowth. Better than forcing through the tangle of vines and thorn laden bushes, they took it, trusting that it would take them to where they needed to be.

At the top of a ridge, it ended, at a wide gap in the foliage that was almost a window, beyond which they could see the steeply sloping side of a mountain, bare and grey, in stark contrast to the lush verdant growth surrounding them.

Elijah was just preparing to leave the jungle when Khizzi grabbed him and pressed one finger to her lips and the other hand pointed towards a small group of people who had just emerged from a wide crack in the rock.

Elijah had to clench his jaws tightly to prevent himself from gasping out loud.

The trio standing whispering to each other like conspirators were Burda, Ranger, and a female who could only be Egreya, his mother.

Hot tears welled up in his eyes and trickled down his cheeks at the sight of her. So tall, and brave, her waist length raven black hair billowing out behind her in the breeze.

The urge to burst out of his hiding place and run into her arms was almost overwhelming him, but then he noticed that she was, in fact, holding what could only be him in those arms.

Swaddled tightly in a yellow blanket, so that all that showed was the jet black top of his head, he realised that this moment in time must truly be but minutes after his birth.

Holding his breath he inched closer, so that he would be able to hear what was being said.

Burda was arguing with Egreya it seemed.

"But there must be another way my Lady, I am not up to the task that you set me!" She said earnestly.

"Oh but you are my faithful Burda, I know your worth even if you refuse to see it yourself, there is no other that I would trust my son to, you and Ranger will know when he is ready to return. Now go quickly before I weaken in my resolve!"

As she spoke, Egreya kissed her son lovingly on his forehead before pressing him into the strong arms of Burda. Turning towards Ranger, she hugged him fiercely and added.

"You are giving up so much for me my friend, I hope with all my heart that I will be given a chance to repay you."

Elijah could see the now familiar blue eyes and sharp angular features of the white haired man struggling to conceal his emotions. All he could muster was a brief nod.

Then, taking the two glowing red stones that were the Eyes of Ula in her hands, Egreya held them aloft above her head to catch the rays of sunshine glancing over the mountain peak.

It was as if they burst into flame in her fingers, and her uplifted face was bathed in scarlet, only her jet eyes remained black. Slowly lowering her hands, she aimed the ball of flame towards a point in space just beside Burda who was gently covering the face of the baby in her arms.

As Elijah and Khizzi watched transfixed, a hole began to appear in the air, ringed by red flames, growing and stretching until it was a portal large enough for even Burda to step through with ease. Startled, Elijah realised that through it he could see a glimpse of their little cabin in the woods!

"Now, take this and keep it safe for him, you will know when he is ready to use it!"

Egreya gasped in a strained rasping voice, as she took one of the pair of stones and pushed it into a leather pouch and then into Burda's hand.

"Go quickly, I won't be able to sustain the doorway for long with only one of the pair, may we meet again!" She cried as Burda and Ranger stepped into the sizzling portal and disappeared, the last thing that was visible before the doorway snapped shut behind them was the waving flag of a white dog's tail.

Elijah and Khizzi stood in their hiding place stunned and open mouthed, Egreya sagged almost to her knees before pulling herself back upright.

"Now you must move Elijah Grey, you must convince her to give you the other Eye of Ula before it is lost to both of you forever!" Whispered Khizzi pushing Elijah forcefully forwards out into the open.

As he came crashing out of the undergrowth Egreya leapt backwards holding the still glowing ember of the Eye of Ula out before her like a shield.

When Elijah regained his feet and stood before her, she let out a loud sob and her face crumpled.

"Um, I don't really know what to say to convince you but-"

Muttered Elijah, hating the distress written all over her face.

"Words are not necessary, I know not how you are here, and I don't need to know, what is it that you want from me Elijah my son?" She said steadily, rapidly regaining her composure as she lowered the Eye and pushed it inside its pouch on a thong around her neck.

Completely taken by surprise by her immediate compliance Elijah stood silent and immobile, with his mouth opening and shutting like a fish out of water.

Khizzi stepped forward and bowed graciously to Egreya before saying.

"We have been brought here by Ayobi the Time Oren, our task is to stop you making the other Eye of Ula unavailable to Elijah, he already has the one that you sent off with him as a baby; he needs its partner in order to defeat Xan, my Lady."

Enlightenment dawned on Egreya's features like a sunrise.

"Ayobi still survives in the future, that is good news indeed! So are you with anyone else?" She asked glancing around hopefully.

"They are all back on the beach, but yes, Matthias, Burda, Brogan and –"

Elijah found and lost his voice in the same breath, as shouting suddenly erupted from the jungle that thrashed about as if an elephant were stampeding towards them.

"Quickly! You must not meet anyone from this time it would be a disaster on a grand scale! Here!" Egreya thrust the leather pouch into Elijah's hand and then began pushing him towards the undergrowth and their previous hiding place.

Behind them, out of the corner of his eye he saw a large group emerge from the trees, darkly clad and heavily built, they were about a hundred yards away and had not seen them yet it seemed.

Once they were safely hidden, Egreya placed her hands on either side of his face and looked deeply into his eyes before whispering urgently.

"My son, it is crucial that whatever happens next, you remain hidden and do nothing save travel safely back to Ayobi as soon as possible." Turning to Khizzi, she smiled briefly and said, "He has chosen well in you, it will be up to you to keep him strong."

Then, she turned and strode out to the clearing with no hint of fear in her poker straight back.

Immediately Elijah tried to follow her, but Khizzi's strong tail whipped around his waist and held him back.

"You must obey her wishes Elijah no matter how much it may feel wrong to you, trust her."

Elijah gritted his teeth, he didn't want to be angry with Khizzi, but he also didn't want to lose his mother now that he had found her, he hadn't even been able to speak to her for goodness sake!

"Watch and stay hidden, that is what you should do now," Khizzi added, but her tail remained tight on his waist.

So he watched as Egreya walked out to meet the approaching hoard.

As they drew close, one figure came to the front, it was small in stature, bent over slightly and clothed in a dark green hooded cloak. Elijah's breath caught in his throat as the figure stopped in front of his mother and a long bony fingered hand whipped out from beneath its cloak and halted the rest behind it. One of the fingers on that hand was elongated to twice the length of the other and ended in a long hooked yellow claw.

"Nax," He whispered under his breath.

Khizzi hushed him.

"Xan!" Egreya said in a loud, defiant voice. "I've been expecting you."

"Good, good, then you will know what I want Egreya, and just in case you're not feeling cooperative today, I have brought a little something to sway your mind."

Xan's voice was thin and shrill from beneath the voluminous hood and he gestured to the crowd behind him.

Suddenly four bound figures were thrust forward to topple to the ground at Egreya's feet.

This time Khizzi had to use her hand to stifle the outcry from Elijah. It was Kwatili, Matthias and Ghelli, and a slim white haired, female version of Ranger.

Egreya did not flinch, she stared steadily at Xan as if they were not there; Elijah noticed that the hand that clutched tightly onto the edge of her jacket twitched very slightly but that was her only response.

"You do not know me well at all, Xan, if you think that I was not prepared for your little surprise reunion." Here she paused to glance momentarily at the three figures sprawled at her feet. Both Kwatili and Matthias met her eyes and nodded imperceptibly.

"Goodbye my friends, until we meet again."

She cried as she threw up her hands and closed her eyes tight against the sudden flare of blinding light that enclosed her in a white sheath.

"No!!!!" Shrieked Xan, lunging forward, both grasping hands outstretched, but he was too late.

As his extended claw like fingers reached Egreya they bounced off as if she were encased in stone.

Matthias hung his head and sobbed openly, Xan screamed like a banshee and pummelled at the now diamond hard surface of the Glidiri Crystal sheath that enclosed Egreya.

There she stood, frozen, with her eyes closed, and one hand raised to touch her neck, exactly as she had appeared to Elijah in the Glidiri Caves.

"Come Elijah, this is the time to leave. I feel, there is nothing more we can do for your mother in this time, and we know that the others somehow escape," urged Khizzi quietly, tugging gently at Elijah with both her arms and the tail that she still had tightly wound around his waist.

For a moment more he hesitated, indecision causing beads of sweat to break out on his forehead.

"Elijah please, before we are discovered!" whispered Khizzi, and the fear evident in her voice was what it took to shatter his stasis. Picking their way as soundlessly as possible, they followed the narrow path back towards the beach.

Every second expecting to hear the sounds of pursuit behind them they moved as quickly as the tangled undergrowth would permit. The temptation to stop and look back almost overwhelming, but a persistent voice in Elijah's head drove him forward.

Suddenly the jungle ended at the beach, and they broke into a run across the shifting sand towards the awaiting Ayobi, who was floating just off shore.

As soon as they broke cover, he rose up from the water surface and hovered inland until he was once again on land. The others spilled out from inside and hastened to meet them, dragging them back aboard so that the Time Oren could once again hover out onto the water.

Just in the nick of time, it seemed, as seconds before Ayobi began to withdraw his head and reseal his shell for the dizzying time travel, Elijah spotted a hoard of dark figures bursting free of the jungle and teeming down the beach towards them. The last sound to reach his ears before the deafening buzzing as they entered the time tunnel was a high pitched scream of pure rage.

# Chapter 28

All sat in stunned silence and deep thought. The return journey back to their time had been anything but smooth and Ayobi now floated on the lake with his long neck extended and his head lolling in the water, utterly exhausted.

The first to rouse was Kwatili, who went first to the neck opening to touch the Oren's neck and ask, "Are you alright Ayobi? What do you need us to do?"

Slowly he lifted his huge head out of the water and turned it to gaze at her with glazed eyes. Smiling sadly, he replied.

"There is nothing for you to do, my time is almost ended, but at least I was able to full fill the ultimate destiny of my kind before it was too late."

Elijah jerked alert at his words and jumped up to join Kwatili.

"What does he mean Kwatili, why is he the last of the Time Oren? What happened to the others?"

She looked at him, her glowing amber eyes brimming with unshed tears, "When Xan reached the beach and saw Ayobi disappear with you on board, he exacted his revenge on the rest of the Time Orens. He hunted them all down and killed them, because they all refused to tell him where, and when, Ayobi had taken you to. Ayobi has hidden on the lake disguised as the Island of Sighs for fifteen years, waiting for this time to arrive, knowing that it would probably lead to his passing."

She paused and stroked the out stretched neck beside her.

"Ah my friend, such courage pays tribute to all of your lost kin."

"But if he rests up, he'll recover surely?" said Elijah.

Matthias had now joined them, and placed a hand on his son's shoulder.

"It's not the exhaustion that will kill him Elijah, now that Xan has seen him, he can identify him, he will not rest until he tracks him down, in helping us, Ayobi has signed his own death warrant."

"But he's the last! Surely if he hides somewhere else Xan won't be able to find him!"

Elijah cried, pacing back and forth in angry frustration.

This time it was Ayobi himself who answered, lifting his weary head higher and trumpeting loudly from his nostrils.

"I will not be caught like a fish in a trap young Elijah, I will deliver you to your destination and then take myself out of all reach and be glad of the final peace, I have had my fill of hiding."

With that he wrenched himself up and out of the water, causing them all to stumble and have to hang on to each other to stay upright.

Surging forward with surprising speed he headed off towards the distant coastline to the North of them.

Before long they reached the grey rocky shore and he stopped just short of land.

One by one, they disembarked in silence, jumping down onto the slippery rocks and scrambling to the more level part of the beach.

As they turned to look back, they saw the Oren rise for one last time, high above them, he began to spin and his outline became blurred.

Just before he winked out of existence, he called down, "Say hello to Juno for me Elijah Grey!"

And then he was gone.

In stunned silence they all stood staring upwards into an empty sky.

"So, is that it? Is he dead?" Elijah asked in a barely audible whisper.

Kwatili coughed to clear her throat before answering. "I do not know Elijah, but I choose to think not."

"Me too."

He replied, rubbing the palms of his hands roughly against his legs and taking in a few deep breaths.

"So, what now, where are we?" he asked looking around him for the first time.

The landscape around them was hard and bleak, mainly rocks, monotone grey with the occasional blob of ochre lichen to break the monotony.

Snapping out of his reverie, Matthias too took in their surroundings, hopping up onto a higher rock to survey further.

Jumping back down, he chuckled.

"Well, I'd like to say that I know exactly where we are, but I haven't got a clue I'm afraid!" he said.

"Surely we should be on the Isle of tears if we're to rescue my mother and…" Elijah couldn't help glancing at Ranger, who was sitting hunched up on a rock, deep in thought.

Elijah walked over to him and sat beside his friend, placing a tentative hand lightly on his shoulder. Beneath his fingers Ranger flinched but he didn't look up.

"Rheyana was okay Ranger, yes she was tied up and a prisoner just like Kwatili, Matthias and Ghelli, but she wasn't hurt and from the ferocious scowl that she gave Xan, she was not afraid." He whispered so that only Ranger could hear.

For a second or two it was as if he had not heard, but then Ranger reached out his hand to find Elijah's and squeezed it fiercely before releasing it.

"Thank you my friend, it was indeed my Rheyana that you saw," He looked up suddenly, brushing his eyes with the heel of his hand.

"She will certainly give Xan as much trouble as she can, whilst protecting Egreya with her life; that I can guarantee!"

He nodded as he spoke, as if trying to convince himself more than Elijah, who said, "I realise now just how much you did sacrifice for my sake Ranger, and, well, I'm sorry about how I was when I first got here and-"

Ranger laughed and swatted his friends head playfully, saying, "Enough Elijah Grey, water under the embankment or whatever you say, come we both need to save our loved ones!"

Ghelli suddenly batted himself on the head and shouted excitedly.

"Of course! I knew this all felt familiar, we are standing on the West coast of the Ice Desert, all we have to do is keep to the edge and we will be safe, plus it will make it very hard for Xan to track us from below using the Drillers!"

"You're right Ghelli, I can't believe I didn't recognise it too, this bodes well for us Elijah Grey, Xan will waste much time searching for our trail on one of the Islands when here we will be, sneaking in through the back door!"

Kwatili was grinning as she gathered together their back sacks and thrust each one into the arms of its owner.

Brogan, however, was not looking so cheerful. "Yay!" he grumbled. "The Ice Desert, perfect for folks with short legs who don't like it hot!"

"Oh Brogan, suck it up, I'm not exactly built for it either but do you hear me moaning?" snapped Burda, rubbing at her damaged leg as she spoke.

"I just know I'm going to regret this but I have to ask, if it's so hot, why is it called the Ice Desert?" Said Elijah, whilst carefully zipping both leather pouches into a pocket in his ruck sack.

Kwatili laughed softly and replied, "I think that will become clear to you within the next ten minutes if we get moving."

Not at all surprised that he didn't get a straight answer, Elijah shrugged his back sack onto his shoulders as he said.

"Well let's get going then, Burda, if you need me to I can carry your stuff too."

A smart retort was on its way from her mouth, but she stopped herself and leaned back on one stout hip to say, "Well about time young man, I've been picking up after you for long enough!"

Ranger laughed, and all three shared a smile at fond memories, back when life seemed uncomplicated and unthreatening; when he had indeed been "just a kid" growing up in a little cabin on the edge of a wood with a dog as his best friend and a mother that no man would be insane enough to mess with!

Together, they scrambled up over the broad flat grey rocks, followed by Kwatili, Ghelli, Khizzi and Matthias, who had been silent since arriving on the shore.

As he crested the ridge, Elijah gasped.

The sight that met his eyes was awesome, even for this crazy world.

Stretching out for as far as he could see, the landscape was mirror flat and white as snow, indeed, if the heat radiating off the nearby edge wasn't already scorching his eyebrows, he would have assumed that it was snow covered. Towering, crystalline stacks jutted like glassy pillars into the yellowing sky, and had an eerily sentient presence, as if they were giant watch towers.

He placed one tentative foot forward off the rock surface that formed the perimeter of the desert.

"Wow, it's really hot!" He gasped, as the tough leather boots transferred heat immediately through to his toes.

"Then you will be glad that I always pack for every situation!" Cried Brogan triumphantly, shrugging his outsize back sack to the ground and grinning widely, displaying his rows of crocodilian teeth.

Turning the bag upside down, he emptied its entire contents onto the ground, to a chorus of laughter.

Contrary to what the others had assumed, given his appetite, the bag was not full of food and drink, but strange flat cork shapes that he proceeded to dole out in pairs to each astounded onlooker.

"Here, they strap on like this." He said, attaching a pair to the bottom of his own bare feet using long leather thongs. He then pranced about on the hot sand, to demonstrate how well his feet were now protected.

"I'm not even going to ask why or how Brogan!" Kwatili chuckled as she tied her own insulating soles onto her long slender feet.

"Hmmph! It's been my experience that it's always best not to know why that old crinkle skin does what he does!" Burda grunted as she struggled to bend enough to reach her ankles, but added, with a wink towards Elijah,

"But I will admit that once in a long while, you're glad to have him around!"

Once all travellers were kitted out appropriately, they set off, taking a straight line across the surprisingly firm surface heading north as best they could figure according to the position of the red sun on the horizon.

Within just a few minutes they were all experiencing the draining effects of the scorching heat. The simple act of drawing in a breath felt as if his lungs were on fire and Elijah could feel his skin dehydrating and burning. Glancing across at Burda he was shocked to see how exhausted she looked already, each agonising step threatening to be her last. The others were faring no better, Brogans short legs meant that he had to take two steps to Kawatli's one, and sweat trickled freely down the rugged bumpy surface of his head and neck before evaporating into the desiccating atmosphere. Matthias had stripped off his thick leather jacket and tied it around his waist, exposing a muscular torso, thickly coated in grey hair.

The only one, in fact not displaying any outward signs of the heat was Kwatili who strode forth at the front of the company, slender neck stiff and stretched, nose tilted upwards sniffing the air continually, her whole body was as tense as a spring.

In an attempt to distract his mind from the thirst now making it hard for him to swallow because his tongue stuck to the roof of his mouth, Elijah stared at the ice column that they were just passing, noticing that he could see no shadow in any direction thrown by the towering shape and that as they drew nearer he thought that he could see blurred shapes within its crystalline purity.

"Do not, under any circumstances be tempted to touch them Raven Boy, it would be as disastrous as when you touched the trees in the Forest of Souls, when I told you not to."

Ghelli panted as he spoke and his voice was a hoarse whisper but Elijah still felt the sting in it.

He wanted to retort that his communion with the trees had in fact saved their lives multiple times, and he was so tempted to stomp over and touch the ice column just to show him, but decided that it would be more sensible to  restrain himself.

A gentle tingle at his waist made him jump and looking down he blushed even redder when he realised that it was Khizzi's chestnut furred tail curled around it. She left it there just for a second more to sooth away the irritation that her brother had caused, then withdrew it, with not a word spoken. He couldn't meet her eyes but smiled broadly to himself when he spotted the puce flush of annoyance that spread over Ghelli's scowling visage.

Ahead, Kwatili halted and crouched down low like a sprinter on a starting block, holding her hand up for silence she froze like a statue as did they all.

Elijah held his breath as he watched her nostrils twitching and her delicate ears flattened against the downy side of her head.

He released the breath as she slowly rose erect and turned to say softly.

"The sun will set within the hour, we are not being pursued at this time so it will be safe enough to stop here and spend the night."

"Aren't we a bit out in the open Kwatili? We could be spotted so easily, especially from the air."

Matthias's question sent shivers down Elijah's spine and he instinctively searched the burnt orange sky above. He saw nothing but still couldn't shake the feeling that eyes were watching him.

"That won't be a problem Matthias, not when we're hidden by this!" said a grinning Burda as she emptied out the tightly rolled contents of her back sack onto the burning sand, having relieved Elijah of it's burden.

Kwatili tipped her head back and howled, then cried,

"You two have to be the best at surprises that I have ever had the pleasure to travel with! By the Eyes of Ula it's a Shrink tent!"

"Well, much as I'd like to take the credit, it's all down to that renegade Ryufu, he insisted that we brought these, must have a sixth sense or something!"

Burda chortled as she began carefully unrolling the soft wrinkled fabric, which closely resembled a crumpled butterfly wing as it emerges from its chrysalis.

Once spread out, it formed a large circle that was the same colour as the white sand beneath it. Elijah was desperate to ask how on earth they were all going to get inside this thing let alone fit, when Kwatili caught his eye and winked, saying,

"Wait Elijah Grey, in just a few moments the heat from the sand will work and you will understand Ryufu's gift."

Behind him Elijah heard Matthias grunt, but decided to keep his attention firmly on the Shrink tent, and he was rewarded almost instantaneously.

As the sizzling heat of the white sand hit the white disc it began to swell like bread dough in a bowl. Before their eyes it rose up from the surface of the ice desert like a ghost, filling out to form a hemisphere of billowing silk fabric that expanded until it was stretched taut and head height, easily now large enough to accommodate them all.

"Wow, that's so cool!" Cried Elijah leaping forward, to be halted by a strong arm across his chest.

"Wowah there Raven Boy, it needs to harden first."

It was Brogan, and he had vastly underestimated his own strength, Elijah bent over winded and coughing.

"Sorry mate, take a minute eh?" He added, patting the boy as gently as he could on the back, and looking greatly embarrassed.

Breathing more normally now, Elijah stood up and shook his head as Burda moved to fuss over him.

"So, how long does it take to harden?" He said to distract her.

"Just watch, you will see." Answered Kwatili, who was actually studying the nearest ice column rather than the Shrink tent.

Suddenly they all heard a soft rustling sound coming from the fabric of the tent, as it began to stiffen and expand as the softness disappeared to be replaced by a rigid shiny white surface that looked just like a giant table tennis ball set into the sand.

"Now you can touch Raven Boy, it's cooked!" Laughed Brogan as he strode towards the Shrink tent, "And not a minute too soon if my skin's not lying to me!"

"It's not oh warty one, we have just a few minutes to get inside before the freeze." Matthias said, ushering them all towards it. As he approached, he bowed his head and muttered some strange words, which it seemed the tent was waiting for. A circular aperture opened up in the previously flawless surface and expanded until it was large enough to admit even Burda's bulk.

"In we go, after you Burda, once you're installed we'll know how much room there is left for the rest of us!" He chipped, playfully slapping her on the rear as she squeezed through the hole.

"Watch your hands and your mouth or you'll be the one left out to freeze!" She grunted from inside.

"What are you all talking about? How could anyone freeze here? It's so hot that we have to protect our feet from burning off." Elijah said frowning up at the still red sky. Then he realised that the sun had disappeared below the flat white horizon, and then he heard another sound that seemed to be travelling towards then across the sand, like the hissing of a million crawling ants.

Louder and louder it got until it was more a sizzling, combined with a strange creaking and groaning.

"Quickly Elijah, inside the shrink tenet before it reaches us!" Cried Kwatili, urging him in through the entrance, they were the last two outside, and as he looked back he gasped.

Spreading over the white sand, like flood water was a thick layer of pale blue ice. It snapped and crackled as it raced towards them, the air temperature had dropped dramatically and was now so cold that it froze his throat as he breathed and he could feel ice crystals forming on his eye lashes and brows.

As Kwatili leapt through the opening she pulled his head inside and uttered the same strange words that had opened the entrance to close it with a snap.

As they huddled inside their shelter, the crust of ice could be heard creeping voraciously over the top of the Shrink tent and then advancing onwards across the desert, the aptly named Ice Desert, Elijah now decided.

Inside the protective shell, it was warm and dry, just large enough for all of them to lay down to sleep, although fairly snug, with no room for movement.

As he lay on his back, staring up at the curved white ceiling above, Elijah couldn't stop images of searching creatures with snuffling nostrils and clawed feet scrabbling over the ice surface all around their hiding place, invading his mind. He forced himself to breath, as he realised that he had been holding his breath from the second that he lay down.

A butterfly light touch on his arm burst the bubble of fear in his chest and turning his head, he met the glow of Kwatili's amber eyes mere inches from his.

She smiled and whispered,

"They may be there Elijah, but they will not detect us in here, trust me, you are safe, sleep."

Strangely, the confirmation should have made him even more afraid, but the truth in her words was palpable and he did indeed trust her implicitly, so he smiled back, closed his eyes and remembered no more.

Until the voices.

Whispers that said nothing understandable at first began to break into his dreamless slumber. Then they grew in volume and clarity until the three words "Answer us Elijah," became a ringing inside his head that finally prized his eyes apart.

In the cool darkness of the Shrink tent, he lay panting and sweating as waves of panic washed over him.

Out of the gloom flared two amber lamp lights, Kwatili was staring straight into his face and his soul.

Slowly she raised one finger to her lips and then sat up silently and gestured for him to do the same. Inching painstakingly past grunting sleeping bodies, they reached the outer wall of the tent where they donned warm clothing and their foot protectors. Then Kwatili leaned her forehead gently against the hard surface of the wall and whispered the opening words.

A small circle opened up at first, so that Kwatili could peer out and check that they were alone before it expanded just enough to allow them to squeeze through. As the blast of frozen air hit them Elijah heard it snap shut again behind them.

Within seconds their breaths formed icicles hanging down from their chins and Elijah could feel thick layers of ice crystals coating his eye lashes, making them so heavy that he could hardly keep his eyes open.

"Come Elijah Grey we will survive for only a few minutes out here we need to be quick!" Kwatili shouted over the howling wind that whipped across the desert surface.

Tugging him behind her, she bent into the wind and walked as fast as possible towards the nearest Ice Column.

The closer they got, the louder the voices became in his head until he could no longer tell if they were in fact still inside his head.

"I do not hear them Elijah, but I know what they are saying!" Kwatili shouted over her shoulder as they approached the column.

"You have to touch it Elijah, you have to send the signal whether it reaches unfriendly ears as well as Ryufu or not, it's the only way!" She cried, pointing to the sheer smooth surface.

"But Ghelli said-"He cried, his hand hovering hesitantly inches from the column side.

She shook her head, and said

"Ghelli means well, but his fear of the unknown blocks his understanding, trust me Elijah!" She replied, her golden eyes fringed with ice crystals.

Before his own fear could prevent it, Elijah reached out until his frozen finger tips met the slick surface.

Instantly his world became blinding light. It was as if he had become one with the Ice column, his body soared upwards inside the column like he was in a lift, and he felt as if he was flying, as light as a feather, up towards the sun.

As he reached the top, he was above the clouds, bathed in steel bright sunshine that melted his frozen exterior and soothed his aching head.

Hovering just above the exit to the Ice Column, he realised that he was suddenly no longer alone. A ring of faces surrounded him, some familiar, some not, some friendly, some definitely not! One face came forward until it hovered so close to his own that he was sure he could feel his breath.

"Well done Raven boy, we know where you are now, go back before it is not possible for you to do so, wait for us at the Northern edge of the Ice desert, we will find you!"

The voice and face were those of Ryufu, his huge round eyes bored into Elijah's before his visage dissolve into the pulsating light show that now surrounded him.

"Return quickly Elijah, others are beginning to be aware of your presence!"

Kwatili's voice seemed to be coming from a vast distance away, and bared touched Elijah's awareness. He was lost in the whirling kaleidoscope that surrounded him, transfixed like a toddler at their first firework show. As his eyes began to feel heavy, he was suddenly overcome by an intense desire to lie down and sleep, to surrender to the soporific effect of the soft melodious humming that filled his head.

"Elijah! Do not close your eyes, wake up and come back to us now!"

The sharp note of fear in Kwatili's tone jarred him slightly out of his dream state, he shook his head in an attempt to regain control over his body, which felt dull and heavy, as if it no longer belonged to him.

"Come to me boy, come see your mother, she misses you."

This time the voice had a distinctly threatening tone, and out of the swirling mist that surrounded him, a new face began to materialise.

Two huge, bulging, puss yellow eyes with a tiny pinprick pupil, skewered his brain and mesmerised it. He felt the warmth draining from his blood as the small, thin lipped mouth slowly curved into a sly, smile, exposing long corn colour teeth.

Out of the mist Xan was calling Elijah to him, closer and closer the thin bony fingers came to Elijah's throat, they twitched with anticipation, making a sickening clicking sound that filled the boy's ears, shutting out Kwatilli's desperate cries.

"You know its best boy, give in to it, reach out and touch my hand and all the problems will be done with."

Xan's words were wrapped in silk and Elijah found that all he wanted to do was let himself drift away and never be afraid again. Slowly he fought to move his limp arm out towards the outstretched fingers, he was mere inches away when suddenly he felt himself being yanked downwards by his waist, so viciously that it squeezed all the breath from his lungs with a loud grunt.

"No Xan, you will not take my Elijah!" Shrieked a small voice out of the air around him as Elijah plummeted downwards at an alarming speed.

His senses rapidly returned to him and just before he crashed heavily onto the ground, he realised that what was coiled around his waist was, of course, Khizzi's brown tail.

In fact, his landing was cushioned by both Khizzi and Kwatili, and the three ended up in a tangled heap on the frozen crust of the Ice Desert, at the foot of the now blackened column.

Before he could completely gather his wits, Elijah felt a set of strong arms lifting him up and then holding him tightly against a barrel chest as their owner ran back to the warm safety of the Shrink tent.

Only when the others were inside and the opening sealed tight did he dare to open his eyes and draw in a deep breath. Brogan was still panting from his run across the ice, and Khizzi and Kwatili were nursing bruises and looking dazed. Ghelli glowered at Elijah from the far side of the tent, and launched into an angry tirade.

"What were you thinking boy? Did I not tell you not to touch the Ice Columns, now Xan knows exactly where to find us, you may as well have lit him a beacon, and you sister-"

He turned his scowl on Khizzi now who visibly flinched away.

"Why would you risk your life for this child who brings with him nothing but chaos and destruction?"

Matthias reached out a large hand to rest it ominously on Ghelli's shoulder.

"Have a care Ghelli, you may be my loyal friend of many years, but that is my son you are speaking of." His voice was quiet but none the less silenced Ghelli instantly.

Khizzi looked up at her brother and answered softly.

"He is important, to Greylea, and to me, I would gladly give my life for him."

Silence closed over the group, as they all realised that her words echoed how they all felt towards Elijah, who had no idea how to respond, so sat with his head hung down, avoiding all eye contact.

"I took Elijah to make contact with the Ice Column, I felt that it was worth the risk of Xan learning our location if it also meant that Ryufu did, we need to be rescued before tonight Ghelli. I have to confess that I under estimated Xan's powers to bend wills to his own even across such a distance; for that I am truly sorry."

Kwatili said, and as if to reinforce her words, the Shrink Tent around them suddenly began to wrinkle and collapse.

"Quickly! Out before it gets worse!" Shouted Ghelli ushering the others out of the rapidly widening opening.

As Burda tumbled out onto the ice, the last out, the Shrink tent sank to the ground like a burst balloon and proceeded to bubble and crackle like an egg in a frying pan before dissolving into the crust of ice leaving no trace that it had ever existed.

"Now what do we do? We'll freeze solid in seconds out here with no protection."

Asked Elijah, wrapping his arms round his chest and beginning to shiver instantly.

Kwatili smiled enigmatically and said.

"Wait Elijah Grey."

171

As they all stood breathing out clouds of steamy breath, the red sun peeked above the flat white horizon. This was immediately followed by a loud sizzling hiss that spread across the icy expanse towards them, and with it the ice crust evaporated into the rapidly warming air.

By the time the sun was fully visible, the ground beneath their feet was once again scorching hot and any dampness remaining in their clothes was steaming off.

Quickly adjusting their sole protectors the company shouldered their back sacks and stood in a circle waiting for someone to take the lead.

"What did Ryufu say to you Elijah? Where are we to head for?"

Asked Kwatili, tightening the waist strap around her slim waist.

"Um, he said the Northern edge, and then that he would find us there." He answered, also tightening his own waist strap, his stomach rumbled loudly as he did so.

Brogan laughed heartily, and reached inside his deep pocket, and tossed its contents to Elijah.

"What's this, or is it best not to know?" the boy chuckled as he turned the brown, somewhat dusty looking, object around in his hand.

"It's called Long Bread, not exactly tasty but it lasts weeks and will line your stomach when there's nothing better going!" Brogan answered, fishing deeper into both pockets and retrieving similar lumps for the others.

Chewing a dry and somewhat tasteless mouthful, Elijah noticed that Brogan was in fact the only one not doing so.

"Oh Brogan, here have some of mine!" He cried tearing off a hunk and offering it to the Crocodilian, who grinned a toothy grin and said,

"Hah! Thanks but no thanks Raven Boy, I carry it for others but wouldn't touch the stuff myself!"

"But aren't you hungry?" Elijah asked swallowing the still dry wad of Long Bread with great difficulty.

"Now that's where my one crocodile gene comes in real handy, I can go weeks on one decent stomach full, don't you worry about me!" Brogan replied, slapping the boy rather too hard on his back so that Elijah choked and spat out the mouthful that he had just about managed to get past his throat.

"Best thing to do with this stuff!" spluttered Matthias, his long nose wrinkling up.

"I don't know, the ingratitude of some people!" Brogan grumbled as he stomped off in the direction of the now hollow looking Ice Column.

"Wait, how do you know that's North Brogan?" Ghelli shouted.

"Don't but I'm guessing that Kwatili does and if I'm wrong she'll stop me." He replied without turning or slowing down.

Kwatili laughed softly and in two long sweeping strides, she caught up with the stubby legged Crocodilian and gently nudged him into a slightly altered trajectory.

They all walked in silence, chewing the last mouthfuls of their Long Bread and wishing that one of them had some water left to wash it down with, especially since the temperature had already soared to oven hot.

The white sand crunched like salt crystals beneath their feet and after an hour even the special insulating soles were allowing the searing heat through to the soles of their feet.

Elijah had given up wiping the sweat away from his face, and it ran in rivulets freely down his cheek and dripped steadily off his pointed chin, his long black hair stuck to his neck and hung heavily soaked down his back. Dehydration was making his tongue feel swollen and chalk dry in his mouth and the glare from off the desert floor was reddening his sore eyes.

Around him his companions were faring much the same, the only one not visibly affected was Kwatili, whose downy skin seemed untouched and her pace had not lessened since starting off.

Burda was the first to drop to her knees panting and coughing, so exhausted that she paid no attention to the blisters immediately forming on her palms and knees.

Elijah dashed over to her and dragged her back to her feet, holding her poor ruined hands in his own,

"Oh Burda, look at your hands, we need to bandage them or at least clean them! "He cried, looking from one to the other of the group who had also stopped plodding and were now standing in a dazed circle around Burda.

"But Elijah, we have no water even to drink and nothing to use as a bandage that's not filthy!" Kwatili said inspecting the damage.

"Oh shush fussing Elijah, I'm fine, just needed a bit of a breather, come on mustn't be late for Ryufu!"

Burda yanked her hands from Elijah's grasp, and shrugged her back pack back into place on her broad shoulders.

"No Burda, you've looked after me all my life, now it's time for me to repay some of that." He said, gently but firmly taking the bag from her and pushing it inside his own. She opened her mouth to argue, but seeing the determination on his face as he lengthened the straps so that the bulging back sack would fit on his shoulders, she snapped it shut and blinked fiercely to hold back tears.

"Well, if we're all okay to go on we should do so, we do not want to find ourselves still on the desert for a night without a Shrink Tent, Ryufu won't want to have to pick up frozen bodies!"

Matthias blurted out, ending the awkward moment, none present had ever seen Burda cry.

"So we don't have another Shrink Tent then."

Elijah said as he fell into step beside Kwatili.

"No Elijah, unfortunately not." She replied staring fixedly out into the distance.

"So how long would we last if we did have to spend another night out here?"

Without looking aside, she said quietly.

"Our hearts would stop within a matter of minutes once the sun has set, it is not an option Elijah Grey."

Even with the added burden of Burda's luggage on his back, her words spurred speed into his legs and he too fixed his squinting eyes on the far horizon, desperately searching for signs of an end to the Ice Desert.

After what was probably another hour of trudging, Kwatili gave a short cry and pointed her long slender arm out towards the sizzling line of the horizon.

"What? What do you see Kwatili? I see nothing but more sand!" Matthias muttered, rubbing the grit from his yellow eyes.

Brogan laughed and slapped Matthias on the back saying,

"Me too mate but I for one am totally willing to trust in those peepers of hers, if she says there's something there to be pleased about, I'm gonna be pleased!"

Kwatili turned to them grinning with such obvious relief that they all felt a weight lift from their hearts.

"Thank you my warty friend, I do indeed see the edge of the desert, no Ryufu at the moment but he said to wait there so let's get there."

Taking a collective deep breath they wearily continued on their way, each step now taking them closer to an end to their ordeal, they hoped.

Another tortuous hour later, they seemed no nearer to the edge at all, even Kwatili's sharp eyesight could still not in all honesty say that it was any closer.

Looking up at the sky, and the position of the sun, Ghelli broke the silence.

"No one wants to hear this I'm sure, but I would estimate that we have probably an hour left before the sun sets."

"You are right Ghelli, we don't want to hear that, any ideas Kwatili?"

Matthias asked, rubbing at his aching back.

Suddenly Elijah stopped and slapped his own forehead and cried.

"Of course, why didn't I think of him before?"

Offering no explanation he stepped away from the group, took a deep breath and called a name.

# Chapter 29

Within a heart beat the surface of the desert around then began to vibrate, sending a glittering shower of sand grains jiggling towards them.

Kwatili laughed and bumped her own forehead with the heel of her hand.

"Why Elijah Grey, you are a genius!" She gasped.

The others were still somewhat bemused but as a whirl pool seemed to erupt out of the desert at Elijah's feet, they all had an "ahah" moment.

"Well, Elijah Grey, we meet again, I was wondering how long it would take!"

The large horse like head wore a huge grin as it reared up out of the desert, silver grey coat shedding sand as if it was water, and the whipping reptilian tail stirred the desert behind it like a whisk.

"Hi Juno, boy are you a sight for sore eyes!" said Elijah, grinning widely at the Sand Oren.

"Hop aboard my friend, we have a sunset to beat." Juno said going down on his knees to allow Elijah to climb up on his back.

"But my friends-"Elijah began, but the sudden eruption of six other Sand Oren from the desert answered his query.

Juno lurched forward into a loping gallop, gripping a handful of mane to help keep himself in place Elijah quickly settled into the "saddle" that Juno's back had created for him and was able to look over his shoulder at the others as they caught up with them.

Even Kwatili had taken up the offer of a fresh set of legs this time, and poor Burda was bumping up and down like a sack of potatoes, completely out of sync with her mount's gait. As he watched, Ghelli drew up beside her and shouted instructions that Elijah couldn't catch, but they seemed to do the trick, because Burda stopped bouncing enough for her Sand Oren to remodel his back to fit her somewhat wider and heavier bulk.

Smiling as he turned back to face the distant horizon towards which they were now travelling swiftly, he was about to ask Juno how long before they got to the Northern Edge when the answer popped into his head.

"We should be safely off the Ice desert surface before the sun sets, only just but that's all that counts."

"I forgot about that thing you do, pity you didn't read my mind earlier, I guess we were too far apart?" Elijah said out loud but knew that he didn't really have to.

"Oh I knew that you needed me but it doesn't work like that I'm sorry to say Elijah. We Oren's have to be summoned, we can't just arrive; it is an Oren thing."

Nodding even though it really didn't make any sense to him. Elijah thought the words.

"No worries Juno, I'll remember that for the future, though!"

"Please do Elijah, you were cutting it a bit fine this time."

Elijah chuckled, and pinned his eyes on the visible line of dark grey rocks that he could just about make out now, and willed it to approach as quickly as possible. Behind him he could sense more than see the red sun beginning to dip below the southern edge of the desert and he could already feel the temperature dropping.

The first ice crystals were forming under Juno's pounding feet as the rocks came within reach.

"Hold on tight Elijah!" Juno cried out loud as he bunched his hind quarters and put all his remaining power into one gigantic leap. Ice seemed to almost try to grab at his splayed toes as he soared through the air to land heavily and roll over onto the broad flat flag stones at the edge of the desert. One by one the others did the same, last of all was the struggling Oren carrying Burda, but he just about made it, sending her sprawling onto rocks, bruised but relatively intact.

As they all got to their feet, behind them they heard the now familiar sound of the sheet of ice as it spread out over the sand, sealing it in for the night in its icy embrace.

"Yes, that was definitely what I would call cutting it a bit fine Juno!"

Elijah whispered, trying not to imagine what would have happened to them if they had still been on the desert surface when the ice struck.

177

"Oh my poor brutalised butt!" Groaned Burda as she struggled to her feet rubbing her behind and then wincing, she had forgotten about her blistered hands.

"Hah! My poor brutalised back needs more sympathy! You are definitely not getting any lighter Burda!" Moaned the Sand Oren who had so courageously carried her.

They all laughed, as the two scowled at each other.

"Okay, so now what?" Elijah asked of no one in particular, looking around him at the white desolation, punctuated only by the towers of ice that glowed blue in the fading light.

"Now, we wait I suppose, that is what Ryufu told you to do is it not Elijah?" Kwatili asked, as she paced slowly up and down the grey flag stone shore line, looking anything but ready to sit and wait.

"Well yes, but how is he going to find us? It could be ages and we don't have long before Xan beats him to it!" said Ghelli as he fell in beside Kwatili.

"If I might make a suggestion?" said Juno.

"Of course, go ahead, any ideas are welcome at this point!" Kwatili replied, turning on her heel and striding to stand before the group of Sand Oren.

"Well, it has come to my hearing that Elijah Grey is now in possession of both of the Eyes of Ula, if this is indeed the case, should he not be able to use them to create a doorway to take you all to where Ryufu is, rather than wait here, somewhat exposed, for him to find you, it was just a thought."

Silence fell over the company as his words sank in, and none could meet Elijah's eyes.

He stood motionless, desperately trying to control the bubble of fear that was threatening to burst in his chest.

Staring around at the exhausted and hungry group of loyal companions that had got him thus far, he knew that he had to try.

Taking a deep breath, he said softly, "What do I have to do?"

It was as if an elastic band that had been holding them all tightly had snapped. Six sets of shoulders sagged and Kwatili placed a cold hand on his shoulder and smiled.

"Ah, Elijah Grey, now you make me regret never finding out from Egreya exactly how she did it, all I can tell you is that she used to think of where or who she wished to find, and hold the two stones together, and, it happened."

Matthias sighed and added,

"So many times she used them so that we could meet in secret, but I was always so intent on making the most of every second spent with her that I too have no advice to give you my son, other than to trust your heart."

Elijah nodded slowly, this was not a lot to go on but one glance at Khizzi beginning to shiver uncontrollably as the temperature plummeted was enough to strengthen his resolve.

"What about you Juno, are you going to go back into the desert or come with us?"

Juno laughed loudly and replied,

"We are Sand Oren not Ice Oren, so we will wait here for the morning sun, we're tougher than we look Elijah, worry not."

"Right then, here goes nothing." Said Elijah as he took both stones out of their pouches and held them clasped together in his palms. Startled by the instant heat radiating from them, he faltered and almost dropped them as a bright red light began to illuminate his hands and face. Closing his eyes tightly he conjured up the best image he could of Ryufu, surrounded by a throng of Yehana as he had last seen him. Beads of sweat appeared on his forehead as he focussed all his energy into the desire to be there, with Ryufu.

After what seemed an age, he sagged and opened his eyes in frustration and muttered.

"It's no good, I'm sorry it's just not going to work!"

But he stopped as his vision cleared and he saw the expression on the ring of faces around him.

Wheeling around he gasped and almost dropped the now cold stones onto the rocks.

Behind him as if it was a rip in the air itself, shimmered a doorway, through which he could just make out blurry dark figures moving around a huge fire.

"Quickly, you have but seconds before Xan becomes aware of the power of the Eyes, go Elijah Grey, we will meet again!" Juno was gently nudging the stunned boy in the back with his forehead towards the doorway, as were his brethren.

As his foot passed through the glowing aperture Elijah felt a strange tingling spread over his skin like a million ants crawling but as soon as he stumbled through to the other side all he could feel was the sudden warmth and soft grass beneath his feet.

One by one the others tumbled through, the last being Kwatili, who, once through turned quickly to salute the Sand Oren who could be seen gathered around the shrinking doorway.

"How do I close it?" stammered Elijah suddenly realising that he had no idea.

But no sooner had he spoken the words, than the ragged aperture snapped shut like a camera lens and the Oren and the Ice Desert were gone.

Sinking down onto the grass, Elijah lay flat on his back, staring up at the steel bright sky above waiting for the world around him to stop spinning. He felt drained and lifeless and would have happily stayed thus if Matthias had not urged him up onto unsteady feet.

"We can't stay here, it's too open; we need to find somewhere to hide away from prying eyes until that renegade finds us."

"You are right Matthias, Xan will have felt Elijah using the stones and will waste little time tracing our whereabouts. Those trees will offer cover, should he send Silff to search for us."

Ghelli was already gathering up his bags and heading towards a small copse of low growing trees about a hundred yards from them.

With his father's assistance, Elijah managed to stagger over and collapse panting and dizzy in the cool dark shade beneath the canopy of leaves.

No sooner had the last of them gained the protection of the trees, than they saw small black specs gathering together in the sky then wheeling in ever increasing circles.

As the Silff glided over the small copse, they all held their breath and kept completely still, not even daring to look up.

When the clicking sounds of the bat like creatures had been absent for some minutes, Ghelli crawled silently and stealthily on his stomach out to the edge of the copse to check the sky.

A thumbs up sign told them that for now, at least, they were safe.

"Now what?" Elijah asked, easing his bag from his shoulders and leaning gratefully back against the smooth trunk of the tree behind him.

"Well, we have two options, we can sit here and wait for Ryufu to find us, or we could try to open up another door way, this time to take us directly to Ryufu's camp."

Replied Ghelli, who had re-joined the group.

"We? Paleface, that sounds like putting me on the hot seat again, not you!"

Elijah snapped, the prospect of using the Eyes of Ula again so soon filled him with fear, and he was still weak from the last attempt.

"We would never ask that of you Elijah!"

Said Kwatili, scowling at Ghelli, who merely shrugged his shoulders adding.

"I was just answering the boy's inquiry Kwatili, not giving orders."

"We should give Ryufu until morning, and then decide, we are safe here after all and I for one could do with a good night sleep."

Said Burda, yawning widely to emphasise her point.

Matthias chuckled and patted her on the shoulder as he moved to sit cross legged at the outer fringe of the trees.

"I will take first watch, I'll wake you up when I can't keep awake any longer Ranger."

Ranger nodded as he curled up on the soft leaf strewn ground, using his back sack as a pillow.

Smiling gratefully, Elijah settled himself beside his former dog, tucking the two leather pouches safely inside his jacket, next to his skin, surprisingly, the slight tingling that he felt from contact with them was comforting.

Grunting with the exertion, Burda slumped down on his other side so that he felt incredibly well protected, so much so that he fell asleep almost immediately.

His slumber was haunted by drifting images of his mother, her eyes wide and frightened, calling to him with no voice, clutching long fingered hands reaching for him as he ran through endless doorways, each one promising to take him to Egreya, but every time he stepped through thinking that this time he had found her, all he found was another long empty tunnel, with her pleading face at the end, but never any closer.

"Elijah, wake up!"

Words filtered through into his brain, it was Egreya's voice. He tried desperately to obey, willing his limbs to move and his eyes to open but they wouldn't co-operate.

"Elijah, you must wake up!" The tone was much more urgent now, and the voice was changing. The sensation of a hand tugging at his arm broke the sleep stasis and he yanked himself upright, gasping in a terrified breath.

A large hand immediately clamped over his mouth to silence any sound. Flicking his eyes from side to side he realised that he was surrounded by his companions, who were all crouched low to the ground looking ready to run.

Matthias carefully removed his hand from his son's mouth when he was sure that he was fully aware of the situation.

"We are not alone Elijah, keep absolutely still and silent until I'm sure of the nature of our company," he whispered, his sulphur yellow eyes wide and intense in the half light.

Elijah nodded, and only then did he hear the definite sounds of rustling around him in the undergrowth.

"It's okay Matthias, it's Ryufu." He whispered, with absolute conviction and no idea how he knew.

Matthias replied with a frown and an even more intense stare.

"How can you possibly know that Raven Boy?" Ghelli hissed out of the gloom, but his answer did not come from Elijah.

"You should trust the boy Ghelli, and as for you, Matthias, we won't talk about the sharpness of your senses!"

It was a familiar voice and the raucous laugh that came afterwards was without a doubt that of Ryufu.

Out into the clearing he stepped, followed by a party of eight Yehana, all were clad in long, charcoal grey coats, buttoned to the hems, and carrying large curved knives, drawn.

Ryufu made some small hand signals and all eight virtually melted into the trees to form a protective circle.

"We haven't seen any signs of Xan's degenerate mercenaries but that doesn't mean they're not there." He said, sitting down next to Elijah and squeezing the boy's shoulders roughly.

"So, how's it been hangin' young man? Learnt how to open doors yet?" he asked, his huge round black eyes twinkling wickedly.

Elijah suddenly found the close proximity of Ryufu's mouth full of sharp teeth and hot breath very unnerving, and he flinched away involuntarily.

"Ryufu yet again you forget the effect that you have on those who don't know you as well as we do!" Kwatili chided, as she squeezed in between them.

"Ah Kwatili, the boy knows I would have eaten him long ago if I was that way inclined!" He replied, then added.

"And he was the only one to sense that it was me just now, even the great tracker Ghelli didn't get there before him!"

Ghelli grunted but did not reply, Khizzi was steadfastly staring at the ground in front of her.

"Diplomatic as ever I see Ryufu!" Chuckled Burda, rubbing her painful knee and grinning.

"Sixty years old, not gonna change now, looks like that wound is still not healed maybe it's due to all the weight those pins have to carry!"

Kwatili sighed and held her head in her hands in despair but Burda merely play punched Ryufu in his chest, sending him splayed onto his back.

"Any way, back to the somewhat serious business in hand if we could?" Matthias said, his obvious dislike of Ryufu evident in the look he swung his way.

Ryufu sat upright and brushed himself down before saying, "I have an encampment about a day's travel from here, at the foot of the Glass Cliffs, there are no signs as yet of Xan and his lot, a flock of Silff went over and are now due West following a decoy band of my Yehana, we have hot food, clean clothes and a special surprise waiting, will that do Matthias?"

He too made no effort to disguise his hostility towards Matthias, Elijah made a silent promise to himself to question Kwatili until she told him the origins of such animosity.

It was Kwatili who answered, saying "I must admit that the sound of hot food is very appealing Ryufu, should we start out now or wait for daylight?"

Before he could reply, one of his Yehan emerged from the shadows and bent down to whisper in his ear, he nodded and stood gracefully.

"We need to be on our way immediately, it seems that the Silff are no longer fooled by my decoys and are heading back this way, we can beat them to the camp if we hurry."

As he said this he was looking pointedly at Burda, who was stiffly rising from the ground.

"Don't fret about me laughing boy, if you lead, I will follow," she muttered, making a grab for her back sack.

"Oh no you don't!" Said Elijah grabbing it out of her hand and shouldering it along with his own.

"Good lad, let's go." Ryufu said in a low voice, glancing up at the sky and placing a stubby forefinger against his wide mouth.

"Best go quietly too, just in case." He whispered and set off into the trees.

Creeping so quietly that even their breathing sounded loud, the company travelled through the undergrowth. Four of Ryufu's Yehana took the lead, and four brought up the rear, Elijah was behind Matthias and he could read the tension in his hunched shoulders as if it were written in letters a foot high. He didn't know exactly what the source of the open hostility was between his father and Ryufu, but he could probably guess that it had something to do with his mother. He only hoped that they would be able to get along for the sake of, well, for the sake of whatever was going to happen next. A hot flush of fear rushed up from his stomach to engulf his whole upper body at the thought of facing Xan and whatever army of hideous monsters he'd accumulated, but he took a deep breath, clenched his jaws together to stop himself whispering out loud, that he was only a kid, and focussed his frightened mind on making sure that if any of them gave their location away by snapping twigs under foot, it was not going to be him!

Night was lifting as they reached the outer edge of the trees. Silently they gathered under the cover of the last one, all staring out at the next challenge.

Stretching out before them, flat and totally featureless was a grass savanna, hot and dry, already beginning to sizzle in the rising temperature.

"Oh buggar, that's not going to be easy with them flying clickers still around!" whispered Brogan.

"Too true my wart covered friend, but cross it we must and waiting for the sunshine would not help so if everyone is ready?" Ryufu asked, glancing from one exhausted face to another.

"Elijah, you need to be in the middle, that way if we are attacked you can be protected from all sides." Kwatili said, arranging the group around him in a tight circle.

As they stepped out from the cool shade, the instant blast of heat almost made them all stagger, and the crisp wiry grass beneath their feet crunched deafeningly loudly.

"Keep moving, the sooner we reach the camp the better, but keep one eye on the sky," said Ryufu, hunched and close to the ground.

Moving forward like a rugby scrum, the group progressed at a fair speed considering how tired they all were, and how rapidly the heat drained them of what little energy they had left.

After what was probably only a matter of minutes but felt like hours, Ryufu halted and signalled that they could all have a rest. Immediately slumping to the ground, Elijah began rubbing the cramp away from his strained neck muscles.

Burda gently nudged a leather water bottle into his hands and he gratefully took a few large mouthfuls before offering it round the glass eyed circle.

Still instinctively glancing up at the cloudless sky every other second, Elijah suddenly noticed that Kwatili's peach fur covered ears were twitching.

"What is it Kwatili?" he whispered softly. He didn't want to startle Burda if it was nothing.

Turning her head just enough to meet his eyes, she pointedly looked upwards, then blinked hard.

As casually as he could muster Elijah too glanced up. He could see nothing but knew that his eyesight was nothing compared to hers.

As he looked down again he realised that both Matthias and Ryufu too were squinting into the harsh sunlight and they exchanged worried looks with Kwatili.

"Well, that's enough rest, I happen to know that a belly full of food, soft bed and clean clothes are waiting just another hour away, and lets not talk about copious quantities of head soothing Sand Beer!"

They all recognised the falseness of Ryufu's cheery tone, but chose to ignore it, hauling their aching bodies back into action in their scrum formation again.

It didn't take long for Elijah to begin to feel rather than hear, the characteristic echo locating clicks from the flock of hunting Silff high above. The closer they got, the more each click that they sent downwards seemed to be actually touching him physically, as a faint tap at first but it soon became as hard as a punch.

All around him he could hear the pain racked breathing of exhausted and cramped bodies, these people, his friends, were all laying their lives on the line for him, even Ghelli, ever critical of him, was willing to place his own body in between the Silff and Elijah.

He suddenly had a vivid image of Maylan's silvery skinned face appear in his mind. She was saying something to him, he could clearly see her lips moving and her eyes were urgently pleading, but he could hear nothing.

Thinking of the moment when even a being as powerful as she had been destroyed in his defence lit a fuse in his chest.

"No more dying for me, I will not allow it!"

He whispered under his breath at first, then it became a mantra that grew in strength and volume until he could no longer hear the ugly clicking of the Silff as they now swooped low over their heads, so low that he could feel the rush of hot wind from their skin covered wings.

He flinched and closed his eyes, waiting for the raking of claws across his back.

It did not come, in fact the Silff merely continued their circling flight right over them, then banked off to the right, heading back over the savanna.

They all hesitated momentarily in stunned disbelief.

"What just happened? We were done for and then, it was like they suddenly lost sight of us completely." Whispered Brogan, grunting softly as he eased his aching back upright.

"I don't know exactly, all I do know is that whatever it was, it has given us a chance to reach safety in one piece, let's keep moving," Kwatili replied, her amber eyes never leaving Elijah, who was steadfastly staring at the grass at his feet.

Escaping what they had all thought was an inevitable attack, seemed to give them all a second wind; even Burda was managing to keep up easily. Suddenly, one of the leading Yehana gave a soft whoop, and pointed ahead.

Relief washed over Elijah like a cool wave, distant still but definitely visible was a collection of large grey tents sitting like hunched spiders at the foot of a sheer cliff face that shone so brightly in the sunshine the glare made him flinch.

Ryufu whooped in reply and grinned widely.

"Yaha! There you see food, drink, and soft beds my friends, keep those stumpies going Brogan, Sand Beer beckons!"

Brogan merely grunted but it was definitely a happy grunt.

Elijah poured the last vestiges of his energy into his cramping, aching leg muscles; he was more desperate than any of them to reach a place where he could rest and think through what had happened, at the moment his exhausted brain was frying slowly in the scorching heat and not able to process anything at all.

As they neared the encampment, a cry went up and a number of small figures emerged like ants and headed out over the savanna towards them.

Within what seemed an impossibly short time the rescue party reached them. Most were Yehana, but there were many others that Elijah had not seen before, all of the weary travellers were scooped up and placed gratefully onto stretchers and carried the rest of the distance, staring dull eyed up at the blank sky.

As soon as they reached the encampment they were surrounded by a bustling, buzzing flurry of activity. Gentle hands helped them stand and guided them all to the largest tent.

Elijah was so drained that he felt as if he was half asleep, snippets of murmured conversations drifted in and out of his hearing.

"So where had they disappeared to?"

"No one's asked, they're in such bad shape."

"But they just appeared again once the Silff had gone right? That's strange you have to agree!"

"I'm saying nothing these folk are unknowns especially the boy, who knows what he's capable of."

"Yeah but they won't hurt us - we're on their side, right? I mean—"

A loud shushing cut the last snippet off, and Elijah was peripherally aware of being laid down on something incredibly soft, warm and so welcome that he felt himself smiling widely just before he knew no more.

# Chapter 30

Once more, it was the gentle features of Maylan that floated before his eyes, once more her mouth was moving and her eyes were urgent and imploring but his head felt stuffed with cotton wool and he could only hear soft muffled sounds.

Desperately he tried to make his lifeless limbs obey his command to sit up, but he was gently but firmly pushed back to the bed, all he managed was to prize apart his eyelids.

Sitting beside him, her round chocolate brown eyes brimming with alarm and relief in equal quantities, was Khizzi.

When she registered that he was truly awake and looking at her, she hastily removed her hand from his shoulder and grinned down at him, a soft flush coming to her downy cheeks.

"Is he finally awake Khizzi? About time sleeping boy!"

Brogan was bending over him, holding out a steaming cup.

Elijah struggled drowsily to sit up and took the cup thankfully, he didn't care what it was; he had suddenly been attacked by a raging thirst.

The first tentative sip tasted slightly salty but he drained it anyway and felt an amazing surge of warmth and wellbeing that initiated in his stomach but flooded his entire body within seconds.

"And now you'll be hungry." Brogan said, offering him a huge chunk of unknown meat squashed between slabs of dark brown bread.

Elijah nodded enthusiastically and devoured the food as if he hadn't eaten for days.

Brogan chuckled, and patted him heartily on his back.

"Yep, that's Sand Beer for you, revives and rejuvenates in one go!"

"Brogan! Tell me that you did not just corrupt that boy's body with that vile brew!"

Burda came charging over like a bull Rhinoceros, Brogan winked at Elijah before making a quick exit.

"I'm fine thanks Burda, how is everyone else?" Elijah asked, rising to his feet, brushing dust from his clothes and hands.

"Oh they're all safe thanks to you Elijah Grey."

The soft voice came from behind him and sent tingles racing down his spine, he recognised it but didn't dare trust that he was correct. Wheeling around his jaw dropped open.

Leaning heavily on the supportive shoulder of her friend Kwatili was Maylan, both were grinning.

"So it was you, and you didn't die!" He cried.

"Yes and not quite, although those Lurchins tried very hard to make it so." She replied.

As she spoke she pushed back the deep hood that had been almost completely obscuring her face, Elijah gasped as he saw the raw red scar that traversed diagonally across her face, narrowly missing her left eye.

"Close your mouth Elijah and stop blaming yourself, I am just happy to be here, a few missing parts are a small price to pay, besides, you should see the other guy!" She laughed and it sounded like bells ringing.

Elijah was about to ask what missing parts but decided that he probably didn't want to know.

"So what exactly did happen out there Maylan? The Silff were so close to attacking one minute and then, it was as if they stopped being able to see us."

She tilted her smooth head slightly and studied him with her pearl white eyes.

"Come, I think that we need to talk together, "she said, holding out one long slim white arm towards him.

Too shy to actually take her hand he nodded and allowed her to guide him over to a smaller tent, into which, they entered, through a barely visible opening that seemed to seal itself behind them.

Inside it was dark and warm, lit by one soft lamp hanging suspended in mid-air. The floor was covered in soft animal hides and a circle of cushions were arranged around a large oval shaped stone.

Maylan motioned for him to sit, and then passed her hand over the stone. It instantly burst into life, an aura of flickering purple flames playing across its surface without actually touching it, spreading a delicious warmth through his body and creating a dancing purple pattern across the curved roof of the tent.

Maylan eased herself into a seated position, with barely concealed pain, and as she did so, the voluminous cloak that she wore fell back to reveal that she was, in fact, missing her entire right arm.

"It is nothing Elijah, my snake gene will allow me to eventually grow it back, but it will take some time." She said in reply to his obvious shock.

He shook his head, and the words "I'm sorry" were just on their way out when she added.

"You have nothing to be sorry for Elijah Grey, an arm is a small price to pay for preserving the most important being in Greylea, now, to answer your previous question, what happened out there on the savanna was simple, the pressure of an imminent attack on people that you care about, brought about a rapid development in your powers, that, it seems are truly unique to you; as to my knowledge, there has been no other who can do what you did."

"But what did I do? All I remember was a sudden burning sensation and then the Silff disappeared off as if we didn't exist."

He cried, placing his hand over his stomach where the burning sensation had initiated from.

"I think that is exactly right Elijah, what you did was create a shield that concealed you all from the Silff, to them it was as if you had all ceased to exist. A skill that could be extremely useful in the near future I feel, as long as I can teach you to control it."

Maylan replied, pausing to breathe in short racked gasps, before taking a long deep breath and continuing.

"It has to be a result of your mixed parentage, call it a wild card if you like, and there may well be more surprises in store, you are, after all as you keep telling us, just a kid!"

He couldn't help but chuckle as she had said it in a very good imitation of his voice, sounding distinctly whiney.

"Okay, so when do we start the lessons?" he said, finding the prospect now much more exciting than scary.

"Oh soon, but there is one task that you must fulfil before we even think about that, you need to revisit your mother, and rescue Rheyana and her son if you possibly can."

"Oh, right, that means I have to open up another doorway." He murmured, secretly dreading the thought.

"It does, but just as before, you will not be alone, Khizzi will accompany you, since it appears that you two have struck up what seems to be an extremely good partnership."

Maylan smiled at the instant red flush that spread over his cheeks.

"Well, erm, yes we er get on and of course that tail of hers comes in useful!" he stuttered.

"Exactly, so, no time like the present I'm afraid, the luxury of time is not bestowed upon us, we need to know Xan's whereabouts and Ranger needs to have his family back, especially the son that he's never met. Are you ready Elijah Grey?"

He answered by standing up.

# Chapter 31

As Elijah and Maylan walked towards them, it was obvious even at a distance that something about the boy had changed.

To Burda particularly, he seemed to have grown, both in height and in confidence, there was such determination in the way that he held his head, and a strength in his stride, this was definitely no longer the innocent and naïve young man that she had watched whisked upwards into the sky just weeks ago.

"Our boy has grown Burda."

Ranger too was looking at Elijah with a lump in his throat, remembering the carefree days back at the cabin.

"He's still only a fifteen year old child that we are entrusting our lives to, an alternative plan would be prudent as far as I'm concerned!"

Muttered Ghelli, not enough under his breath for his sister not to hear and dig him viciously in the ribs scowling fiercely.

"So, you're going to try to rescue Egreya and Rheyana, I will go with you." Matthias said, very matter of factly bending down to repack his bag.

Maylan reached out with her one good arm and touched him lightly on his shoulder, he froze immediately.

"It will be Khizzi who accompanies Elijah, for the same reasons as before." She said gently.

Beneath her hand Matthias stiffened and then sagged in acceptance.

"So does that mean that we're travelling back in time as well?"

Elijah tried hard not to allow his sudden surge of panic seep into his voice.

"It does indeed Elijah, in fact you will aim to arrive moments from when you left before, so you must be extra vigilant and make sure that you do not accidentally run into, well, yourselves."

Elijah breathed deeply, and risked a quick glance in Khizzi's direction, utter confidence glowed from her brown eyes.

"Okay then, talk me through it Maylan, because the last time I really had no idea how I did it!"

Maylan managed a half laugh half cough and beckoned for him to come closer.

With Khizzi by his side, Elijah stood before Maylan, holding the twin stones in his hands.

She reached out and clasped her one hand around his, he could feel its coolness enclosing the growing burn from the stones.

Closing her pearly eyes, she whispered softly.

"Close your eyes and picture your mother as you last saw her Elijah, take yourself back to that moment, shut out everything else, with each breath take yourself closer."

At first he struggled to focus, he could hear the noises of the camp around him, his friends breathing, and his own mind telling him that what he was attempting was impossible.

But suddenly, it was as if he had sealed himself into a bubble of silence, and the only sound that he could hear was Maylan's murmuring voice inside his head, it was saying open your eyes Elijah."

Fear kept them closed for a second, then he felt the sudden warmth of another hand holding his.

Prizing his reluctant lids apart, he had to take a second to calm himself, as he was staring into a bright rip in the darkness, through which he could clearly see the stiff figure of his mother imprisoned in the Gladiri Crystal, exactly as he had seen her before retreating into the forest before. Beside him, Khizzi squeezed his hand and whispered,

"Go quickly Elijah Grey, I will remain here to keep you safe."

With that she wound her tail tightly around his waist.

The instant feeling of security that it provided, gave Elijah the courage to step forward through the doorway. As his body passed through, a strange sensation like icy fingers clawing at his skin made him shudder, but as soon as he was standing on the other side, the warm sunshine bathed it away.

Glancing over his shoulder, he smiled and nodded at Khizzi who was still just the other side, tethered to him by her long tail, anchoring him, and filling him with courage. Her lips moved but made no sound, he knew what she had said though, and he nodded again.

A sudden rustling to his left caught him by surprise and he ducked behind a dense thorny bush just in time to see himself, running in the opposite direction into the undergrowth.

"Wow that was close!" He whispered to himself, then voices attracted his attention back over to the clearing at the foot of the mountain.

"Get after him, he must not be allowed to escape whoever he is he has seen too much!"

It was unmistakably the voice of Xan, sending his minions after him, that meant that he might just be in time to save his mother from being imprisoned in the crystal, if he was quick, and careful!

Creeping as silently as his shaking limbs would allow, he inched closer to the clearing where he could now see the figures of Xan and Egreya.

His heart sank as he realised that he was too late, Egreya was already encased in the Gladiri Crystal and Xan was ranting loudly.

"Damn you Egreya, you can't hide in that thing forever, I'll find a way to open it, I swear!"

Then he stomped away followed by two stumbling Maigrey.

Elijah's head was spinning, he had always assumed that it had been Xan who had imprisoned her, but she had spun the crystal herself, to protect herself from him, or –"

"She did not want Xan to know that you had the other Eye of Ula to make the pair Elijah Grey, for she knew that whilst he remained ignorant of that fact it would give us an advantage."

The quiet voice inches from his ear would have made him yelp out loud had she not placed a small white hand gently over his mouth.

He found himself staring into a pair of sapphire blue eyes that were so much like Ranger's he knew who it was immediately.

"Rheyana?" He whispered.

"It is, and this," She gestured slightly behind her, where a small version of Ranger cowered,

"This is Rhelan, son of Ranger."

She paused and her eyes took on such a heavy expression of sorrow that Elijah spluttered out.

"But Ranger's alive, he's waiting for you right now!"

Now it was her own gasp that she had to smother, with both hands, before she leaned forward to plant a kiss on his cheek.

"Thank you Elijah Grey you have made my life worth living once more. But you must commune with Egreya before we leave, she will need much strength to endure the times to come."

She pointed towards the Glidiri Crystal.

"Okay, wait over by the doorway, Khizzi will keep us all safe."

As they crept off towards the flickering doorway, Elijah himself, edged towards the clearing.

To his relief, for the moment, there was only the tall milky shard standing in the clearing, as he neared it, the figure inside became clearer.

He felt a huge lump rise in his throat as he saw her face, terror was written all over the finely formed features, the dark deep set eyes stared unseeing out at him, her lips were frozen in a cry.

Not knowing what else to do, he reached out and laid his hand palm down on the cold surface of the crystal.

"Elijah, my beautiful son!"

Her voice came straight into his mind, inside the crystal her face remained in it frozen expression of fear.

"Do not fear for me Elijah, I am safe inside here, and here I must stay until you have destroyed Xan and his army, if he knew I had already given the other stone to you, your life would be in danger, as it is, he thinks that I have it and he cannot get to it through the crystal. This must continue it gives you and Matthias a huge advantage, and is a small price to pay trust me!"

Elijah absorbed her words, and was about to form an argument when the tail around his waist gave a sharp tug.

"Khizzi is doing as you said, she is keeping you safe, go my son, we will be together soon I promise."

The communication link snapped shut in his head, he was alone, looking longingly into the crystal when he heard sounds of arrival and felt an even more insistent tug at his waist.

Tears rolled freely down his cheeks as he forced himself to leave her and, keeping low, made his way back to the doorway where Rheyana and Rhelan were waiting.

He gestured to them to go through which they did, shimmering as they passed over the threshold. With one last look backwards, he too passed through and felt the sizzle as the doorway snapped shut behind him.

Debilitating weakness sucked him to the ground as he returned to Ryufu's camp and the anxious group that awaited him.

Helping hands came out of the fog that seemed to surround him, urging him gently to his feet and supporting arms cradled him as he attempted to walk on unresponsive legs.

Snippets of conversations wafted into his awareness and slowly he began to be able to make sense of them.

"He must not be allowed to open time doors again until he has full control, no matter how useful it might be in the fight against Xan, that was a close one and I do not intend to lose him!"

It was his father's voice and he sounded both angry and concerned.

"Forgive me Matthias, but he will recover fully and the risk was worth it I assure you."

Elijah shook his head in an effort to clear his thoughts and he mumbled through numb lips.

"I'm glad I went Father, at least my Mother knows that we're coming for her soon, and Ranger has his family back."

The stunned silence that followed drew his own attention to the fact that, for the first time since meeting him, he had referred to Matthias as his father.

Rubbing at his eyes to clear the mistiness that still remained he peered around him.

He was seated beside a fire that by now was just glowing embers in the largest of the tents, but even in the dim light of the lamps set high in the roof, he could now see seven grinning faces, and a group of three hugging figures ignoring them all.

"Well of course, um, son, you did an amazing thing for Ranger, and, um your mother, how was she?"

With his eyes firmly on his friend who was still locked in a fierce embrace with his wife and son, Elijah hesitated before turning his attention to Matthias.

"Well, she was okay, I mean I couldn't see her very clearly, the Glidiri Crystal is kind of difficult to see through you know but she told me that we'd be together soon."

In his mind he couldn't get rid of the expression of fear that had been frozen onto his mother's face, but he couldn't bring himself to shatter Matthias's illusion.

Maylan stepped in at this point to hold her cool palm against his forehead.

"Elijah needs to recuperate so I am ordering everyone away to allow him to eat, drink and then sleep, Ranger, could you bring food and Sand Beer perhaps?"

Almost instantly Ranger was at his side with a steaming bowl of something that resembled porridge and a cup of Sand Beer, the rest retreated into the shadows.

"My friend, how can I ever—"

Elijah halted Ranger with a hand on his arm.

"Not another word Ranger, just go and enjoy being with your family."

With his blue eyes glowing as Ranger returned to Rheyana and Rhelan, and Elijah took just a few sips and swallowed one mouthful of porridge before sinking down onto the soft blanket and falling into a deep sleep.

# Chapter 32

A familiar sound drew him out of his slumber, it was Burda's rattling snores, reverberating around the tent.

Propping himself up on an elbow, he yawned and looked around.

They were all scattered around him, except for Maylan and Kwatili who he could just make out in the gloom at the far edge of the tent. They were deep in conversation with a Yehana, and something about their body language sent tremors of alarm throughout him.

Rising quietly to his feet, he tiptoed past the sleeping bodies to speak to them. Kwatili and Maylan turned in unison to greet him, the Yehana took his leave with a bow to them both, and then, to Elijah's astonishment, to him also.

"What is it, and don't baby me by telling me nothing's wrong, I'm not stupid!"

He said, making them both smile wryly.

"We do not have as long as I had hoped to prepare for battle. Xan is gathering his forces rapidly and they will be upon us within two days according to that scout."

Well he had told them not to sugar coat it!

"Perhaps now is the time to give you this Elijah Grey, your mother entrusted it to me and said that I would know when you were ready to receive it."

Yet again, the quiet voice of Rheyana seemed to come out of nowhere, that woman sure could move silently!

Standing beside him, she placed a large bag onto the sandy floor and began to pull something out of it.

Both Maylan and Kwatili gasped and exchanged a look that Elijah couldn't read.

As it unfurled, it rustled softly like leaves in a breeze.

"The Raven Cloak, I thought it was lost when Egreya was captured, oh Rheyana, you have no idea what a difference you have just made!" Cried Kwatili, leaning forward to gingerly take the cloak from Rheyana.

"Elijah behold your birth right." She said as she placed it around his shoulders.

Elijah expected it to feel heavy as it settled onto his body, it was covered in long blue-black feathers and draped down to the ground at his feet but he was amazed to discover that once it was in place, he couldn't feel it at all!

"So, how does it work Maylan, what do I do to, make it work?" He said quietly, running his fingers over the silky surface of the feathers.

The silence told him everything and his heart sank.

"Since there has never been one such as you before in the history of Greylea, I have no knowledge to give you, other than, wear it and it will probably tell you itself?"

She replied smiling weakly.

He nodded and pulled the Raven cloak more tightly around his body, expecting some sort of reaction or revelation but all he felt was rather too warm.

Wordlessly he headed outside, suddenly feeling claustrophobic inside the tent and desiring the fresh air and open sky.

Matthias went to follow him but Kwatili placed her hand on his shoulder.

"He needs to figure this out on his own Matthias, show trust in your son."

"I don't like the idea of him out there on his own with Xan so close, who knows what is in the sky looking out for him." He replied, but he stayed where he was. Ranger on the other hand darted out of the tent entrance, a flash of long white hair.

Elijah glanced around as Ranger drew close.

"Old habits die hard!" He said, grinning at his former canine companion.

Ranger shrugged and fell into step beside him as he strode up the steepening slope of the mountain. When they reached a wide ledge some fifty feet up above the camp, they stopped and sat down, backs against the warm rock, lifting their faces to the rising sun and closing their eyes.

"I have not taken the opportunity to thank you for saving my family Elijah, I had given up all hope of ever seeing them again."

Elijah smiled, and replied softly, his eye lids still bathed in rosy sunlight.

"Least I could do Ranger."

A cool breeze stirred the blue-black feathers around his neck, they gently tickled the skin of his jaw and reaching up he brushed them away with his fingertips.

"Oh, that can't be good."

Ranger's quiet voice sent chills of alarm shivering through Elijah whose eyelids flicked open instantly.

"Oh crap, and don't tell Burda I said that!" He muttered.

As his eyes focussed, he saw a long black crawling line that stretched the extent of the horizon.

"Guess there's no point in hoping that's just a lot of Sand Oren coming for a party!" He said, chuckling mirthlessly past a huge lump of fear in his throat.

"I would estimate slightly less than the two days we were told before they reach the outer edges of the desert. If we are to hatch a plan Elijah, now would be a good time."

Ranger's composure helped calm the churning in Elijah's stomach enough to allow him to find a normal voice to ask.

"How many do we have on our side Ranger?"

Ranger shrugged slightly, and answered with his eyes still fixed on the horizon.

"Ryufu has gathered around three hundred Yehana, and apparently is expecting other reinforcements to arrive any minute. I'm no battle expert, but I would guess that we do not stand a chance without an element of the unexpected."

"By that I suppose you mean me, and this thing!" Elijah muttered, suppressing a sudden urge to get up and throw off the cloak and watch it flutter uselessly to the ground.

Ranger placed his cool hand on his friend's arm.

"Don't judge yourself so harshly Elijah, I for one have faith that what you need will come to you if you leave your mind open, and I'm not the only one who believes in you either!"

He glanced down at the campsite, where the small figure of Khizzi sat, patiently waiting for Elijah to return, her long, sinuous tail swaying gently side to side in the sand.

"Come Elijah, you need food, drink and sleep, maybe that is when you will find enlightenment, if nothing else you'll be ready for battle!"

On the slippery way back down to the camp and the awaiting Khizzi, now joined by the others, Elijah deliberately concentrated on keeping his footing rather than give in to the temptation to stare out at the darkening throng blackening the horizon.

No words were exchanged as they reached the tent mouth and entered into its warm embrace.

Ranger fetched food and drink that Elijah consumed obediently before laying down by the freshly stoked fire.

Refusing the offered blanket, he wrapped the cloak around him and pulled it up so that his face was covered by the feathers.

Breathing in their musky scent he closed his eyes and relaxed his mind.

# Chapter 33

As soon as his eyes were closed it began. Disjointed images flashed like a movie trailer through his mind.

Mostly it was memories dredged up of his childhood with Burda and Ranger, in the cabin in the forest. He saw himself, a small dark haired boy, running after Ranger, pulling his tail and laughing, the three of them squeezed into the porch seat, swinging slowly and watching as the forest darkened into night and the dancing glow worms turned it into a world of magic.

Then he saw himself walking back from the little village school, trailing his feet in the dust to leave billowing clouds in his wake. In his sleep he smiled, these were all pleasant and cherished memories of a childhood spent, he now realised, in blissful ignorance thanks to the constant vigilance of his two guardians.

Suddenly, the whole image took on a completely different tone as the battered old taxi cab that he now knew belonged to Xan came crawling along the road behind his six year old self.

Instinctively his heart began to race, he had no memory of encountering Xan at any time other than the incident when he had been much older, outside the school gates, he watched with his heart in his throat as the car drew closer to a seemingly unaware and completely defenceless child, how could he have no memory of this?

And then he saw it, and he knew what he had to do and how to do it, the only question that remained was did he have the courage to carry it out?

# Chapter 34

"I have a plan, but you're probably not going to like it," Elijah said as he shook Ryufu awake.

A low rumbling growl rattled in his throat as Ryufu shook his head and heaved his bulky form up onto his feet. He opened his mouth to reply but snapped it shut again when his bleary eyes focussed on the intense face before him. Somehow, in the hour or so that the youngster had been asleep, a drastic metamorphosis had taken place. Standing in the place of a frightened fifteen year old was now a stern young man with determination blazing from his deep set eyes and the stance of one who finally knew his purpose.

Nodding slowly Ryufu replied, "Okay Ra-Elijah, let's get the others awake and hear it."

Huddled together around the dying embers of the fire, the group listened silently as Elijah outlined his plan. It was a sign of their new found respect for him that no-one said a word as he spoke, nor when he had finished. Even Burda, who he had expected to be the first to tell him that it was an insane plan and refuse to allow him to take such a risk, merely nodded, with reluctant resolve in her sagging shoulders.

"Well, we'd better get moving then, Xan certainly won't wait for us to be ready that's for sure!"

Matthias allowed his hand to brush feather light across his son's shoulder before walking away towards the waiting Yehana, the others followed.

Kwatili and Maylan remained beside Elijah, one either side of him. Maylan waited until the others were out of earshot and said quietly, "Are you sure Elijah, there may be other solutions, we still have—"

"I'm totally sure, Maylan, and you know very well that we don't have any alternatives. Xan's army is almost at the edge of the Ice Desert, and the plan won't work if he gets off it onto the beach, it's now or never."

# Chapter 35

Out on the Ice Desert, his weak eyes protected from the searing sun by red tinted glasses, Xan felt his pulse quicken as he realised that he could now actually see the outer edge and the grey tents of their encampment.

His breath whined past his chisel shape teeth as he drew in a deep breath of satisfaction.

"Finally I have you, all of you in one nice neat package, no more interference from you half breeds and mutants. The Eyes of Ula will finally be held in the hands of one who deserves them!"

Slowly he raised a trembling hand to wipe the drool from his thin stretched lips, the one elongated digit waving in the air across his face like a wind screen wiper.

A measured cough beside him jerked him from his reverie.

"What is it? Don't even think about giving me anything but good news!"

"No my Lord Xan, I merely wished to report that the extra four hundred Maigrey have joined us from the West, and that your army now numbers two thousand and forty."

"That will do, what was the last reckoning on Ryufu's pathetic rabble?"

"Oh the latest Silff report was no more than a few hundred with no sign of reinforcements on the horizon, we should crush them with no effort what so ever!"

Xan smiled and flicked a hand at the cowering creature dismissing it without a word, gratefully it scuttled away, knowing that it had been lucky to be delivering good news; as it passed by the charred remains of the one who had been allotted the task of informing Xan that the party containing the Raven Child had successfully joined Ryufu at his camp.

Grinding his teeth as he walked, he muttered oaths of vengeance against them all, but especially the mutant child, that one he would deal with himself, no more slip ups the child had to die this time.

Yet again he was disturbed by a cough at his shoulder.

"What now?" He snapped but then whipped away his protective glasses to squint towards the far edge of the Ice Desert.

"Never mind I see him, tell the men to continue forward, but I will speak with him first alone."

Striding forward towards the lone figure silhouetted against the shining wall of the mountains he fought to control an inexplicable bubble of fear that had expanded to fill his chest.

"What are you doing now child? And why am I afraid of such as you?"

He muttered under his breath as he closed the gap between himself and Elijah Grey.

# Chapter 36

As the stick thin figure approached him, Elijah fought to silence the voice in his head that was screaming for him to turn around and run as fast as he could, he was only a kid!

But the breeze coming off the desert softly ruffled the ink black feathers around his neck and it was as if they were whispering to him saying.

"You are Elijah Grey and this is your moment."

He repeated the words over and over to himself as he stood and waited now for Xan to reach him.

"I am Elijah Grey and this is my moment."

At a distance of about twenty feet Xan halted sending a billowing cloud of sand like a ghost to hover momentarily over the two dark figures before dissolving back into the desert.

"So, the offspring thinks he can face me alone eh? Not a wise move but then brains aren't in abundance in your family now are they Raven Boy?"

Xan's voice held a shrill tone of fear to belie his words.

"I am Elijah Grey, and this is my moment."

The quiet calmness in Elijah's reply was totally unexpected and therefore all the more unnerving.

Xan tried to cover his reaction by laughing and throwing back the hood of his cloak.

"Your moment to die you mean, who are you to stand before me and my army so cool and collected, you are either very brave or very stupid child!"

Elijah merely smiled sweetly back although if Xan had been any closer he might have spotted the tiny beads of sweat beginning to blossom from his forehead and trickle down the sharp contours of his face.

"Actually Xan, it is you who will die today, but I'm willing to give you the chance to surrender and live, all you have to do is go away, oh and return my mother unharmed of course, easy, much better than dying along with all your Maigrey, you maybe should take a minute to consider it?"

The bubble of fear instantly burst and erupted like a volcano of fury out of Xan's eyes.

"How dare you threaten the mighty Xan! How dare you insult me by asking me to bargain for my life? You are a mutant child, alone in the desert, with powers that you cannot begin to understand, let alone control. I will crush you into the sand and then send your darling mother behind you, Hah, even your renegade father has abandoned you to your fate. Where are your so called friends and allies now eh? They've all retreated like frightened rabbits and sent you to meet your death alone!"

There was something about the smile that curled into Elijah's lips that suddenly deflated Xans bluster and clogged up his throat.

"Alone? Oh, I'm not alone Xan, whatever made you think that?"

As he spoke, Elijah exhaled a huge sigh of relief and released his hold over the power he had been struggling inwardly to control.

Instantly to either side of him a vast army appeared, at least two thousand heavily armed Yehana, their sickle shaped swords clinking like bells in the stunned silence that fell over the desert.

For just a moment Xan's thin shoulders sagged, as he watched Matthias, Ryufu, Kwatili, Maylan, Burda, Brogan, Ghelli and Khizzi emerge  from the ranks to assemble around Elijah, bloodshed in their stone steady eyes.

So the boy had evolved, he must have used his power of concealment to hide the true size of the gathered army from his Silff too, clever.

But Xan had come too far down this road to alter the destination now, so, even though his thin arm shook with fear, he raised it above his head to signal his army to attack.

From that instant all the world around Elijah changed.

According to the plan, as soon as the two armies impacted in an eruption of sound, blood and fury, Elijah slipped behind his fortress of friends, who slaughtered and maimed whilst protecting him completely from not only harm but with their bodies they also fought to shield him from witnessing the carnage.

Somehow he found the sound and smell almost as terrifying and sickening as anything he thought he might see but they had charged him with staying behind them, so there he stayed, waiting, and ready.

Achingly slowly they forged forward, forcing Xan and his army steadily backwards over the desert and towards the setting sun.

Peeking out from behind the blood soaked back of Kwatili as she swung her huge curved sword and sliced off another Maigrey head that bounced like a soggy football over the sand, Elijah saw what he was waiting for. His heart beat quickened and he tried to swallow but his tongue and mouth were so dry they stuck together making him choke. Glancing briefly over his shoulder, Ryufu nodded to him and held his eyes in a fierce stare until Elijah nodded back.

"NOW!" Ryufu screamed above the mayhem and the entire army turned and ran as fast as they could in their exhausted state, leaving behind just Kwatili, Ryufu and Matthias to protect Elijah.

"Hah! So your so called followers are as unreliable as ever Ryufu!"

Screeched Xan triumphantly, waving his dripping sword aloft, seemingly unaware of the fact that his left arm was no longer attached to his shoulder and lay at his feet.

Ryufu said nothing, the smile that parted around his long pointed teeth should have told Xan to beware but Xan was delirious with blood loss and blood lust.

The three parted to allow Elijah to step forward, both hands clasped together against his chest, eyes out of focus as if he was sleep walking.

Only at the very last minute did the wide grin droop on Xan's thin face, and his arm slumped to his side sending the sword clanking to the already hardening surface of the Ice Desert.

Glancing over his shoulder he realised that the ruby face of the Sun was just about to slip below the horizon. He opened his mouth to shout the order to retreat off the desert but the words never left his throat.

Elijah spread his arms apart, holding one pulsating Eye of Ula in each hand, as he brought his hands together again a booming detonation exploded from his hands, sending a visible shock wave forwards to sweep Xan and his Maigrey tumbling like leaves in a gale, further out over the rapidly freezing surface of the desert.

Kwatili scooped Elijah up in her arms as he collapsed like a stringless puppet to the ground and sprinted to safety closely, followed by Ryufu and Matthias.

As they reached the safety of the grey stone beach, they turned to watch as Xan and his army met their doom.

One by one, as the ice touched them they froze, before shattering into showers of crystals that sparkled in the last red light of the sunset.

"You have not won mutant child!" Xan screamed as his body exploded into stars that settled slowly into a dark shadow on the Ice.

As the echo of his voice died, an eerie silence descended like a fire blanket leaving just the sound of the survivor's heavy panting and the soft rumbling sound as they sank exhausted to their knees on the cold grey pebbles.

Stinging tears trickled unfettered down his cheeks as Elijah Grey stared out at the devastation and destruction he had wrought.

"So many lives." He murmured.

A warm hand settled on his shoulder.

"He would never have surrendered, or listened to reason Elijah Grey, this end was inevitable both for Xan and for those who blindly followed him, you are not to blame; you are to be thanked by all those who will now live on in peace in Greylea."

Turning his head slowly to meet the gentle eyes of Maylan he said nothing but managed a weak smile, too stunned to properly register that the hand resting on his shoulder was the one that she had been missing and that the skin covering it was mottled grey and black scales, not the smooth pearl white skin of the other.

Another pair of hands slipped under his arms and pulled him to his feet.

"Put those carefully away now Elijah, and come back to camp, you need to rest and recover your strength in order to complete the days tasks."

Shaking his head to try to dispel the horrific image of the thousands of frozen figures exploding into ice crystals, he stared down at his trembling hands, still tightly gripping the twin stones that had unleashed such awesome destruction.

Turning towards Kwatili behind him he thrust his hands towards her.

"You take them Kwatili, I don't want them!"

The tall warrior woman flinched away from the Eyes of Ula as if they were her own death.

Recovering her composure she smiled gently, closed her own hands over his and firmly pushed them back towards him.

"They are yours by birth right Elijah Grey, trust me when I tell you that just as you fear and loath those at this moment, there will come a time when you will be glad that you possess them, they do not always have to bring death."

"But- I'm just a ——" He began to stutter, but the steady gaze suddenly turned upon him from Kwatili and the rest of the group now assembled around him cut off his words.

Burda huffed loudly and stepped forward, matter of factly brushing dust and battle residue from his shoulders, not meeting his gaze but he spotted the tears trickling down her craggy cheeks.

"Enough chatter young man, rest is what you have been prescribed and rest is what you will have, off with you to the tents."

As he had done all of his short life, Elijah obeyed, knowing that she was right and knowing also that there would be absolutely no point in arguing with her.

Staggering and stumbling on legs that felt like they'd had every ounce of strength sucked out of them, he made his way towards the first grey tent, ducked beneath the skin covering the doorway and collapsed onto the nearest heap of blankets, his head buzzing with exhaustion.

"How long will it take for him to recover enough?" Were the last words his conscious mind heard, he was asleep before the answer.

# Chapter 37

"Matthias you must be patient, he cannot attempt the rescue until he has the strength, to do otherwise could prove fatal for them both!"

"I know, I know Kwatili, but I have been without her for so long, this is agony, and those last words of Xan's are haunting me, what if-"

"SSShh he is waking up, let him do so peacefully Matthias."

As Elijah's senses fully returned to him he opened his dry and encrusted eyes to see the fast retreating back of Matthias and the large concerned amber eyes of Kwatili.

"I'm fine before you ask." He croaked. "Although I could use a drink please."

Almost instantaneously a beaker was pushed into his hand and he felt himself being lifted from behind into a sitting position.

Gratefully he drained all of the contents feeling the sweet smoothness sooth his roughened throat and mouth.

"Food he will want food as well!" Burda's voice came from behind him and was so loud that it made him flinch.

"No Burda, I'm fine now, really I am." He said as he saw her mouth preparing to disagree.

For a second or two they just looked at each other in silence, and then she smiled and nodded.

"Yes, yes you are Elijah Grey." She whispered softly before heaving her great bulk up off the ground with more curses and swear words than he had ever heard come from her mouth, and shuffled away, rubbing her back and shaking her head.

As he watched her go he had to clench his teeth together in order to resist the urge to call her back and say yes, okay, what was I thinking, of course I'm hungry. But, with a sinking heavy sensation in his chest he let her go, knowing without doubt, that the days of safety within Burda's bubble of protection were over.

Taking a deep breath he rose to his feet, tested their steadiness, and then turned towards Kwatili.

"Right, I'm ready to go rescue my mother now."

"Are you sure that you are strong enough Elijah?" Maylan queried as she joined them.

"No, not really but if I wait and something happens to her, I'll never forgive myself will I?"

He answered, gingerly removing the twin stones from inside his jacket.

"Well said Raven Boy, maybe I will be forced to change my opinion of you if you keep this up!" Chuckled Ryufu, slapping Elijah roughly between the shoulder blades hard enough to send him staggering forward.

"Careful you ruffian, you don't know your own strength." Chortled Brogan as he deftly caught Elijah and set him onto his feet again.

"Take care young Elijah, and know that if it all goes belly up, it's not down to you okay?"

Brogan whispered into his ear, giving his shoulder a firm, emphatic squeeze, before walking away towards the fire to join the hunched figures of Burda and Ghelli.

His words suddenly conjured up the dying words of Xan as he exploded into ice out on the desert.

"You have not won mutant child!"

What had he meant by that?

Icey fingers drew sharp nails of apprehension down Elijah's back now as he turned to seek out Kwatili's eyes.

"Give those thoughts no mind room Elijah, you will find what you will find, but to do so you must go as quickly as possible." She responded, ushering him over to the base of the sheer grey cliffs where Maylan and Khizzi were waiting.

As he reached them Khizzi glared defiantly and said

"Yes I'm coming with you, no there's nothing you can say to change that!"

Elijah grinned and answered

"Actually all I was going to say was, can everyone here read my mind or what?"

212

She giggled nervously and blushed, covering her embarrassment quickly by busying herself with unnecessarily wrapping her long tail tidily around her waist.

"Right then, we will begin." Said Maylan, holding out her mismatched hands to Elijah.

"Wait!"

Matthias appeared beside Elijah so silently that the boy almost jumped out of his skin.

Running his huge hand over his thick coarse grey hair, Matthias stood looking awkward and indecisive, before clearing his throat loudly and saying.

"Bring her back to me son, but bring yourself back too."

Then he wheeled around sharply and retreated before Elijah could respond.

"Okay, Dad." He whispered anyway, even though he knew that he wouldn't hear.

"Right, how do I do this Maylan?" He asked as he took a determined step towards her still out stretched hands

"Hold the Eyes together so that their surfaces are touching, close your eyes and try to picture your mother as you last saw her as clearly as you possibly can, empty your mind of all else and I will do the rest." She replied, taking hold of his two hands and holding them pressed together, with the Eyes of Ula already becoming warm and pulsating, cupped in his palms.

As he closed his eyes he was aware of Khizzi's tail gently winding around his waist, and was not surprised to experience a wave of reassurance at its touch.

Conjuring up the image of the tall shard of Gladiri Crystal that imprisoned his mother he tried to focus completely on wanting to be there, the Eyes of Ula began to vibrate in his hands and become almost too hot for him to continue to hold them without his skin being charred, but he held on, somehow knowing that the sensation was an illusion created by the stones, or at least that was what he earnestly hoped!

Suddenly it was as if he had been sucked out of his body and yanked skywards at mind numbing speed, clamping his jaws against the instant nausea, he realised that he was actually able to look down and see their three bodies standing together far below. Maylan with her hands tightly clasping his own, and

Khizzi pressed close to his back; all three encapsulated within a bright sphere of scarlet light.

All around him whirled misty, blurred shapes that orbited him but never came close enough to come into focus, and somehow he knew that he should be glad that they didn't, because they shrieked and howled like banshees and the air around him had chilled to icy cold.

"Find your destination and hold fast to it Elijah, or you are lost!"

It was his mother's voice inside his head but the screaming of the banshees around him almost drowned out her words. He tried to reach up and cover his ears with his hands but he couldn't move, blind panic threatened to over whelm him, he could feel himself weakening, drifting, succumbing to the urge to just give up fighting.

But she would not let him.

Suddenly the breath was almost squeezed out of his lungs by a fierce tightening around his waist and he felt himself descending back downwards with the same dizzying speed as his ascent.

Down into his body he plunged, and then she pushed him forward, so abruptly that he thought he would surely flatten Maylan into the ground as he fell on top of her; but instead he flopped heavily on his stomach onto soft green grass, with Khizzi on top of him!

Winded and dazed neither moved for a second or two, then Khizzi let out a small squeaking sound and rolled off his back, scrabbling to her feet brushing non-existent grass from her clothes and looking anywhere but into his face.

Elijah remained seated on the grass until he had managed one deep breath without pain in his bruised ribs, then he rose slowly to his feet and looked around.

They were once again at the foot of the smooth grey stone cliff face where he had last seen his mother before she had imprisoned herself within the Gladiri Crystal, just after she had watched Burda and Ranger take her new born son away to hide him in another dimension from Xan. Now Xan was dead, and his threat had died with him along with his army of mutant Maigrey, she was safe, and once he had told her that, she could release herself and come back with him to Matthias and the others.

So where was she? He glanced at Khizzi and her expression did nothing to quell the surge of fear now flooding throughout his body.

Stumbling on shaking legs, Elijah moved closer to the place where her Crystal had been standing. The grass was flattened and yellowed to its shape but it was gone, she was gone, he was too late.

Letting out a loud gasping sob, Elijah sank to his knees and ran his fingers through the limp grass, hot tears coursing freely down his cheeks to drip off his chin and soak into the soil.

Too much, it was too much. He was just a kid, who had thought he was an ordinary kid, living an ordinary life with his ordinary, if quirky, mother and dog.

And now, now what was he? Who was he? He didn't look the same, he didn't feel the same and he certainly wasn't the Elijah Grey who was a bit slow at maths and liked to skip games lessons if he could.

Burda wasn't even his mother, and now he'd lost his mother without having even had the chance to see her and touch her to know that she was real!

Buzzing angry bees of frustration, fear and sorrow threatened to burst his head apart, and he didn't care, he'd had enough now, he was just a fifteen year old who didn't want to play this game anymore he wanted to curl up and give up.

But again, she would not let him.

From out of the grey thunder around him reached in a small soft hand that gently took hold of his and squeezed.

"She's gone, he knew and he's taken her somewhere so that I couldn't find her."

"It does not matter Elijah Grey, because together we will find her."

Rocking back onto his heels he looked at her, and frowned.

"But I have absolutely no idea where to look Khizzi, hell I don't even know how to get back to the others without her!"

She smiled and held out her other hand, fist closed. Slowly her slender brown skinned fingers uncurled and nestling in her palm was a perfect curl of jet black hair. It fluttered like a fragile battered bird as the breeze caressed it.

Leaning her head to one side she whispered.

"We have this, Egreya must have cut it just before her crystal was taken, she too knew that you would come Elijah Grey, she and I have faith in you, even if you are, just a kid!"

Gingerly he reached out and picked up the lock of hair, holding it reverently between his fingers, before closing them protectively around it.

Ignoring the rapidly increasing vibrations from the Eyes of Ula tucked away inside his jacket, he got to his feet and walked over to the spot where the Gladiri Crystal had been standing. Khizzi moved to stand beside him, long tail still wound around his waist, linking them together like pearls in a necklace.

"You don't have to come you know Khizzi, who knows what we'll find and where we'll end up, it's my fight now, you could try to get back to Ghelli, I'll be fine."

In answer she punched him in the ribs and laughed.

"You don't think I'm going to choose my grumpy brother who stops me doing anything even remotely fun over an adventure with you do you Raven Boy?" She chuckled, her cheeks flushed pink with excitement.

"Well, I had to offer!" He replied, then, taking a deep breath, he removed both glowing red stones from their leather pouches and cupped them together in his palms with the black curl of his mother's hair wound between them.

Immediately his mind was filled with a jumble of flashing images, disjointed and terrifying.

Strange, dark, brooding landscapes, with huge screaming winged creatures filling the sky, whirlwinds of sparkling particles danced like wraiths across shifting dunes of black sand. And in the centre of it all, still and silent, stood a slender black cloaked figure. Amidst all of the chaos and confusion it was the only thing that remained steady.

He couldn't see a face but he saw a long white arm as it was raised into the air to point towards him, as if the figure could see him, and then it spoke one word into his mind.

"Son."

Closing his eyes, with Khizzi beside him, Elijah Grey stepped forward and the world around him winked out like a light switch.

Milton Keynes UK
Ingram Content Group UK Ltd.
UKHW021146130524
442628UK00014B/688